Welcome to Sycamore Hill

VOLUME 1 OF 2

SYCAMORE HILL

STACEY WEEKS

ISBN: 978-1-7381668-6-2

Grace and Love Publishing

Praise for Stacey Weeks

One of the things I enjoy about Stacey Weeks' writing is her ability to present a powerful & touching gospel message organic to the story, without it feeling forced or preachy. Instead of stopping an entertaining story for a sermon, Weeks uses the faith-centered elements to enhance the characters' journeys on the page and point to the Source of peace, strength, and courage.

— CARRIE ~ BOOK REVIEWER, READING IS MY SUPERPOWER

Weeks is a writer I count on for sweet contemporary romances with faith messages to make me think. She combines sympathetic characters with heartening take-aways about the freedom of living in grace and the power of community.

— AUTHOR EMILY CONRAD

The town of Sycamore Hill is warm and welcoming. The heart of God shines throughout the story.

— JULIA - BOOK REVIEWER, CHRISTIAN BOOKAHOLIC

More Fiction by Stacey Weeks

SYCAMORE HILL

To Sweet Beginnings in Sycamore Hill

The Sycamore Standoff

His Sycamore Sweetheart

The Sycamore Slopes

One Sycamore Sunday

A Sycamore Secret

MISTLETOE MEADOWS

Mistletoe Melody

Mistletoe Mission

Mistletoe Movie Star

STAND ALONE TITLES

Fatal Homecoming

The Builder's Reluctant Bride

In Too Deep

Contents

HIS SYCAMORE SWEETHEART

Free Short Story
Download at StaceyWeeks.com

When sweet peppers and jalapeño mix,
anything can happen.

Addison avoids visiting the city. He hates the crowds, traffic, and pace. He especially hates the compact vehicle the rental company insists he'd reserved. But then he runs into Sarah. Or, more accurately, she runs into him, mixing sweet peppers and jalapeño with burnt metal, petrol, hot pavement, and her desperation to not merely survive life in the city but find a place to thrive. Addison isn't looking for a weekend thrill or a romantic entanglement anymore than she is. They both want to go home. Maybe, together, they'll find their way.

SERIES INTRODUCTION

TO SWEET
BEGINNINGS IN
Sycamore
HILL

A SHORT STORY SEQUENCE

STACEY WEEKS

To Karen, Sandy, Heather, Tara, and Deirdre.
You believed these characters had more to their stories. The Sycamore Hill Series continues beyond this collection because of your faith in them and in me.

So, whether you eat or drink, or whatever you do,
do all to the glory of God.

1 Corinthians 10:31

To Sweet Beginnings in Sycamore Hill

WELCOME TO SYCAMORE HILL, WHERE HEARTS MEND, REDEMPTION IS WITHIN REACH, AND LOVE'S BLOSSOMS ENDURE EVEN THE HARSHEST STORMS.

When a whistleblower speaks up, she sets off a chain reaction that unfolds over a single, unforgettable day just as Sycamore Hill prepares for its biggest holiday celebration. As the dominos fall, a baker lands a life-changing opportunity, a journalist chases the truth, a woman faces her greatest fear, and a missing child finds their way home.

In the heart of this close-knit town, five couples stand at the edge of sweet beginnings filled with endless possibilities. This compelling short story sequence is just the beginning. Each couple's journey continues in a full-length novel filled with romance, redemption, and the promise of fresh starts.

Thursday 2:00 p.m. Owen and Gloria

This wasn't quite the triumphant return Gloria Sycamore had always imagined. She tugged up the hood of her winter coat with one hand and tipped her chin down. She clutched a file folder to her chest. Her downcast gaze made the likelihood of being recognized slim.

Gloria pointed herself in the direction of the library and merged with the foot traffic on Main Street. The archives should have copies of the newspapers from when her life imploded. Not that she wanted to relive those moments, but she needed to look at the articles with fresh eyes and a clear head. She didn't trust her memory. Or maybe she didn't want to believe what she suspected.

She'd be in and out, and no one would be the wiser. If she was wrong, no one would know she was here. But if she was right, everyone would know. Her chest tightened, and she swallowed a lump swelling in her throat. She knew what really happened that day, and more importantly, God knew the truth. But if that was right, why did she feel like a scolded dog slinking into town with its tail between its legs?

"Good afternoon," a cheery voice called from the doorway of a bakery.

Trepidation tightened her core. Her grip on the folder stiffened as she lifted her face. A man with a white apron tied around his waist rested his gloved hands on the handle of his snow shovel.

Relief loosened the knots in her belly. Her face relaxed into a smile as she flicked her eyes to The Muffin Man's gilded sign. Cute.

He bent at the waist, whistling a holiday melody as he resumed his chore. She knew the minute the proprietor noticed her heeled, leather, took-an-entire-paycheck-but-she-deserved-them boots. His whistling faltered. Gloria flattened her lips. Apparently, some fashion trends hadn't trickled down to Sycamore Hill. She buried her mouth and nose under her scarf and avoided making eye contact with anyone else as she hurried away. Every click of her booted heel seemed to scream; you don't belong, you don't belong.

"Look out!" A group of teenagers brushed past her and bumped her shoulder. They knocked the file from her hands, and she turned her ankle in her ridiculous heels, landing palms down on the pavement. The breeze snatched the loose papers.

Sycamore Hill: One. Gloria: Zero.

As one page scraped and danced down the sidewalk, she pinched her eyes shut. Dampness seeped through her knees, and her palms burned from the cold. She inhaled a deep, slow breath, but it didn't slow her racing pulse. Her imagination was on overdrive. They were just kids. She hadn't been targeted. No one even knew she was back. Sycamore Hill had been one funeral away from claiming ghost town status when Gloria shook its dust from her feet. It would seem that the sleepy settlement had woken up during her years away.

Sycamore Hill: Two. Gloria: Still zero.

"Is this yours?" A hand extended the rescued newspaper page waltzing with the wind.

Gloria skipped over the headlines. She had them memorized. *Experimental Drug from Emergence Pharmaceuticals Shows Promise. Income Opportunity Knocks at the Door of Life House.* Her attention lingered on the picture of her former bio-medical lab partner. Tiff's confident grin stared back at her. She always did take a good photo. With her arms folded across the front of a starched white lab coat, she looked every bit the part of a trustworthy professional. But Gloria knew better.

"It is. Thank you!" Gloria pushed herself to her feet, but she crumpled when she put weight on her ankle.

The man cupped her elbow. "Let me help you."

Gloria fumbled out another thank you. It had been a long time since anyone offered her assistance. If enough new blood pulsed through the town's veins, maybe her scandal was ancient history? Lord, please let it be so!

A gust of wind blew back her hood as she lifted her face to her Good Samaritan. Little wisps of blonde curled out from under the edge of a dark knitted cap with a brown leather label. Her mouth fell open.

Recognition dawned in his eyes. "Gloria?"

Owen Mason's once lanky frame had filled out during her absence. His shoulders were broader than before, and even in a winter jacket, she could tell he narrowed nicely at the waist. The twinkle in his eyes dimmed as her delay in responding lengthened.

Say something. Anything.

She bit the inside of her cheek. She couldn't seem to push words around her suddenly swollen throat and thick tongue. Once she confirmed her identity, he'd walk away. She hadn't just abandoned Sycamore Hill; she'd rejected everything the small town stood for, including him. It was the only way she could cope.

A vertical line etched between his eyebrows as he drew them together.

Say words. Any words will do.

Heat burned her skin as she recalled their last interaction. His smile faded. She'd left Owen with only a letter to explain why.

"Hi, Owen." It came out deep and raw. Then, as if her eyes had a mind of their own, her gaze trailed down all the way to his bare ring finger. Her stomach hopscotched. When she lifted her face again, the corner of his lips twitched.

He inhaled a large, deep, savouring breath.

Sycamore Hill: Two. Gloria: One.

Finally, she was on the scoreboard.

———

It'd been three years since Gloria had left Sycamore Hill. Still, a spark shot through Owen when their gazes met and held with a magnetic force. For a millisecond, her whole face lit up, and it erased any lingering bitterness he'd carried over her abrupt departure. But then she slid on a guarded look, and tenseness filled his gut. No one had handled the scandal well, least of all him.

Doubts about his reception evaporated when her attention lingered on his bare ring finger. She blushed and looked away when he rubbed it with the fingers of his opposite hand. Interest or curiosity? Her face brightened, giving him his answer. Thank you, Lord, for spilled hot coffee! He'd left his gloves at the church to dry and returned to The Muffin Man to grab another cup.

Owen leaned forward, and lightness filled his limbs. The cold wind pushing at his back battled with an uncontrollable flush of internal heat. Gloria wasn't back in Sycamore Hill to impress anyone. Her covert actions and wavy blonde hair pulled into a sensible ponytail at the nape of her neck told him that much. The colourful scarf covering her long neck meant she still preferred vivid colours to neutral, even when trying to blend into the crowd. Her silly boots said that she still followed fashion. His brain ticked off these observations in an unsuccessful attempt to stop him from imagining how her neck curved into her shoulders or obsessing over what fragrance she wore. One nuzzle into that curvature would satisfy both needs. Just the thought made his insides buzz.

He forced his gaze away. Objectifying her wasn't only inappropriate, but it was unkind. It was hardly what she needed right now. Still, he couldn't help but note that if he'd combined all the post-Sunday-morning-sermon handshakes from hopeful mothers parading their single daughters by the unmarried pastor, he still wouldn't feel as alive as he did right now. A quiver rippled down his spine at this unexpected opportunity from the Lord.

Gloria's pink lips folded inward, and she touched them with her gloved fingers. Her hesitation speaking to him was a fresh knife to the heart. A million questions filled his mouth, but he bit them back. After all their years together, had she really planned to come back to Sycamore Hill and not call him? Sure, they shared childhood years, but their friendship still counted. Was she going to see her parents? Did she know how much her year after year refusal to come home had hurt them? A snappy comment joined his lengthening list of questions, but he swallowed it. What kind of pastor would it make him if he voiced every thought in his head?

Human.

He'd learned a little something about the grace found in second chances, and the way Gloria's chin trembled made him think she needed one. And maybe a friend, too.

"It's nice to see you again." She finally spoke. The words were right, but her tone and facial expressions contradicted them. It wasn't nice to see him again. Not even close. In fact, if he had to guess, it was probably as nice as digging into a brussels sprout sundae when you were expecting hot fudge.

He gave her a weak smile. His attention dropped to the newspaper she had yet to take from him. The gears started to turn. If she was finally returning to town, why would she bring the past with her?

Her face paled as if she'd followed his thoughts. She leaned back subtly and fortified the wall around her.

Owen relieved Gloria of the rest of her papers, tucked them under one arm, and offered her his hand to help her up. If she wasn't ready to talk, he could wait. He'd waited years for this reunion. What were a few more hours? He discarded all his questions except one.

"Back for long?"

———

A heavy sigh slipped out as Gloria accepted Owen's offered hand. "I planned to be in and out." And avoid being seen, she didn't add. Gloria slid a glance his way from the corner of her eye. She didn't have time for this, yet she instinctively smoothed the front of her jacket. She refused to answer her inner critic asking why she felt the need to be perceived as put-together by her high school boyfriend.

She hobbled alongside Owen. "I didn't count on a twisted ankle slowing me down." According to the paper, the drug trial was set to begin next week, and no one but Gloria knew of Tiff's pattern of bending the rules or the ruthlessness tactics of her employer, Emergence. She cut her gaze back to Owen. Why wasn't he asking her about the article? She saw him read the headline. Why was he making mindless chit-chat? Why was he carting her belongings around as if they were two teens between classes at the high school?

Owen shortened his stride so she could easily keep up, despite the hitch in her step. "Why the clandestine arrival?"

She was about to argue over his word choice but stopped. Clandestine about summed it up.

Sycamore Hill: Three. Gloria: One.

Gloria nodded at the papers under his arm. "Tiff and I were lab partners at Grander University. Since Grander Hospital is a teaching hospital, they work with students all the time. This drug study is big news for them." Even bigger than the news that framed Gloria for Tiff's actions.

Gloria pointed at the library across the street to indicate her destination. She needed to find out if Emergence was the same company that Tiff worked for while they were in university. The old articles on file should contain the information she couldn't find online.

Owen steered her toward the quaint one-room building with a wide porch and white pillars. The library had always reminded Gloria of a church. Despite its small stature, it projected a stately feel, like once you entered, you'd crossed into a sacred space.

"Is this going to be a happy reunion?"

Gloria snorted. "Hardly." She paused at the base of the library's steps. There were only five, but it might as well have been a million with her bum ankle.

Owen's arm slipped from her elbow down to her waist. Her face, neck, and ears felt impossibly hot over how well they still fit together. She briefly closed her eyes, and memories of high school dances, movies, and football games spent snuggling close to Owen's side assaulted her. But just because he wasn't married didn't mean he was unattached. She started to pull away, but she needed his help to climb the steps.

Owen supported her one step at a time until they were at the front door. The heat blower blasted, warming her skin. At least that's what she blamed for her temperature spike. She paused under the balminess, partly because she was cold, and partly because her ankle screamed.

Owen led her to a wooden table and pulled out a chair. Gloria collapsed, closed her eyes again, and inhaled the faint and familiar scent of pinewood oil, old paper, books, and knowledge. Her eyes prickled unexpectedly. She wasn't prepared for nostalgia to overwhelm her.

"Can I check your ankle?"

Her eyes popped open. She nodded.

Tender hands lifted her foot and rested it on the seat of a nearby chair. Owen prodded her ankle. "You're going to need to stay off it, keep it elevated, and ice it for a bit. I hope you didn't plan to drive back to the city tonight."

Gloria groaned.

"What's so important that it can't wait a day or two?" His head tilted to the side as his fingers continued to press into the tender spots of her injury.

"Ouch!" She jerked her leg back. The prickles in her eyes dampened her cheeks.

"Sorry." He puckered his lips. "I don't think it's broken. But sprains can be just as painful as a break."

Gloria inhaled through her nose. Owen retreated to a chair across from her. He stacked her newspapers on the table, folded his hands, and leaned onto his forearms. Waiting. She supposed she owed him some sort of explanation.

"When Tiff and I were lab partners, she falsified the results in our final culminating project."

Owen's expression did not indicate how he felt about that statement. As a pastor, he'd probably heard lots of scandalous confessions and had learned not to react. Or maybe he didn't connect the dots to how Tiff's lack of ethics could impact Sycamore Hill.

"She begged me for the time to make it right," Gloria continued. "But she ran to her employer—who I now suspect had put her up to the scheme—and they framed me for the discrepancies in the study."

Owen nodded.

That part wasn't a surprise. It was all over the Sycamore news. *Faults in the Founding Family Exposed! A Sycamore Scandal!* Or her all-time favourite, *Prestigious School Expels Prestigious Family.*

"They tied such a perfect bow on the lie that even I began to doubt my innocence."

"Why do you suspect her employer was involved?"

"Because she got a huge promotion after graduation. I think this new drug trial coming to Life House is based on that falsified study. I think Emergence is the same company under a new name. I'm sure I read that in one of the follow-up pieces. I've also been emailing a nurse at the hospital who has evidence that the trial is unsafe. But I don't have his name. He doesn't want to be identified. I need to go to the hospital and find him or find the evidence."

"The first one's easy enough. I'll grab what you need." Owen hopped up and strode to the library's computer to search for the location of the old papers. He still had the same gait from when he was younger. Long steps. Chest out. Confident.

Muffled shushing came from the back corner. Sitting on a bright red area rug, a mother tugged her squirmy toddler back into her arms. The little girl squealed and pounded her palm on the colourful board book her caregiver held open. She rolled off her mom's lap, flipped over on the floor, and stuck her bottom in the air and her thumb in her mouth.

There was a time Gloria thought she'd have babies by now. Her palm fell over her hollow middle. But if infertility ran in families, she might never have kids. Her sister, Jessica, had been trying to get pregnant for almost a year.

Owen moved away from the electronic catalogue and disappeared down an aisle opposite the kid's corner. Gloria always thought Owen would make a great father.

A tiny tug on her jacket sleeve jolted her. Huge blue eyes blinked, and the little girl extended a drool-covered index finger and babbled.

"I'm sorry," the mother gushed, scooping up the child. "She tends to wander. She just started walking and is forever getting into things." The mother retreated with her daughter again to the kids' corner.

"She's beautiful." Even Gloria heard the longing in her whispered reply. She cut her gaze to the aisle into which Owen disappeared. The tips of her ears burned.

Owen emerged from another row of books and dropped a stack of papers on the table. He sat back down.

"You're helping?" Gloria's heart pushed against the confines of her ribcage.

His smile stiffened. "Of course, I am." He opened the first paper and bent over it.

Why did she ever think she had to do this alone? Deep down, she knew that Owen and her parents would have stood by her had she fought the accusations, but she'd lived her whole life in the Sycamore family shadow. Sycamores set and reached high goals. They made the honor roll at prestigious schools. They grew up, married locals, and had great careers in fields that benefited the town. They didn't get sucked into scandals. She was supposed to stay local and maybe move into politics like her parents. It was all so decided. Neat and tidy. Until it wasn't.

"Dad's re-election campaign for mayor was just around the corner," she blurted. "If I pulled out of school before they could expel me, then I wouldn't be the Sycamore that dragged the family's name through the mud."

Owen didn't look up, but his hands stilled, and the newspaper stopped rustling. "The news still leaked."

Her stomach hardened. "But it died quicker with me gone."

His frame stiffened, the only indication of his emotional state. "You could have come back before now. It's been years."

She reached across the table and rested her hand on top of his. She waited until he looked up. "When I couldn't poke holes in Tiff's airtight accusation, I felt like I couldn't breathe. I spent my whole life trying to be a perfect Sycamore like Jessica, and then some jerk of a company swoops in and tells everyone I'm a horrible cheat. I couldn't fight it because I didn't know who I was."

"I knew you." His quiet words were a balm to her soul. "And I would have believed you."

She squeezed his hand. "I'm here now."

He flipped his hand over so her palm nestled in his, and he threaded their fingers together. "Yes, you are, and you still need to get into the hospital. But unless you plan on going in as a patient, I don't see you sneaking by security with that ankle. I can call a guy. Ben. He's a reporter. If we tell him what you know, he'll take it the rest of the way."

The burden she'd been staggering under slipped off her shoulders. She really didn't have to do this alone. If Owen could accept her so readily after so long, maybe her parents would, too. Maybe they hadn't chopped her branch off the family tree and fed it through the woodchipper to save their political careers. Maybe all their invitations to return were sincere and not attempts to force her into the Sycamore mould.

"Okay. I need your help. Thank you."

Owen took out his phone and tapped out a few messages. His phone pinged with instant responses.

"Who are you texting?"

"Don't worry." His steady, comforting tone wrapped around her like a gentle hug. "I know exactly what needs to be done." He lifted his face, and his jaw's determined set made her feel safe. She wasn't in this alone. "We'll end this together so you can finally come home."

She nodded. The tension in her muscles slackened, and she inhaled a full, slow, and easy breath. Her heartbeat slowed to a calm and steady rhythm. Her glass was no longer half empty or half full; instead, the cup was refillable.

Sycamore Hill: Three. Gloria: Two.

It was anyone's game.

————

Getting Gloria to accept help had always been like chipping ice off the windshield with a silicon spatula. Impossible. But the way she melted into his offer told Owen that she was weary—weary of the scandal and weary of facing it alone. She needed more than just his help.

"Let me take you to your parents' place. Ben can meet us there. He'll know the best way to stop the drug trials."

"I can't just show up unannounced at my parents'. Not after all the times I've refused them. Besides, we don't even know if they're at home."

He drummed his fingers on the tabletop. "How about the church? We'll meet with Ben and figure out the rest."

She nodded, and he fired off a few more messages.

It took them longer to hobble to his truck than it did to drive to the tiny church that sat just on the outskirts of town. As he pulled into the gravel lot packed down with snow and ice, he tightened his grip on the steering wheel. *Please, Lord, go before us. Help Gloria accept what I've done.*

The second he parked the truck, two figures emerged from the double arched doors.

Gloria whipped her head around to face him. "What did you do?"

Owen cut the engine. He picked up Gloria's hand and held it loosely. The fact that she didn't rip it from his grasp was a good sign. "There have been a lot of changes in Sycamore Hill," he said. "A dying town found new life and got a second chance. I made a lot of mistakes, and the people here gave me a second chance. Now I'm their pastor. I've learned a lot and grown up, but the most important thing I've learned is that some things—the most important things—never change."

Like his feelings for her.

Gloria turned her head to the passenger side window. Her parents stood, bundled up in winter coats, mitts, hats, and scarves. Her dad had one arm around her mom, holding her back, waiting for Gloria to make the first move.

Teresa Sycamore's lip trembled, and a tentative smile wobbled.

"You think you need to clear your name," Owen said. "You came back to protect the people of Life House. I think the Lord has something even bigger in motion here."

Gloria's mouth gaped slightly. One hand moved to the door handle, and dampness filled her eyes. Owen didn't know what to make of her throaty words, "Sycamore Hill: Three. A second chance: Priceless."

A wide smile overtook her face, and Gloria opened the door.

Thursday 11:59 p.m. Ethan and Kathryn

Ethan Roberts wasn't Santa Claus, but he did have a good reason for breaking into Kathryn's house in December. She'd taken something that belonged to him, and he needed it back. It wasn't stealing if it was his. And it wasn't breaking in if he found her hidden key. At least, he was pretty sure it wasn't breaking in . . .

The Sycamore family could no longer prepare the menu for the Life House gala. Gloria's return had thrown the entire family into chaos. In their absence, Ethan's bakery snagged the career-making opportunity. The entire town was about to dine on a coconut herb salad, cedar-plank salmon, roasted asparagus, and mini potatoes. His grand finish was a chocolate liqueur souffle. He'd ordered all the necessary ingredients, and while he waited for them to arrive, he had to wrap up the details on his upcoming Christmas promotion highlighting his great-grandma's secret trifle recipe. But when he looked for the recipe, it was gone. Failing to deliver on this promotion would tarnish the reputation he was trying to build, but thanks to internet television, he knew just where to find it.

Ethan ran his hand along the rough grout lines surrounding the red bricks to the left of her front door. The chipped-out section over the third brick from the corner snagged his fingertip. *Gotcha!* He shoved his finger into the hollowed-out groove and felt for the key.

Yes! He palmed the key and glanced up and down the street.

Kathryn should've listened to him. He'd told her to change her hiding spot a long time ago. She was lucky it was him coming in and not some crazy fool looking to score easy Christmas gifts. The front door shut behind him and closed with a quiet click. He chuckled. Well, maybe lucky was a stretch.

If everything went the way he'd planned, Kathryn would never know he'd been here. He'd get in, get the recipe, and get out. Nothing to it. With one eye on her closed bedroom door, he crept toward the kitchen. He needed an altercation with his ex-girlfriend like Santa needed another plate of cookies and a glass of full-fat milk.

He opened the cupboard where she stashed the recipes she used on her cooking segment of Sycamore Hill at Sunrise. He flipped through the collection until he found the one that belonged to him: his great-grandma's secret recipe. *Bingo!*

The baker in him loved that she was old-school enough to keep paper copies of her recipes instead of filing them electronically. But the businessman in him couldn't believe she'd steal the recipe she knew he was planning to use to kick off his Christmas promotion at his bakery. Between that and catering the Black-Tie Gala for Life House, he'd end the year in the black. If his shop was going to make it, he needed to close the month strong.

He unfolded the faded paper on the countertop. Not only had

Kathryn used his recipe, but she'd butchered it. Everyone who saw her ruined version of his great-grandma's Christmas trifle would assume his individually sized portions were just as bad, making the one thousand dollars he paid in upcoming holiday advertising wasted.

A camera poised on the tripod in the corner caught his eye. His stomach churned. Kathryn's kitchen disaster had gone live yesterday, and it already had thousands of hits because who didn't like to see a pretty girl covered in powdered sugar present a disaster? The internet thrived on failed attempts, and Kathryn's ability to laugh at herself only endeared her viewers to her all the more.

Did she mess it up on purpose? Did she think that substituting a common ingredient for great-grandma's special—Wait. He squinted at the recipe. A slow smile stretched his face. The bottom of the page was torn. She didn't know the secret ingre—

"Move an inch, and you're dead." The command came from behind him, accompanied by the sound of a gun cocking.

Ethan stiffened, raised his hands above his head, and slowly turned around.

"I mean it!" Her voice raised in pitch as he ignored her instructions to stay put.

"You don't have a gun, Kathryn, not unless a lot has changed in the last two months. You can't even squash a bug. Never could, not even when we were eight, and we spent summer afternoons catching insects. You'd catch them, set them free, and mumble something about all God's creation deserving to live."

"Ethan?"

He dropped his arms and scooped up the recipe on the countertop. He flicked a glance at the paper. "You don't have a gun, but you do have my great-grandma's recipe."

Kathryn lowered her cell phone, which had been pointed at him.

Did she think the app that replicated the sound of a cocking gun could miraculously shoot out bullets? He shook his head. "What would you have done if I'd been a real intruder?"

Her hand pressed over her heart, and she sagged, but only briefly. "What are you doing in my house at midnight? I should call the cops."

"Go ahead, call them." He flipped the recipe box lid closed and put it back in the cupboard. "I'm just taking back what's mine. When they get here, I can tell them how you stole this," — he shook the paper— "and used it as comic relief on your morning show."

Her mouth dropped open, but no sound came out.

"That's what I thought." He folded the recipe and stuffed it into his front pocket, feeling a little bit smug for striking her mute. After years of knowing her and never winning an argument, he finally had the last word. "I'll be going—"

She reached out to stop him. "I didn't steal your recipe! I found it. I'd never steal from you."

He shook her loose. "Yeah, you found it." He put air quotes around the words "found it". "You found it in my bakery about three months ago when I showed it to you."

She paled even further. Was it from guilt and shame, or from remembering the kiss they'd shared that day? Heat filled his chest. For a minute, he couldn't remember why they'd broken up. All he could remember was how good they were together, how good they'd always been together. Like pork 'n' beans. Barbie 'n' Ken. Break 'n' enter. She was definitely prettier than B—

"I found the recipe!" She stomped over to the door that led into her attached garage, threw it open, and stabbed the light switch. "Last week you put that old hutch on the curb." She jabbed her finger at the hutch sitting on a blue tarp. "I picked it up to refinish it."

He felt his eyes widen. That was his mom's old hutch. He'd hauled it to the curb himself. "You took that?"

"Yes." Her expression softened into a tentative smile. "I remember your mom giving us cookies from that ugly cookie jar she sat on the top. Seeing it made me think of her, you, and—" She stopped abruptly, broke eye contact, and cleared her throat. "The recipe was stuck in the back behind a drawer. I didn't even connect it to the recipe you had shown me a few months ago."

"Still, you knew it wasn't yours. I could charge you with stealing."

She flicked the light switch off, re-entered the house, and pressed the door shut. She rested her forehead against the door like she was exhausted. "And I can charge you with breaking and entering."

"Kathryn—"

She swung around to face him, her fierce expression cutting off his words and challenging him to test her threat. They stared at each other for a solid minute, neither blinking, both refusing to budge an inch, like a strange version of the childhood game chicken.

He looked away. "It doesn't count as breaking in if we dated. Besides, I have a key." He dug the key out of his pocket and held it up for her to see.

She snatched it from his fingers. "An officer might say that strengthens my case. Ex boyfriend finds the hidden key and breaks in at midnight. The headline writes itself." She stuffed the key into the pocket of her faded bathrobe and tightened the belt.

"Look, whether you knew the recipe was mine doesn't matter. You know now. It's the recipe I featured in all my Christmas promotions, and you've gone and—"

Understanding dawned on her face. "Ruined it with my silly

show." She felt behind for a chair and sank onto it as the reality of her online mishap hit fully. She held his gaze, her expression filled with genuine sorrow. "I'm sorry. How can I make this right?"

"You can't."

She stared off into the distance with a familiar look on her face. Her mind was churning. Suddenly, her gazed locked back onto his, and her eyes lit up. She bolted upright in her seat. "What if we recorded a segment together for my show? We demonstrate the right way to make Grandma's trifle. It'll be more promotion for your business. The timing is perfect. I can schedule it to post first thing, and with tomorrow's show taken care of, I won't have to hurry through the morning to get to the road race in time. I promised to cover it live."

She sucked her lower lip into her mouth and bounced in her seat while she waited for him to respond. Could they do it? Could they work together one more time and turn this disaster around with clever marketing?

Her eager expression sparked a place inside of him that hadn't burned since their relational fallout. What had gone wrong between them?

"You can teach me the correct way to make it," she said. "We can recap my disasters and highlight each mishap I had. Then, we can plug your store and end with a link for pre-ordering individual servings by the dozen that'll be ready for pick-up the week after the gala."

Her enthusiasm was contagious. It always had been.

She jumped to her feet and scooped up both his hands. A current zipped from his fingers to his heart. "We can film it now." She tugged him toward her, and they stood so close she had to tip up her face to look in his eyes. She waited with a look of expectation.

It was so brilliant he could kiss her. His gaze dropped to her lips. He would only have to move a few inches. She had always been the Barbie to his Ken, the pork to his beans, the—

"It's gonna be great!" She squeezed his hands once more before she dropped them and bounced toward the camera.

He jolted out of his reverie.

"I get the most hits over the breakfast hour. We better get started." Her eyes glittered. The faint flush of pink in her cheeks and tousled hair made her look more like a teenager than an adult, more like the girl he remembered from his childhood who always knew just what to do to get him out of trouble.

He remained motionless, just following her with his gaze. "Why did we break up?"

She froze. All the joy drained from her expression as her posture wilted. "You couldn't handle my success. Remember?" She avoided his eyes by pretending to set up the camera.

He took it like a fist to the gut. When Kathryn's morning show, Sycamore Hill at Sunrise, went viral, she landed a cookbook deal, and his dad used her success to drive a knife through Ethan's heart. *Only women belong in the kitchen. Be a man and hang up your apron and join my construction crew.* His old-fashioned dad kept rubbing salt in the wound until Ethan couldn't stand it anymore. He forced distance between him and Kathryn, him and his Dad, him and, well, everyone. Now, Ethan was spending Christmas alone, and he had no one to blame but himself.

In less than an hour, he and Kathryn stood in her kitchen, now lit up like daytime with the help of stage lights. He couldn't believe how she'd made her own success. She didn't let the limitations of a small town stop her from pursuing her passion for film. She created her own station online and then gave it everything she had. She always did.

They faced the camera together, and he counted down in his head as the red light blinked faster and faster until it turned green.

"Good morning, Sycamore Hill!" Kathryn beamed at the camera. "I'm Kathryn Withers, the host of Sycamore Hill at Sunrise. Many of you tuned in and watched the episode where I debuted a Christmas recipe that I couldn't get quite right. Let's face it," she laughed. "I was like Mrs. Claus on cough syrup. I only had part of the recipe, so I invited you, my viewers, to help me figure out the final steps and ingredients. As a result of that episode, a local baker, Ethan Roberts from *The Muffin Man*, has stepped forward to help me. It turns out that the recipe I found stuck in the back of an old drawer has been in his family for generations. Ethan's great-grandmother passed this recipe down, and Ethan's grandmother taught him the secret to this delicious treat. Today, Ethan will walk us through preparing the trifle in muffin cups step by step. Afterward, I'll tell you where you can save yourself the trouble of making it, and order them by the dozen from Ethan himself."

It took them about three hours to get it just right. After some editing, tweaking, and laying down a soundtrack, the episode uploaded. They fell onto the couch, exhausted.

———

"We're at twenty-five thousand hits so far," Kathryn called from the kitchen where she poured coffee into two mugs. "I knew it'd be huge!"

He scrolled through his website sales receipts. "My orders are the highest they've ever been this early in December. I can't believe it worked."

"My ideas always work." She winked at him as she put the coffee cream back in the fridge.

"Okay, then I can't believe that you did that for me, especially after I snuck in here and pretty much accused you of espionage."

She handed him a mug and shrugged like it was no big deal. "Did you see the comment your dad made?"

"My dad?" Ethan nearly choked. He set the coffee cup on the end table and mopped his face.

Kathryn stood in front of him and swiped up on her phone screen and read, "*My grandma made this recipe every Christmas. When she died, my mom took over the tradition. Seeing my son make it today has brought back so many good memories. Christmas is a time to remember. It's a time to remember our Lord who came to earth to live a perfect life and then die in our place. It's a time to remember family and the traditions that honor family. It's a time to repent and mend rifts. It's Christmas, and I'm proud of my son for reminding me of what matters and for keeping our traditions alive. I'm sorry I didn't believe in your bakery, Ethan.*"

Kathryn had to be making this up. Ethan tugged her down onto the sofa beside him. Her back nestled nicely against his chest, and he looked over her shoulder to see the phone screen. He couldn't believe it. His dad wrote that? His dad, who started calling him Betty Crocker, and who mockingly danced around him singing, "Here comes the muffin-man, the muffin-man, the muffin-man," wrote that? His dad had never, not once, in his whole life ever said "sorry."

"It's a Christmas miracle!" His lips brushed her ear with the whispered words.

The corners of Kathryn's eyes crinkled as she laughed. She leaned back into him. "Your dad's been coming to my church since we went our separate ways. I think he's softened quite a bit. Do you want to respond to him?"

"In a minute." Ethan jostled her, forcing her to turn and face him. He gently wiped away sugar granules from the tip of

Kathryn's nose. "You are amazing. Do you have any more surprises for me?"

The corners of her lips turned up, and she nudged him with her shoulder. "I'm not as amazing as you. The camera loves you. Look at all the heart emojis the girls are leaving you in the comments." She held up her phone again.

He bumped her phone down. "Those aren't the hearts I'm interested in."

She stilled. He heard her soft intake of breath. She pulled her bottom lip into her mouth and looked—hopeful?

Did this mean— Was she—

He leaned in and tipped his head so his forehead touched hers.

"I've missed you," she whispered.

He studied her eyes, needing permission. When he found what he was looking for, he feathered his lips against hers. "Last night I remembered all the reasons I loved you. All the reasons I still love you."

The images of Barbie and Ken were long gone. He only had thoughts of Kathryn, the peanut butter to his jel—

His phone rang.

She tossed it an angry look. "Whoever that is can wait."

Ethan glanced at the screen and straightened up. "It's my supplier. I gotta get this." He tapped the call. "Hello? . . . There's a problem with what?" Ethan stuffed his index finger into his ear, trying to hear better. "Thanks for letting me know."

"Ethan?" The pressure from Kathryn's hand on his arm reminded him he wasn't alone.

He lifted his face hers. "My supplier can't get the chocolate liqueur that I need for the souffle. That was supposed to be my grand finish on the Life House menu."

"Can you get it somewhere else?"

He shook his head.

Her eyes twinkled with that look. The one that meant she was up to something. "Then it's a good thing we cooked up a winner last night." She showed him the most recent stats from her show. The trifle was a hit.

"Grandma's Trifle to the rescue."

Friday 3:00 a.m. Emma and Ben

⌒⌒

Emma Powles's chin slipped off the palm of her hand, and her forehead smacked the kitchen island counter-top. "Ow!"

She brushed her fingertips over her tender brow, forcing her thick hair out of the way. The clock on her microwave glared 3:00 a.m. She was going to look like a mess at the fundraiser tonight, not that it mattered. She didn't have a date for the black-tie event.

She gripped the counter edge with her fingers, jerking her slender frame in a sharp twist until a satisfying crack vibrated up her spine. You'd think with all the advancements made in the world, someone would create a kitchen island stool that combined style and comfort. She massaged her fingertips into the small of her back. Well, if someone had, she'd never found it in her price range. A newly completed nursing degree and six months of home renovations forced her to pinch every penny.

She loved her new kitchen island stools, however impractically designed. She loved her cottage style rowhouse. It was cozy, full of character, and after months of constant renovations, finally, everything she had hoped it would one day become. She had everything she ever wanted. Well, almost everything. Her focus on becoming a nurse practitioner had made dating impossible, and now at thirty years old when she finally had time to think about a relationship, the pickings were slim. Especially in a small town like Sycamore Hill.

She tipped her head back and gazed up at her new skylight. A coating of snow blocked her view, but she closed her eyes and imagined the stars in the sky. She inhaled deeply, filling her lungs to capacity and then slowly exhaling. She made a wish. Not exactly a wish. More like a prayer. Some might call it bad-mannered to ask God to usher Mr. Right through her front door, but a girl could ask.

The glow of her laptop screen darkened, and her computer went to sleep. Good idea. She'd been studying up on the Emergence drug trial set to begin Monday, but she wasn't going to learn anything with one foot in dreamland. She folded her laptop shut. She'd revisit the material in the morning when she had a clear mind. She owed the residents of Life House—the test group—her best attention, since she would be overseeing their care.

The barstool legs scraped across the ceramic floor as she stood up. Soft warmth brushed against her calf. Lola, her aged, long-haired, ginger cat, had finally come out of hiding. She wove herself between Emma's legs. Loyal to a fault, old Lola purred for no one but her. Emma bent down and scratched behind Lola's ear just the way she liked it. "Hey there." The cat had only recently come out from hiding. Despite being declawed, Lola had managed to paw her way inside Emma's box spring and mattress set. She made a little hideout inside the wooden frame and escaped to her safe place throughout the renovations.

Emma scooped up her empty coffee mug and moved toward

the sink when a cataclysmic crack shattered the quiet. The skylight rained down shards of glass and snow.

Emma thrust up her arms, instinctively protecting her head and face. The mug smashed onto the tiled floor. She scrambled backward and sliced open her bare foot, smearing blood across the tiles.

A still body slumped on the floor like a heap of rags. The rags moaned and rolled over.

A scream ripped through her. Emma scampered backward and slipped on the snowy floor and landed on the cat.

Lola yowled and streaked off.

The man sprang up and sprinted out the front door into the wintery night.

What just happened?

The wind banged the front door against the house and coolness swept in from the porch and broken skylight. Flakes of white swirled in her entryway. She limped toward the front door. A crack sliced through the silence and an ice-laden tree branch hit the ground. The streetlights flickered and cut out, blackening the neighborhood. Great. The branch must have taken down a power line. She peered down the street. There was no sign of the man, and no sign that her neighbours heard the commotion. She softly closed the door, and the bottom of it caught something and sent it clattering across the floor.

A key? She picked it up and turned it over in her fingers. He must have dropped it. It looked like the locker keys at the hospital. She stuffed it into her pocket. She'd clean up and then call the police. They could figure out what the key was for.

Lola had left a trail of small wet footprints leading to her bedroom. The cat was most certainly holed up inside her box spring under her bed again. Lola wouldn't come out until she was good and ready.

With only the moonlight to guide her, Emma examined the damage. A pile of snow melted on the table, glass covered the floor, and a long smear of blood marked her path. She felt for the shard of ceramic piercing her foot and plucked it out. It looked worse than it was.

What first? A broom or a tarp? She hobbled to the closet. Should she call the police or clean up? She reached for the broom with shaky hands. As she wrapped her fingers around the handle, a second set of feet landed with a thud and a grunt. She froze.

The man rose in the shadows and then collapsed to the floor.

She pressed her back against the wall. *Did he see her? Thank you, Lord, the lights are out!*

She slipped inside the closet fumbling with her cell phone. No service. The branch must have damaged more than a power line. Her rapid breathing wheezed loud to her ears. Pressing her ear to the door, she held her breath, hearing nothing but her heartbeat.

She knew the moment he hovered on the other side. The scent of faint pine aftershave wafted through the slats. Her heightened awareness intensified every second. She turned her head away from the crack where the door met the wall. *Is this it, Lord? Is this how I go?*

The door jerked open.

A half second of paralyzing fear stunned her before her body reacted in desperate defense. She charged and landed an elbow to his gut.

"Ommph," he whooshed.

She stomped down on his injured foot, and he howled in pain. It was hurt or be hurt. But he was more than twice her weight and quickly pinned her to the floor, holding her arms down with his knees.

"No!" She squirmed under him. "No!"

———

Ben froze. As the body beneath him writhed and whimpered, her high-pitched voice registered. "You're a woman!" He scampered back as if struck.

"Yes, I'm a woman!" She scrambled to her knees and crawled across the floor, putting as much space between them as possible. She eyed him warily. "What did you think you were attacking— my cat?" She pulled her knees into her chest and huddled into the corner.

Loathing shot through him. He'd never hurt a woman. Never. He flicked on his flashlight and aimed the beam at her face.

Wild fear leaped in her blue eyes. He held out his hands in front of him in a gesture of surrender. "I'm sorry, I thought you were—" He dropped his hands. "It doesn't matter what I thought. I'm sorry."

"It doesn't matter?" Her shrill voice rose one decibel with each word, drowning out the pounding in his skull. "It matters to me very much!"

The power flicked back on, flooding the home with light. Ben got a good look at his captive. Her waist-length auburn hair and creamy skin made a striking combination against her bright eyes. Her slight frame quivered in shock. It was no wonder he had no trouble pinning her down. She was as thin as a reed.

She stood on shaky legs. "Lola?" she called. "Lola?"

"Who's Lola?"

"M- m- my ca-a-at." She limped toward the hall.

"Are you hurt? Did I hurt you? I'm sorry. I didn't mean—" He took a step forward, and the minute his weight shifted to his bad leg he crumpled to the floor. A sharp piece of glass sliced through his sleeve like a warm knife through butter. Bright red gushed.

She jumped into action, snagging a dishcloth from the kitchen and pressing it into the gash. Jitters long gone, she was all business. "Hold this. Elevate it."

His dark eyes caught hers. She was helping?

"It will slow the flow of blood." She leaned in for a closer look. "Then we can see how serious it is." His gaze never left her face as she expertly treated his injury. He jerked when she shifted her attention to his injured leg and prodded his knee.

"I think it twisted when I fell through the skylight."

She clamped her lips together.

"I don't think you'll be walking comfortably any time soon." She turned her face away from him. "I'll get my kit." She scurried down the hall, leaving behind a trail of tiny red droplets.

"You're hurt," he called after her, stating the obvious.

"No kidding." Sarcasm colored her voice as she toted a large Rubbermaid container down the hallway. She laid out enough supplies to perform surgery.

"Are you a doctor?"

"Something like that," she murmured.

"What's your name?"

Nothing.

"I think I should know the person treating me, don't you?"

She spun around and thrust her upturned nose in his face. "I'm sorry. Am I being rude? Two men just dropped through my skylight. Forgive me if I've lost some social graces. Were you hoping for tea?" She ripped open a large bandage and slapped it on her foot. Then she grabbed an even larger one and sized it up for his arm. "Roll up your sleeve," she commanded.

He complied. She frequently moistened her lips as she worked. Her jaw clenched, and a muscle twitched in her cheek. He could have counted her heartbeat in that twitch, but her hair tumbled over her shoulder and partially blocked his view.

She continued to treat him, rolling up his pant leg, wrapping his knee, and activating a cold compress. Her glossy fingernails were neatly filed and clean. Her hands moved with an elegance that sent his heart thumping. His throat grew thick. He'd never considered how beautiful a woman's hands could be until today.

Not once did she threaten to call the police, ask him his name, or demand an explanation for his uninvited presence in her house. It piqued his journalistic mind. Ten years as an investigative reporter had taught him a lot about reading people. He'd become a sort of unofficial expert at interpreting expressions and gestures. It'd been both a blessing and a curse. His knack for seeing if a person was telling the truth came in handy with his job at Sycamore Hill's newspaper, but it also took the mystery out of relationships.

Her brow furrowed as she focused on her task. A subtle bump in the middle of her forehead held a bluish tinge. She'd have some battle wounds from tonight. That's too bad. Most women want to look their best for the holidays.

As she gently clipped the end of a tensor wrap snugly around his ankle, he'd decided that he'd like to get to know her better. Her saucy temperament and fiery retorts were a refreshing change from the type of women he usually met at church. Most were too obvious, too eager to gain their M.R.S. for his taste. Several had indicated they'd welcome an invitation to the Life House gala, but until this second, he had planned to attend alone. Would it be in poor taste to ask her on a date after damaging her house?

She wiped her hands on her thighs. "That's the best I can do." She sat across from him on the floor and finally met his eyes. "Are you going to tell me what's going on?"

"That's it? No threat to call the police?" Her matter-of-fact mannerisms were madly appealing. He shifted to the right and dug his left hand deep into his pocket.

She stiffened. "Would you like me to call the police?"

"I'm a reporter." He handed her his credentials. "I'm chasing a story. I'll pay for the damages to your house."

———

Emma took his credentials and examined them, little good it would do. She wouldn't know if they were false. She handed them back. "So, Ben Sawyer, what's the scoop? How did you end up on my roof?"

"I'll trade you details for a name." He winked.

She hesitated, hating how his playful wink flooded her with warmth. Common sense dictated she should call the police, but common sense wasn't the engine driving her train tonight. Exhaustion was. She just wanted this over. Whatever this was.

"My name's Emma. And there must have been something wrong with the skylight for it to shatter like that. I'm sure a warranty will cover it." She snagged an afghan from the sofa and perched at the island. "Your turn."

"May I?" He gestured to the seat beside her.

She nodded.

"A source put me in touch with a nurse who can support her claim that Emergence has been falsifying their drug study results. The nurse was too scared to meet in person, and my source doesn't have access to the area."

Her ears perked. She flipped open her computer and turned the screen toward him. "This study?"

"Yes!" His attention moved from the screen to her, and he examined her so closely she started to squirm. A part of her desperately wanted to know if he liked what he saw, but even more than that, she wanted to know if there was trouble with this trial. She was responsible for the people entering it. She'd arranged to have the residents of Life House apply. So many of them needed the extra income, and everything she'd read indicated it was safe to begin human trials. But if she was wrong—she couldn't even go there. She went into health care to help people, not hurt them.

"How did you know about it?" he asked.

"I graduated GU and work at Grander Hospital." Sycamore Hill was too small to have a hospital. Emma drove a half hour to the closest city while completing her education. She hated the commute, but cost-of-living made it necessary. Once she was fully qualified, she planned to start a clinic in Sycamore Hill. Her hometown needed local care. "Do you know the nurse's name?"

He shook his head. "He never gave it to me, but I asked questions that would force him to retrieve the answers from wherever he was hiding his evidence. I was following him tonight, but he got spooked and started to run. He ran into the alley back there." He nodded his head in the general direction of the grocery store on the adjacent street. "I thought I had cornered him, but he climbed up a tree and started moving across the roofs of the townhouses."

"Him?" That narrowed down the options. The hospital only had a handful of male nurses.

"I didn't figure that out until I saw him tonight."

"The key!" Emma sprung up, dug into her pocket, and pulled it out. "He dropped this when he ran out the front door." She turned it over in her hand. "I thought I recognized it. It's from the hospital. It's a locker room key."

His eyes glowed. "This is the break I've been waiting for. If we can find his files, I can break the case without involving him."

"How?"

"The evidence he's squirreled away combined with my source's testimony will bring the truth to light."

"But not tonight," Emma said firmly. "You need to get that leg elevated. Let me help you." She slipped an arm around his waist to help him hobble to the sofa.

"It has to be tonight. The trials start next week."

Emma pinched her lips, inhaling through her nose until there was no more room in her lungs. He was right. Her breath shot out of her. "Then I'll go. I can get in and out of the locker room easier." This was the best decision. Everything would be okay. No one would look twice at her.

If that were true, why did her chest tighten so painfully?

She propped up Ben's foot on the ottoman and added extra support under the knee. "It'll just take over an hour. You can wait here." She didn't wait for his reply. It wasn't like she needed his permission to return a lost key to the hospital.

Emma slid along the hospital corridor. They dimmed the lights in the evening, and the quietness of the midnight hour hummed deep in her ears. *Get in. Get the file. Get out.*

"Working late, Emma?" The head nurse pushed out the locker room doors just as Emma was about to enter. "I didn't see your name on the schedule."

"Just picking up something I forgot." Emma forced brightness into her lame excuse, but her heartbeat hammered against her ribs. What kind of wacko returned to work in the middle of the night? Her nursing career had better work out. She was not cut out for espionage.

Emma made a quick pass through the locker room, checking the changing area, showers, and lounge. Empty. She systematically worked through the lockers, stuffing the key in each one until finding the one that it fit. Bingo! She riffled through a knapsack hanging on a hook without luck. She moved the shampoo and body wash from the top shelf. Nothing. She leafed through a magazine resting on the bottom.

The locker room door opened and muffled voices grew louder.

Emma froze. Her heart thrashed in her ears as the conversation grew in volume. Footsteps padded her way. This was it. This was how she would lose her job. She'd never work again. Sycamore Hill would never get a clinic. The drug trial would start and people would get hurt and—

The footsteps stopped in the nearest aisle. The ting of a metallic door opening and closing vibrated through the room. Then, the conversation grew quieter. She heard the soft whoosh of the locker room door closing.

Emma sagged against the wall. The handle of the neighboring locker dug into her spine as she slid to the floor. What was she doing? She couldn't afford to lose her job.

From her position on the floor, she saw it. The white corner of a paper file jutted out from the very bottom of the locker. It was hidden between two textbooks.

Maybe she could rock a double life?

Emma stuffed the file into her shirt, zipped up her jacket, and hightailed it out of there.

By the time she returned home, her pulse had returned to normal, the swelling on Ben's knee was reduced, and the snow had stopped.

Ben flipped through the papers. His gaze moved over the pages she'd read in her car. He lifted his face, and for the first time, it lacked creases of tension. "Thank you. This will be enough to stop the study until it can be thoroughly investigated." He pulled his phone from his pocket and called his editor with the update.

Emma's skin tingled. Exhilaration shot through her veins as

she listened to his side of the conversation. They'd done something good here. Her insides vibrated as if they'd been hooked up to an I.V. of pure caffeine. "That was thrilling," she said when he had disconnected his call. "I felt like a secret agent."

She crouched down and checked his knee. "Swelling has reduced." She gently prodded it. "That's good." Her fingertips tingled, and a shiver of pleasure tiptoed down her spine.

Ben grinned. "Addicting, isn't it? The adrenaline. But riding it sometimes leads to injury." He lifted his chin toward his knee. "I'm glad you're okay. I wouldn't have been able to live with myself if you'd run into trouble." He hoisted himself up and hobbled to the kitchen.

Emma's chest prickled.

"Got a mop?" He tipped his head back and stared at the damaged ceiling.

They mopped the floor and somehow managed to hang a temporary tarp over the skylight. While they worked side-by-side, they swapped faith stories. She learned Ben had a married sister and a nephew. His parents lived in town, and he had always wanted to be a reporter. He came to faith in college when his roommate invited him to a debate about creation versus evolution. No one had been more surprised than him when God turned his heart. Now, he was passionate about writing truth and exposing lies. Soon they were laughing together like old friends.

The sun peeked over the horizon. Emma flicked her wrist. 7:20 a.m. Whether she wanted to or not, she had to get ready for the day. She'd offered her services as a medical volunteer at a community event that started at 8:00 a.m. She accompanied Ben to the door, wishing she could read his expression. Did he enjoy their evening as much as she did, or was this kind of action-packed night normal for him?

He lingered at the door and leaned in.

Was he going to kiss her? Did she want him to?

His voice dipped, "This may be a strange thing to say considering, well . . ." He gestured to his injured leg. "But I had a great time tonight."

Warmth rushed to her cheeks. "Me, too."

His gaze softened and swept over her. It felt like the gentlest caress.

She lifted her chin and held her breath. The motion swayed her forward, and she nearly brushed up against him. The air vibrated with energy.

He reached out to sweep a strand of hair from her eyes. "You're probably not available, I mean, someone must have already asked you." The way he fumbled for his words filled her with hope. His face and his neck reddened. He cleared his throat. "What I'm trying to say is, are you free for dinner tonight?"

She wilted. Any other night but tonight! "I can't. I'm attending the fundraiser tonight."

A surprising light filled his eyes, and he chuckled. "The gala for Life House? That happens to be where I had hoped to take you for dinner."

"I'd love to." She twirled her hair around her index finger and glanced at her damaged ceiling.

I said the front door, God, but I'll take the skylight.

Friday 7:00 a.m. Eli and Meg

7:05 a.m. Only one minute after the last time Eli Martin checked. He stuffed his hands into the front pockets of his hoodie to stop from obsessively watching the digits change on his watch screen.

"Let's go." His roommate, Addison, nudged him. "You probably freaked her out when you called it a date."

"Meg wouldn't miss this. We've been training for weeks." The fundraising race started in less than an hour. The runners all donned some sort of holiday wear. They raced in Santa suits, Santa hats, elf shoes, reindeer ears, and ugly Christmas sweaters. The Sycamore Hill at Sunrise show even covered the race for its web station. The race had become a big deal, second only to the black-tie gala in raising funds for Life House.

"I didn't scare her," Eli said. At least he didn't think he scared her. They planned to meet on the trail and walk together to the starting point outside The Muffin Man. It was going to be their warm-up. They'd been on-again, off-again jogging together since they met six months ago on the trails. Eli was building up to a friendship so he could ask her out. Sometimes Addison joined them, but more often than not, it was just Eli and Meg.

Addison laughed as he stooped to tie his shoelace. "She probably went to the starting point alone. Didn't know how to let you down easy."

Eli looked past Addison at the mostly-empty running path behind them. A soft dusting of snow covered the trail. The cold weather always scared off all but the most dedicated runners. "No way. She'd never run alone."

"How do you know? You hardly know her." Addison stood and began twisting at the waist to warm up his lower back muscles.

Sure, he didn't know where Meg lived, her phone number, or even her last name. She was pretty tight-lipped about personal details. But he *knew* her. He knew she'd moved to Sycamore Hill almost a year ago to get away from a boyfriend who couldn't handle getting dumped. He knew that dogs terrified her because her ex had trained them to be savage. Eli knew she loved pumpkin spiced coffee, that she was the speaker at the gala fundraiser later this evening, and she was in school to obtain her Landscape Architect Degree. He knew she had a kind heart, because one day she stopped to give her running gloves to a homeless man, and he knew she went to church every Sunday. He sat exactly three rows behind her. Close enough to see her but far enough away to not smother her with too much attention.

But mostly, he knew because of that. Eli nodded to a poster stapled to a nearby tree. Kim Jansen had posted a picture of her missing boxer. Eli knew Baxter wasn't violent, but Meg wouldn't risk running into the animal. Its muscular frame and square jaw would trigger too many memories. "She won't run alone until they find this dog."

And she was never late.

Addison bent forward at the waist and grasped the toes of his sneakers, stretching the back of his legs. "So, she decided to skip the race. You'll catch her tomorrow. Let's go, Romeo."

"She wouldn't skip the race. The fundraiser is too important to her." Eli suspected Meg had suffered some sort of abuse in her past.

Eli stared down the path in the direction from which Meg usually arrived. Any second now he'd see her pounding up the pavement with a half-smile and long ponytail, wearing her favorite royal blue running jacket. She'd apologize for being late, saying she stopped to help a lost kid find his grandma or something like that.

Addison's hand landed heavy on Eli's shoulder. "As your friend, it's necessary to point out that you're moving from concerned acquaintance into weirdo stalker territory." Addison grinned as he said it, but he stood his ground.

Eli did have a habit of obsessing over things, but not girls. Never girls. Despite the fact he'd never had any trouble getting dates, he had yet to meet a woman who would make him happy to give up a late afternoon hockey scrimmage or watching football with the guys at night.

But Meg had potential. She didn't flirt or try to impress him. Meg didn't care that he came from money, or she didn't know that he came from money. Meg was the first genuine woman he'd met in a long time. She enjoyed his attention, but she also appeared utterly whole without it. It was maddeningly attractive.

"Stalker? Pfft," he dismissed Addison with a snort, but he couldn't help second-guessing himself. Had he crossed some sort of line? Is that why she wasn't here?

"She's fine," Addison pressed. "She probably slept in because she forgot to set her alarm."

"The night before the race?" Eli cast another look down the path.

"I'm going." Addison stuffed his earbuds into his ears. "I know I've lost when you get that puppy dog look." Addison lumbered off, calling over his shoulder, "I'll catch you at the start line."

Eli lifted a hand to acknowledge that he heard his friend. He decided to wait five more minutes. He looked at his watch again. The sensation that something wasn't right with Meg increased. Maybe he was crazy. Maybe everything was fine, but he wouldn't be able to live with himself if something happened and he did nothing. He began to jog toward town, praying they'd meet on the path.

About ten minutes later, closer to where the trees thinned and the businesses thickened, a commotion outside The Muffin Man ratcheted up his pulse.

A crowd gathered near the side of the shop in front of the alley. Eli slowed to a walk. His chest tightened.

The Sycamore Hill at Sunrise host stood at the corner of the building and spoke into the camera. "I'm coming to you live from The Muffin Man, the start line for the Home for Christmas Road Race. The race set to begin in thirty minutes will be delayed until animal control contains a dog that has cornered a young woman."

Eli shoved his way through the growing crowd. He reached the edge as a growl overtook the commentary. Then, there was a familiar flash of blue.

"Meg!" He lunged toward her, pushing past the proprietor of The Muffin Man and the local pastor, who'd been inching closer to the animal.

"It's Kim's dog," they called out. "She's on her way. We don't know what has it all riled up."

Baxter advanced, backing Meg deeper into the alley.

Eli snagged a stick from the ground as he approached Baxter

from behind. *Lord, I don't want to hurt Kim's dog. Please bring this to a peaceful resolution.*

————

Meg didn't know if she should feel relief or concern that Eli rounded the corner of The Muffin Man and entered the alley. What on earth was he doing? He crept closer and closer to the dog. "Hey, Baxter, it's me," he crooned. "You know me."

Sweat beaded on his forehead. His eyes, locked on the dog, widened as she moved in his peripheral range of sight. When Eli's gaze darted to her, the dog took another step toward him.

Eli prodded Baxter with the stick.

"I don't think that's a good idea," Meg said. The animal looked nothing like the happy pet Kim once introduced to her. Baxter wasn't just a friendly dog; he was great with people. Especially kids. He needed to be since Kim interacted with so many families in her ministry. Meg didn't particularly like Baxter, but she'd never feared him until this morning.

Baxter gave a yowl at Eli's poke, but held his ground.

Eli lunged for the dog's collar, and Baxter dodged to the right.

"Run, Meg!"

Instead of running toward safety, she retreated. Eli's face contorted into an expression of confusion. She didn't have time to explain. Every time she spoke, the dog refocused on her. She needed Baxter preoccupied with something else. Someone else.

Lord, protect Eli.

The dog regrouped and emitted a low and throaty warning.

Round two.

The animal circled, herding Eli closer to Meg. It blocked their escape, but she didn't care, as long as he could get between the dog and the dumpster. Two men closed in from behind, unnoticed. Maybe they'd make it out of this. All of them.

Meg estimated the distance to the back fence that closed in the alley. Six feet? Eight feet? They'd never get over the chain link fence before the dog got one of them.

Lord, keep us safe.

Eli's lips moved like he was praying, too. "I'll distract the dog," he said. "You get over the fence."

She shook her head. "No."

That single word swivelled Baxter's attention back to her. She clamped her mouth shut. No more words.

Eli's body went rigid at her refusal. She got it. He didn't know her. Didn't have any reason to trust her. A guy should know the woman he's about to die for.

The dog swivelled its head from them to behind the dumpster. It made a move in the direction of the trash.

Meg crouched. It was now or never.

Muscles rippled down Baxter's quivering body. He edged closer to the dumpster, and Eli inserted himself between her and Baxter again. The move was so heroic, so noble, that her insides liquified for a millisecond. But she wasn't the one in need of rescuing.

"Go!" Eli roared at the dog.

That was a bad idea. Really bad. *Lord, help Eli. Help me.*

Baxter showed his teeth.

A muffled sound to the left caught the dog's ear. It cocked its head.

No!

Eli grabbed her hand, but she wrenched free and dove behind the dumpster.

Eli threw himself at the dog, and the cries and screams from the crowd only seemed to exasperate the animal.

Meg peeked from her hiding place. The dog turned toward Eli. "Run!" she shouted.

Eli sprinted toward the back fence.

Three feet... two... Come on.

Paws hit Eli's mid-back just as Pastor Owen and the owner of The Muffin Man snagged Baxter's collar. Meg's breath caught in her throat. Eli's cheek bounced off the concrete, and he covered his head with his arms.

Two others arrived on the scene and looped the snare of a restraining pole around Baxter, pulling him toward a truck. Behind them, another vehicle skidded to a stop, and a volunteer from the clinic jumped out.

It was over. They made. They all made it.

———

When the weight of Baxter failed to land fully on him, Eli peeked. Addison was right; Eli didn't know Meg. He didn't know her at all. His head pounded. He didn't even know he'd been holding his breath until it rocketed out. He rolled onto his stomach. That's when he heard it.

A child's whimper.

Of course! Kim's dog was fiercely protective of children. He wasn't trying to hurt them; he was trying to protect the child from them.

Meg rocked a weeping toddler in her arms, making comforting sounds. "Shhh. It's okay. I've got you. You're safe."

"Amber? Amber!" A woman ran into the alley.

At the sound of her voice, fresh wails ripped from Amber. She reached out her arms for her mother, and Meg relinquished her.

"Thank you!" The woman's entire body shook as she cried. "I looked away for only a second."

Meg's body held rigid for another second, then she sank to the ground, trembling violently. Eli helped her into a sitting position.

"It's not Baxter's fault," Meg called to the men loading him into the truck. "I saw some teens getting into mischief back here. They didn't know Amber had wandered back here. I think Baxter was trying to protect her from them, and I got stuck in the middle."

One officer closed the back of the truck and waved an acknowledgement that he had heard her. His co-worker approached with a notebook in hand.

"I know the owner," Eli added. "It's Kim Jansen, and Baxter is not violent."

He asked a few more questions before thanking them. "We'll contact Kim and make sure the dog gets home."

The medical volunteer crouched in front of them as soon as animal control left. "You guys were lucky. It looks like you're mostly just scratched."

A trail of blood trickled down Meg's forearm. "It's not from Baxter," she assured her.

Meg leaned into Eli as the volunteer turned his palms over and examined the injuries on them. Meg tucked herself under his free arm and looked up at him through ridiculously long lashes.

"You guys look good. Let me grab a few more bandages and antibiotic cream and you'll be all set." The medic hurried back to her vehicle.

Eli wiped away a smear of blood on her cheek with the pad of his thumb, letting his palm linger, cupping her face. Their eyes locked.

Meg's trembling subsided, and her features softened into a smile. Her expression held no regret.

Addison was right. Eli didn't know this woman, not by a long shot. But he sure hoped to get the chance one day.

Friday 6:00 p.m. and Saturday morning, Jackson and Kim

Kimberly Jansen doesn't have an original thought in her pretty little brain.

Kim shoved the insulting memory back. It had been almost a year since she last spoke with her ex and held her baby boy in her arms, but Hayden's words still surfaced in moments of stress. *Useless and unremarkable.*

And right now, unprepared. Kim hadn't yet pulled together her closing comments for the evening. She simply hadn't had the headspace. How could she possibly keep her mind focused on a party when tomorrow she would hold Oliver again for the first time in over a year? But cancelling the gala wasn't an option. The future of Life House depended on it.

Christmas was one of the busiest times for the skeleton crew that ran the organization. The holidays brought out the best—and worst—in people. Their temporary shelter filled to capacity every December. On top of managing all that, Kim organized their annual black-tie fundraiser on a shoestring budget. A budget that didn't allow for an easy menu change when The Muffin Man said an essential ingredient had been recalled or when Gloria's return prompted last-minute adjustments to their seating plan.

She pressed her hand over her stomach. *Breathe. It'll be fine.* She'd put out those fires easily enough, and she'd stomp out any new sparks. And tomorrow, she'd hold Oliver. Kim's arms ached with longing. She folded them over her middle and forced a smile as she refocused on the woman standing in front of her, the reason for the new seating plan.

"Thank you for accommodating Gloria," Teresa said.

"It's my pleasure." Kim would hardly deny the town's founding family two extra seats at their table for the prodigal daughter now returned. "I understand wanting to celebrate her homecoming and keep her close."

Teresa Sycamore's gaze had been moving over the crowd filling the meeting room of Sycamore Hill Community Hall, but now it locked on Kim. The happy buzz of conversation faded into the background. The fabric of Teresa's navy-blue gown rippled like a wave as she cocked her head to the side. "Yes, I imagine you do understand. Did I hear correctly that Oliver comes home tomorrow?"

"Yes." Kim smoothed trembling hands down her front. Oliver hadn't even been a year old when Hayden picked him up for a scheduled visitation and never returned. The police called it a parental abduction, and Kim filed a report that Hayden had taken Oliver out of the country without her permission. After all the years she spent walking alongside women as they navigated family court, she never thought that one day she'd be advocating for herself or her child.

"And still, you managed to pull this impressive evening together. Well done." Teresa lifted her chin appreciatively at the tight groupings of Christmas bulbs that provided a pop of color. Stockings hung from holders spaced evenly along the window ledges, and garlands wound around the perimeter of the room. Kim knew they rimmed the entire large room because she had raced around the space seconds before the guests arrived, plucking all the tiny Santa ornaments from the greenery. Their biggest financial supporter did not *do Santa*, and Life House couldn't afford to lose their donation.

"Thank you." Kim shifted her weight from left to right, uncomfortable under Teresa's perceptive gaze. The hem of Kim's dress dusted the floor and hid, for the most part, well-worn high heels. Kim had snagged the dress on clearance because she put every spare penny toward lawyer fees. But once she had Oliver in her arms, it would be worth every sacrifice. One nice thing about being an unremarkable woman was that no one seemed to notice her discounted frock, worn shoes, or broken heart.

Except for Teresa Sycamore. They were kindred souls. They both knew a little bit about losing a child for a season and the joy of that child's return. Would Oliver's story end as happily as Gloria's? Kim cut her gaze to the Sycamore table. Gloria and Pastor Owen shared a laugh. This was her first Christmas with her family in years.

And it would be Kim's first Christmas with Oliver. Tomorrow, she'd have her baby boy back. Her stomach flipped. She just had to get through tonight.

"Can I ask what will happen to Gloria now the news about Emergence has broken? Will it clear her name and reputation?"

Teresa's eyes softened. "It won't happen overnight, but if everything Gloria suspects is true, an investigation will eventually clear her name. They expect the trial to take about six months."

"I'm happy to hear that she'll be cleared."

Mr. Sycamore, looking dapper in a three-piece suit, tapped the microphone on the stage, and everyone's attention turned to him. Teresa gave Kim's hand a gentle squeeze before rejoining her table.

"Thank you for attending tonight," Mr. Sycamore said. "We know the holidays are busy and there are many extra events filling your calendars. It means a lot that you would set aside a few hours for a shared meal and to hear more about the ministry of Life House. Before we begin, I'm thrilled to announce that the hospital has pledged to make a large donation to the charity of my daughter's choice. She chose Life House. Gloria, with help from Ben Sawyer and Emma Powles, exposed a flaw in Emergence Pharmaceutical's upcoming research study."

Polite applause filled the room.

"Let's also acknowledge Ben and Emma and the risks they took to secure the evidence and save Grander Hospital and Grander University potential millions in future legal settlements." He nodded at the couple sitting at a round table to the right of the Sycamore table.

The clapping continued.

While the entire room looked at Ben and Emma, Kim studied Gloria. Kim wanted to do more to thank Gloria for protecting the residents of Life House, but Gloria wanted none of it. She said being able to come home and hold her head high was enough reward.

Once the applause died down, Mr. Sycamore continued. "You're here tonight to learn a bit more about the organization that so many people in our community hold dear to their hearts. Meg Gilmore is a former resident of Life House, and she's going to share a bit about her experience. Let's welcome Meg to the stage."

More polite applause accompanied Meg as she moved hesitantly from her table where she sat with Eli and made her way to the front of the room. She tucked a long strand of hair around her ear.

Kathryn followed Meg with her camera from the side of the room. She covered tonight's events for her web station.

Kim knew that Meg hated public speaking, but she was determined to share her story so the ministry that helped her would continue to be available for others, even after the debacle with her dog this morning. When Meg's gaze collided with Kim's, Kim nodded encouragingly. Meg had already done the hardest part—she'd told Eli her story. She had been trying to work up the courage to do so for weeks. Eli supported her, but it didn't mean the others in town would. Kim still didn't know how to wrap up tonight's event in a way that helped the town accept Meg's story and continue to support the ministry. Nor did she know how to focus on tonight when tomorrow was the day she'd hold her son again.

Kim gave her head a shake. Meg needed Kim to pay attention and pray for her, not fret about her unprepared closing comments or be distracted with tomorrow's reunion.

Kim struggled to find something fresh to say about Christmas that encouraged their donors to open their checkbooks every year. When she added to that her shock over Hayden's twin brother, Jackson, contacting her about Oliver, it was no wonder she'd slipped in her usual preparedness. If Meg followed the script she'd shared with Kim earlier, Kim had about five minutes to figure it out.

Meg began softly, "I came to Life House because I needed a safe place to stay. They cared for me emotionally, mentally, and spiritually. They were not intimidated by the anger in my heart."

Pressure built behind Kim's eyes. She knew something about anger. She was angry about Hayden, angry at feeling powerless, angry about laws that needed something tragic to happen before impacting circumstances, even angry at God for allowing loss and hardship. When Hayden left, Kim had to work through the very same steps she gave the women at Life House.

"I was not ready to hear what my counsellor told me." Meg momentarily flicked her gaze to Kim. "Still, she loved me. She listened. And when she suggested maybe God was doing something that could only be accomplished by Him helping me endure the trial instead of taking the trial away, I shut her down. I didn't know how to endure. I only knew how to escape."

Meg's hands twisted in front of her body. The skinny podium couldn't hide her discomfort. She shifted her weight from left to right. "In the past, when trouble came, I fixed my *problems* with pills—" Meg put air quotes around the word *problems*, "—and I wasn't sorry. When I finally told my counsellor all the things I had done—the things I had tried to do—I expected her to evict me. I mean, how can a place with the word *life* in the title welcome someone who tried to end hers?" Meg snorted a half laugh and half cry. She wiped her nose and pushed on as the room struggled to decide what to do with her confession.

"That was when I learned what pro-life really meant. Pro-life is caring for all life—including mine." Meg lifted her chin. She met individual gazes in the audience and didn't blink, not even when she locked eyes with Kim.

Kim's insides twisted. Was she pro-life when it came to Hayden and his family? She didn't want to soften toward the people that had kept Oliver all these months. She didn't want to consider their feelings, fears, or position. She'd needed her anger to survive the last year, but now that she was on the cusp of getting her son back, she didn't know what to do with it or how to get rid of it.

Meg's voice strengthened. "I arrived here wearing the labels of foolish, victim, shame, and failure. But now, I have a new identity.

Jesus calls me holy, and when I failed to act accordingly, He offered me His holiness to cover my sin and shame."

Gloria reached across their table and placed her hand on top of her mother's. Teresa's eyes softened as she focused on her daughter. A tiny smile curved up the corners of her mouth. All the hurt and anger caused by Gloria's departure evaporated upon her return. Only joy remained, infusing Kim with hope.

"Because of Christ," Meg drew back Kim's attention, "I can stand here knowing the worst things I've ever done don't define me because *He* defines me." Kim followed Meg's gaze to the back of the room where Eli sat, nodding along with Meg.

Thankfulness for his support swelled in her heart. Meg needed a friend like Eli.

Everybody needed an Eli.

Tentacles of tension spread through Kim's middle and wrapped around her lungs. She held her breath.

Meg bit down on her lower lip. Her chin quivered. The silence grew lengthy enough that several guests shifted in their seats.

Lord, help her. Protect her fragile faith. Give her boldness.

"I'd only been here two months when I learned I was sixteen weeks pregnant, and everything inside of me wanted to just make the problem go away."

The entire room inhaled one collective breath as the meaning of Meg's words registered. The uncomfortable silence shifted into something unidentifiable. Kim couldn't tell if it was good or bad.

"My plans for an education and a new start evaporated," Meg said. "I was angry again. Angry at myself and at God. But after all I had learned about love and sacrifice and what it means to put someone else ahead of me, I couldn't make the same choices I had made before."

Lydia Bretford joined Meg on the stage with a squirming eight-month-old on her hip. She shifted to face the audience and lifted the child, tugging down the blanket the girl pressed to her skin so they could see her tiny face. "Some of you have already met Sonya, our adopted daughter." Lydia's soft words were thick and filled with emotion. "What Meg once viewed as an end to her dreams, we saw as the beginning of something new."

Just like that, indescribable peace descended. Kim had her closing message. Hadn't Mary's world shattered? Weren't her plans for a wedding and a future replaced with confusion and fear? Joseph had planned to leave her quietly and end their engagement. Scripture doesn't say how Joseph felt, but Kim imagined anger was only one of the emotions that must have attached to the confusion coursing through his veins. Mary was pregnant while engaged to him.

Most of the women who came through their doors could relate to how Mary must have felt. But however impossible it must have seemed, God was with Mary. She gave birth to Jesus and named Him Emmanuel, which meant God with us.

At this moment, Kim identified even more with Joseph, the man who held the power to send Mary away yet stepped up and followed God toward the dawn of salvation's advent.

God with us. With Mary and Joseph. Meg and Eli. With Lydia and Sonya. With Oliver. With Kim. God was with them.

The peace in her heart expanded, covering tomorrow's appointment with the immigration officer and Oliver's Uncle Jackson, who was bringing him home. Jackson had stepped up and done what was right despite the personal cost, just like Joseph.

Kim shoved the thought aside.

"One day," Lydia said, "Sonya will ask why she was given to us, and I am prepared to share with her a story about sacrificial, costly love, the kind offered by our heavenly Father and the kind offered by her earthly mother."

Kim climbed the platform stairs as the ladies descended. She pulled Meg into a brief hug and whispered into her ear, "That was amazing."

With all eyes on her, Kim launched into the biblical tale about a great love, a huge sacrifice, and God coming to be with us. Her pretty little brain didn't need a fresh angle on Christmas because the best words of hope come from a story from long ago.

———

Jackson McGregor paced back and forth in the small meeting room at the airport. Hayden's ex would walk through the doors and reclaim Oliver at any minute.

He shifted the sleepy boy on his hip. He was closing in on two years old. He didn't even remember his mother, but that didn't change things. At least, that's what Jackson kept telling himself as he worked with the Canadian Embassy's immigration officer and the Royal Canadian Mounted Police to track Kimberly Jansen to the small town of Sycamore Hill.

Oliver whimpered, rubbing his face into Jackson's shoulder. He pressed his nose into the boy's hair and inhaled. He smelled of sunshine and Indonesian wind.

Had Jackson suspected his twin brother had kidnapped Oliver, he would have made things right a long time ago. But Hayden arrived at their parents' mission in Indonesia with a sob story about the mother's unexpected death and how she had no family. According to his parents, Hayden had hung around for almost a year, playing the part of a doting father, but it was only a matter of time. Jackson's parents waited two weeks before contacting him after Hayden split. It took him another week to arrange a leave of absence from his job as police officer, and then he hopped on a plane. That was four months ago—four months of red tape, courts, and investigations that all led to this moment.

To good-bye.

Stuart, the immigration officer he'd gotten to know so well, wordlessly set a bottle of water on the table for Jackson.

"Thanks." Jackson massaged tiny circles into Oliver's back. Emotion clogged his throat. He swallowed hard, forcing himself to dwell on the truth. Returning Oliver to his mother was the most unselfish thing he'd ever witnessed his parents do, and he'd seen them do a lot of good over his years in ministry.

His parents had started to suspect something wasn't right with Hayden's story long before he left. By the time Jackson arrived, they'd taken the first steps of contacting the Canadian Embassy and sharing their suspicions with the immigration officer there. The RCMP confirmed Oliver's mother was alive and searching for her son.

Stuart's phone vibrated on the table. "She's on her way up."

Jackson stood near the wall of windows that framed the airport meeting room. He kept his eyes fixed on the far corner of the hall. His heart hammered in his chest. She'd round that corner any second now, and his life would never be the same. Three, two—

"Look, Buddy. That's your mamma." Jackson pointed at Kim, whose wide eyes darted left and right until they landed on them.

Jackson hoisted Oliver up a little bit higher. *Lord, we're gonna need your help.*

"Mamma?" Oliver repeated as he plucked his finger from his mouth and pointed it at her.

Jackson tightened his arms around his nephew. This wasn't going to be easy, but the right thing rarely was.

———

Kim's watery gaze latched onto Oliver. He had her eyes and the same heart-shaped face, but it was fuller now. His pale skin had darkened under the Indonesian sun. But, of course, she'd known of these changes already. Jackson had sent hundreds of photographs as they prepared for this day, but seeing Olivier in person instead of on video was . . . was . . . she didn't know what it was.

Surreal. Miraculous.

Her vision clouded, and she nearly buckled at the knees. Her lawyer's arm shot out to support her, but she stiffened against the sudden weakness. She wasn't going to faint. She was going to be present for every second. She'd waited so long for this. Prayed so hard.

Her lawyer held open the door for her.

Her eyes never left Oliver as she entered the meeting room, not even as a roar filled her ears, and her stomach vibrated as if a flutter of butterflies had been set free.

"Let me." Hayden-but-not-Hayden pulled out a chair and motioned for her to sit.

The familiar cadence of Hayden's voice sent a chill down her spine and sparked the anger she'd been working so hard to douse. Jackson sounded—and looked—just like his twin. Talking with Jackson through video chats hadn't triggered her like seeing him in person did. All her unresolved feelings rushed to the surface.

Jackson is not Hayden. If she needed any proof of that, it was sitting on Jackson's hip and looking at her with a curious smile.

"Would you like to hold your son?" A barely perceptible crack in Jackson's voice was the only indication that he struggled with this moment as much as she did.

No, that wasn't right. Not as much as her. No one had struggled through this season as much as she had.

Kim's eyes flooded. She couldn't take in a full breath. She

reached out trembling hands, but Oliver twisted back into Jackson's arms. Pain sliced through her even as logic reminded her that he couldn't possibly remember her. Their video calls couldn't adequately prepare him for this moment any more than they could prepare her. Jealousy spurted like a geyser she struggled to plug.

Jackson squatted down in front of her chair and positioned himself to turn Oliver's face toward her. "It's nice to finally meet you."

His deep timbre dragged her gaze back to his. Bringing Oliver back to Canada meant he'd permanently damaged his relationship with his twin. Pain and sorrow filled his eyes as his attention lingered on Oliver, drinking him in much like Kim, but for different reasons. Kim gulped as a woman denied for too long, and Jackson savoured this moment as one who might never find refreshment again. Hayden's twin brother was identical in every way except the ones that mattered—character, faith, and integrity. Pent-up anger and jealousy melted into hope. This didn't have to mark the end. Kim held the power to create something new.

She smiled briefly, letting the magnet of her beautiful boy with the long, dark lashes, flushed cheeks, and pouty lips pull her back. She held out one finger, and Oliver wrapped his wet fist around it. It took some coaxing, but Oliver eventually came into her arms, and she buried her nose in his downy hair.

A man she assumed to be the immigration officer made a noise in this throat. "When you're ready, we have some things to go over with you."

"Give her a minute," Jackson cut in, his words gravelly and rough.

"I can't believe you've had him all this time." Kim's attention roamed over her son, checking every limb and joint.

"My parents did," he corrected her. "They're missionaries in Indonesia. I'm a police officer in Ontario."

Right. She knew that. Hayden had told her all about them. It was why she'd assumed he was a believer, but she'd learned the hard way that being the child of missionaries didn't guarantee personal faith. There'd been enough red flags that she should have known better, especially when she considered what she did for a living, but she'd been swept into the romance.

"Had I known," Jackson's voice cracked, and he levelled a look at her. He waited until she lifted her gaze to his. "I would have intervened sooner. I'm so sorry for all you've endured."

Her heart clenched like a wrung-out dishcloth. She didn't want to like Jackson. She didn't want to care. All she wanted was to keep Oliver close and all potential threats away. Her son drifted off to sleep, his cheek pressed against her shoulder and his mouth gaping slightly. The weight of his sweaty body against hers warmed places in her soul that had been cold for so long. Her arms were full, but Jackson's parents' arms were empty. The enormity of Jackson's sacrifice—their sacrifice—settled heavily.

A great love. A huge sacrifice. Difficult obedience lived out by God's people. The message of Christmas is the advent of hope.

"We'd like to be part of Oliver's life." Jackson's declaration words scratched at the raw edges of her wounds. "My parents and me."

She tightened her arms around Oliver, and he stirred. When he lifted his face to hers, his bottom lips jutted out and trembled. He reached for Jackson again.

"Hayden knows he can't return to Canada without facing the consequences," Jackson redirected Oliver back to her. He pulled a small toy from the pack at his feet and handed it to him. "You have nothing to fear from him or from us."

Kim pressed her lips together. They'd risked so much to bring

Oliver home. She inhaled and held onto her breath. *Lord, give me wisdom.*

She felt God asking her to trust that this day and every day after was from Him.

"I think having you here would help Oliver settle. And invite your family. Please. Oliver will miss them."

The tightness in Jackson's features loosened. "They're waiting on standby at the airport in Indonesia."

Kim laughed. Of course, they were. They loved Oliver. It was her first real laugh in months. Maybe even all year. God was with her. Had always been with her.

Jackson twisted his lips to the right. "I hear Sycamore Hill is a nice place to live." He locked an adoring gaze on his nephew. "Are the police open to transfers?"

Kim bit the inside of her cheek. "I don't know about that, but Oliver could use an uncle." And she could use a friend. A flutter of possibility filled her insides.

Jackson lifted a water bottle from the table and held it up as if making a toast. "To second chances and new beginnings in Sycamore Hill."

Kim's chest swelled as Oliver popped his thumb into his mouth and nestled his head in the curve of her neck. As his hot breath dampened her skin, thankfulness to the God who provided far more than she could have asked or imagined filled her. She not only had Oliver back, but a whole new family that loved him as much as she did. She gently pressed her lips to Oliver's temple and looked over his downy hair to meet Jackson's gaze. "To sweet beginnings," she echoed.

The Sycamore Standoff

A MAN WITH A PLAN, A WOMAN WITH A PAST,
AND A THORNY ADVENTURE CALLED LOVE.

Landscape Architect Meg Gilmore's past resurfaces, threatening
the harmony she's fought to cultivate. She's forced to confront the
powerful family of Eli Martin, a friend she thought she could
trust. With a 250-year-old tree—the very heart of Sycamore Hill—
at stake, Meg and Eli's goals intertwine. For now.

Eli's roots run as deep as the ancient tree, and his noble intentions clash with familial expectations. He tries to help Meg—the
first woman to see beyond his wealth and status—but only jeopar-
dizes their future. Will Eli and Meg find their way out of the weeds
and let love bloom, or will their secrets tear them apart?

THE
Sycamore
STANDOFF

STACEY WEEKS

Spring

One

Something wasn't right. Meg Gilmore stopped abruptly on the sidewalk in front of her cedar-sided historical home. As she squinted at the tiny one-bedroom bungalow, the hairs on the back of her neck lifted. An unseasonal shiver rippled down her spine. Her backpack slipped off her shoulder and landed on the ground with a thud.

The Canadian flag mounted to the right of the front door rippled in the warm, late-afternoon breeze. The vintage mailbox remained closed. Tulips and daffodils waved a happy greeting from their sunny spot in the front garden. Nothing was trampled. Nothing appeared out of place. Everything looked just as she'd left it this morning.

Yet it all *felt* wrong. The double-check-your-locks, peek-in-the-closet, and look-behind-the-shower-curtain kind of wrong. Meg's legs quivered, and she settled a hand over her midsection. She couldn't explain why. There was no reason for the chill filling her core or her instinct to retreat.

Meg hadn't felt this kind of inexplicable apprehension since . .

. well, she really didn't want to think about *that*. Straightening her spine, she picked up her bag. Things were different now. She sucked in a deep breath, marched to the front door, jabbed her key into the lock, and twisted. The lock clicked open as expected, and she gave the door a trepidatious shove.

Her breath shot out of her. *See. Everything is fine.*

Finding an adorable house in a historical neighborhood in Sycamore Hill had been one more rung on her ladder toward independence. Sure, she didn't own it. And yes, it was the smallest house on the street. But scraping together the first and last month's rent to secure the place while studying as a full-time student at Grander University and working part-time at The Muffin Man boosted her confidence. And she'd done it all by herself.

Her keys clinked against the ceramic rim of the shallow, catch-all bowl on the entry table. In less than a minute, Meg moved through the entire house, tidying a stack of books here and a throw blanket there. She snagged her journal from where she'd left it this morning on the round table in the breakfast nook. Everything was fine. Normal. Just as it should be. Just as it had always been since she arrived in Sycamore Hill. But if that were true, why did an invisible weight press on her chest, making it difficult to take in a full breath?

Meg hugged her journal. Journaling usually filled her soul with a cathartic calm—the kind of peace missing from her messed-up insides right now. Her counselor-turned-friend, Kim—trustworthy from the days Meg lived in Sycamore Hill's local shelter, Life House—would tell her to work it out on paper. But Meg had graduated from their program nearly a year ago, and she didn't want to write. She wanted to talk.

Lord, You say to pray about everything, so here it is. Something feels off. Her eyelids fell closed, and she inhaled a focused, deep breath. *Help me remember that You are with me always.*

A sudden vibration in her back pocket made her yelp, and then laugh. Rubbing her palm over her galloping heart, Meg forced her uncooperative gaze to focus on the text message from Eli. *Meet me at Alfred in 10?*

She gave it a thumbs up, and the reply went out with a quiet whoosh. This was ridiculous. Meg tossed her knapsack onto her bed as she passed the open bedroom door. The smooth, undisturbed quilt sagged under the weight of her textbooks. The bedroom was the only separate space in the house, if you didn't count the restroom. Having come full circle, Meg sat down on the small bench near the front door. There was no logical reason for her rising panic.

But it happened like that sometimes. Coming out of nowhere and gut-punching the breath from her lungs.

A burning sensation scorched the back of her throat. She tugged off the ballet flats she'd worn to school and pulled on a pair of socks and sneakers. Outside the paned glass back door, the sun remained high in the sky, having only partly begun its descent into evening. Hours of daylight remained—not that she needed hours. Every amenity Sycamore Hill offered its residents was within a five-minute walk from her house. Meg shut and locked the door behind her and headed toward the center of town. With every step that put distance between her and her house, the creepy feeling of being watched receded, and her labored breathing eased.

By the time Meg rounded the corner onto Main Street, she almost felt normal again. Her boss from The Muffin Man bakery called out a cheery good afternoon and waved. Meg waved back. Grabbing breakfast-to-go at the bakery that employed her had become part of Meg's morning routine, her one treat on a tight budget.

Her steps hitched. All the articles she'd read advised women with a past like hers to avoid predictability in their schedule, but it had been so long since . . . Her chest constricted. Had she made herself too easy to find?

Her phone vibrated again. *Running late.*

Meg had hardly read the message before someone brushed past her, nearly sending her phone to the sidewalk. Her breath stalled in her throat as she fumbled to maintain a hold on the device.

"Sorry," mumbled a woman, hurrying past her before turning toward the bank.

Meg sagged and sent Eli another thumbs up. Everything was fine. As she crested the gentle incline of Main Street, the magnificent sycamore she'd nicknamed Alfred came into view. The tips of its full crown waved hello, and the quivering in her belly settled. Its rich and familiar aroma soothed her erratic heartbeat. The shade beneath Alfred's protective branches was her go-to place for solace. And today, she needed solace.

But then she spotted a chain-link fence imprisoning it. A padlock. A public notice.

As if a fist had reached into her chest and squeezed, her heart wrenched.

Meg raced toward the tree, hitting the barricade with the power of a gale-force wind. Rattling the locked gate shook a poster loose: *The Future is Yours. Come Home to a New Horizon Property.*

Meg picked it up. Condos? She tore her gaze from the poster to Alfred's patchwork bark that exposed white, green, and cream-colored inner layers. Alfred mattered more than condos. The massive sycamore fig—the singular remnant of an ancient forest from another era—stood as the sole survivor of his community. He was a fighter.

Like her.

"I'm sorry, Meg."

Meg jumped as Eli Martin's hand landed softly on her shoulder. His condolences cut through her grief.

"Did you know?" Meg didn't turn around. Instead, she looped her fingers through the chain link separating her from the first public place she'd ever felt safe. Tucked into Alfred's embrace, under the protection of his shade, she'd begun to believe that if a tree could withstand over two hundred years of progress, if it could fight to survive as the surrounding forest turned to concrete, then she could survive, too.

"I didn't. I swear." Eli's weighty touch seeped warmth. He squeezed her shoulder. Of course he didn't know. Eli wouldn't let her be surprised like this. He would have told her. Warned her. Prepared her. An unexpected tingle made her feel like a schoolgirl again, and she smiled.

She was a schoolgirl. A pupil. A *mature student*, according to the university admissions department. Obtaining her Landscape Architect Degree was another Life House assignment tackled with gusto. Meg was only a quarter way through the four-year program, but soon, her future would be secure, and she'd be able to prevent horrible decisions like this, and she'd never have to depend on another person again.

Meg stepped away from Eli's touch. Slowly, the tightness in her chest subsided, until the only remaining effect of her grief was her heartbeat throbbing deep in her ears. Eventually, it, too, slowed. She finally turned and faced her friend.

Eli held out his phone screen for her to read, emotion welling in his eyes. "New Horizon Properties bought this place and that one." He pointed to the neighboring property, and the two houses across the street. "They want to tear them down to build condos."

A tremble rocked through her with such force that it knifed her gut anew. Pressure built behind her eyes. Alfred was a part of Sycamore Hill's history, and they were just chopping him down as if the only good he had to offer was firewood. Even after the newspaper published her opinion piece on the importance of preservation and conservation and how the town did one well but lacked in the other, nothing had changed. The community shared responsibility to limit the environmental impact of harmful human activity on the land. Would they never learn?

Eli's face softened. He caught her hands, and, gently unfurling her fist, threaded their fingers together. They'd known each other for over a year and had been casually dating since last Christmas. He didn't say anything. He didn't need to. His presence was enough.

She straightened her spine and lifted her face to Alfred. Scattered beams of sunlight streamed through the breaks in Alfred's foliage. His branches no longer waved hello. They bid farewell. Even the sun, previously bright, ducked behind a cloud to convey the gravity of the moment. "I'll save him," Meg whispered, more to herself than to Eli.

But he'd heard, and his wrinkled brow peeled Meg's bark. She tugged her hands from his grasp and lifted her chin. The fence around Alfred had nothing on the fence around her heart. Eli thought he knew her, but he only knew the parts she had been willing to share. He knew when she'd moved into Life House two years ago, she'd been pregnant. After having the baby, she arranged an open adoption. Meg had eventually graduated from the one-year program at Life House and promptly enrolled at Grander University. Meg had been on her own for nearly a year now. No, that wasn't quite right. She'd been alone her whole life.

But he didn't know the rest. Few people did. She retreated and hid behind her motivational chant: *Trust no one.*

Meg pushed her tongue against the back of her teeth. *Focus.* "Alfred was here before Sycamore Hill. Who knows? He might even predate confederation." An idea germinated, sending shoots of hope through her fertile mind. She and her classmates had discussed the challenges of designing around significant landmarks and how people in other towns had rallied to save trees. She could do this. Would do this. Because if Meg knew anything, it was how to survive when the odds were stacked against her.

Meg turned and faced the direction of home and bounced a curled knuckle against her mouth. "I need to go."

Eli matched her stride for stride as she retraced her steps back to her tiny house. They covered several blocks in silence before he spoke again, but what he said warmed her heart. "I'll help in any way I can."

She smiled. "I know you will."

They paused on her front porch, and a tentative curve tipped up the corners of Eli's lips. "Maybe one day, you'll invite me inside?"

"Maybe," she echoed, all the while knowing the unlikeliness of it. Growing up in an abusive home and repeating the damaged pattern in her early dating choices only reinforced the idea that bad things happened behind closed doors. She didn't entertain men inside her house. Ever.

Besides, from what she could tell, there were any number of single women in town that would welcome Eli's affections. It was odd how the more available they made themselves, the more Eli seemed to pull away. The only conclusion that made sense was that Eli liked a challenge.

As enjoyable as it was to be the object of his affection and attention, Meg refused to be a challenge to conquer. It's why she kept things casual.

They said goodbye. Meg closed the door behind her, leaning her back against it. What were the odds that someone like Eli Martin would be genuinely interested in someone with as much baggage as her? What would it be like to come home to him and be the sole focus of his attention?

Her eyes drifted closed. A delicious curl turned her mouth as she quietly tested the waters. "Honey," she wistfully called out, just pretending. "I'm home."

The floorboards creaked. She smelled him before she saw him, and her stomach recoiled. The man Meg never wanted to see again stepped from the shadows.

"Did you bring dinner?"

Two

Eli was nearly at the road when it occurred to him that the Historical Society might be a resource for Meg. He retraced his steps, bounding up the porch stairs two at a time, and rapped his knuckles on the wooden door. Matching rocking chairs groaned as the wind nudged them back and forth. A tiny table separated the two rockers, the perfect size for holding lemonade. The curtains in the window rippled.

Meg opened the door a crack. A chain lock drooped across the opening. She didn't smile.

"I forgot to mention the Historical Society might have some information on Alfred. They set up shop in the museum." Eli stuffed his hands into his front pockets and rolled onto the balls of his feet and back to his heels. Meg didn't invite many people inside. Usually, she stepped onto the porch and visited with her guests in the rocking chairs. They'd spent many evenings chatting about life, faith, and the future in those seats. But instead of swinging the door open, the knuckles on her exposed hand whitened from her grip on the door edge.

His scalp prickled.

"Good idea. Thanks." Meg's chin trembled, and she lifted it a notch.

Her gaze bounced around, avoiding his. Eli dipped his head, unsuccessfully trying to make eye contact. A tendon stood out in Meg's neck and pulsed. It sent a tightening sensation seeping through his chest and limbs. Something was wrong.

"Do you need a ride to school tomorrow?" He'd started driving her to the city on the mornings her carpool got a later start.

She shook her head. "No, I'll walk. But thank you for asking." Meg started to close the door, but Eli wedged in his toe.

She moistened her lips and lifted her gaze slowly, one agonizing inch at a time. She blinked rapidly, her eyes damp.

He frowned. The school was a half hour away by vehicle. "Walk?"

Her complexion emptied of color, and the rest of his reprimand died on his lips. Her head remained still, but a sidelong glance to her left made his stomach churn.

"Hey." He brushed the back of his fingers against hers. "Are you okay?"

She jerked. A gurgle sounded from her throat, and she glanced quickly to the left, then back at him. She cleared her throat. "Yes, walk. I could use the fresh air. I gotta go. I'll see you tomorrow."

He nodded slowly. It all landed wrong. Very, very wrong. Before he could say or do anything else, the latch closed, and a bolt rattled into place.

Eli scratched the back of his neck. He'd spent the last year getting to know the skittish, tight-lipped woman who arrived in Sycamore Hill to escape an abusive past. He respected the boundaries she'd drawn around her life, understanding enough about her troubled history to know a friendship with her was going to take some time. Did the news about Alfred trigger something? Did she just need some space? Eli pressed his lips together, and his core squeezed.

The curtains in the front window billowed as if someone watched from inside. All the hair on Eli's body sprung to attention. This didn't feel like Meg withdrawing to get some space. It felt different.

He meandered down the walkway as if he planned to leave. As soon as he moved out of view, he doubled back. The neighbor's backyard connected with Meg's. It was only separated by a small hedge. He shoved Mrs. Brisbane's side gate open, and the loud groan made him wince. He stayed close to the house and rounded the corner to the backyard. Mrs. Brisbane reclined on her back porch, sipping from a tall glass. He waved as he jogged by.

She half-rose from her chair as Eli hurdled the trimmed cedars that divided the properties. He'd explain later.

Eli landed in a crouch and stayed low. The breeze nudged a hammock strung between two trees in Meg's well-tended backyard. A plastic patio set with four chairs sat undisturbed near the back door, just a few feet from the closed barbecue. Eli soundlessly relocated one chair to directly underneath the kitchen window. Meg never hung curtains on this window. She loved the light that streamed through it too much to filter it.

He climbed on the chair and immediately whacked the side of his head against the bird feeder, sending it swinging. Seeds dropped and bounced off the chair seat and scattered on the patio. His stomach rolled. If Meg caught him like this and nothing was wrong, their friendship would never recover.

A radio droned in a neighboring yard. Somewhere, someone hammered away on a home improvement project. But not a peep from the house.

He cupped his hands around his eyes and avoided the still-swaying feeder. He pressed his face against the lower right portion of the glass. Did the police arrest Peeping Toms? Maybe they only charged stalkers.

It wasn't stalking if concern drove the action.

Except that's exactly what a rejected, obsessed, narcissistic, stalking Peeping Tom would say.

Meg stood stiffly in the center of her living room with her arms clenched across her middle. She wasn't facing Eli, but he could tell, even from this angle, that she was unhurt. Relief shot through him. But just as he was about to turn away, a man stepped into view, and Meg bent into herself. Every protective instinct inside of Eli reared.

Meg shrank back, one motion of retreat for every menacing step the stranger took toward her.

Eli whacked his head against the feeder again. He ducked, holding his breath. His head suddenly felt like a million-pound golf ball perched on the tee of his neck. *Lord, help me.*

A few months ago, Meg had twisted her ankle while they were jogging the Sycamore trails. Eli had helped her home, and she'd told him where to grab her extra key that she hid in the backyard. A ridge of field stones lined the edge of a garden, but one was fake. Eli climbed off the chair and studied the stones. Bingo. He wiggled the third rock from the left. It only took two or three attempts to loosen it. He palmed the key.

This wouldn't be the first time that Eli helped Meg out of a scrape. In fact, he was pretty sure the only reason their friendship progressed from running partners to dating was because Eli once jumped between Meg and a dog, essentially saving her. As dangerous as that was, this felt worse.

Eli slid along the cedar siding on the back of the house toward the back door. He slid the key into the lock. As gently as possible, he turned it. He was just about to twist the knob when someone tapped on his shoulder. He bit off a yelp as he whipped around, fist raised, ready to strike—Mrs. Brisbane?

Meg's feisty, silver-haired neighbor crossed her arms over her front and stared at him with the practiced eyebrow raise of an experienced grandmother. Her right orthotic tapped the patio stones. "Just what do you think you're doing, young man?"

"Shhhh!" Eli pulled her aside. "Meg's in trouble."

Mrs. Brisbane's over-plucked eyebrows rose into the sausage roll curl stretched across her forehead. "What do we do?" she whispered.

Eli flexed his twitchy fingers. The last thing Meg needed was a busybody like Mrs. Brisbane getting in the way. "I'm going in. You stay out here."

"I'll keep watch." Mrs. Brisbane's hair bobbed with each word. She tucked herself behind the corner of the exterior wall. This was probably the most exciting thing to happen to her in years.

Eli returned his attention to the door, but he couldn't see Meg or the strange man anymore. He poked his tongue into his cheek and inhaled a long breath through his nose. Meg's place was too small for them to be hiding. If they weren't in the great room, that left the bathroom—highly unlikely—and the bedroom. Deep inside his ears, a steady pounding intensified.

He turned the knob and slid into the kitchen. He left the door slightly ajar in case they had to make a quick getaway.

Meg's voice carried from the front bedroom. "I swear, I don't have any."

Eli's pulse spiked. A robbery? Of all the massive, historical homes on the street, Meg's—as the smallest and most modest—was the least likely to be hit.

"Don't lie to me," a deep voice rumbled. "You've got a stash somewhere. Now get it." Frustration oozed from the man's voice.

"How did you find me?"

"I googled your name and some article you wrote about the environment popped up. It wasn't hard after that. Now move. You owe me."

"I owe you?" Meg's incredulous and shaky tone raked nails down the chalky tension. "I owe you nothing. *Nothing.*"

Eli's stomach cramped. This wasn't the time for Meg to assert herself. His gaze darted around the kitchen. There had to be something suitable to use as a weapon. Would they hear if he opened a drawer to get a knife?

"Come on, baby."

Eli's gut flipped at the man's shift from forceful to overly familiar.

"If I hadn't taken you in," he continued, "you'd be on a slab in the morgue. I fed you and sheltered you. That's gotta count for something."

Eli limbered up his shoulders.

"You want acknowledgement for what you did? You tortured me. You enslaved me. You made me believe my life wasn't worth living. You shamed and controlled me. And you are not welcome here. Get out."

"Not until you give me what's mine."

Something crashed, and Meg yelped.

Go time. Eli shook his hands to loosen them, and the movement knocked the table against the wall. He froze.

Eli couldn't hear Meg's muffled words over the growing pounding in his ears. He grabbed a broom leaning in the corner by the backdoor. He unscrewed the bristled end and wielded the stick like a baseball bat.

"Leave, Jake. I mean it."

It has a name.

"Or what?" Jake cackled like a cartoon villain. "Is your

boyfriend coming back? Have you put all your hope in a new man?"

Eli's fingers flexed on the pole. He was about to rain down a world of hurt.

"I can take care of myself," Meg snapped.

Springs groaned as if someone sat on the mattress. "Come on, Meg . . ."

Oh, no you don't. Eli soft-footed it to the edge of the bedroom door.

"Please," Meg croaked.

Eli rounded the corner and Meg's wide eyes stretched further.

"The lady asked you to go." Eli loomed over Jake for about five seconds.

Then, Jake stood.

Eli had to tip his head all the way back to maintain eye contact. It was like David facing Goliath. Was he supposed to show dominance and stare Jake down?

He's not a dog.

Jake had to outweigh Eli by at least fifty pounds and his cocky posturing made Eli's knees lock and his stomach clench. In a fair fight, Eli didn't stand a chance.

But then again, this wasn't going to be a fair fight.

Jake's nostrils flared. "You need to mind your business." He flicked the tip of his middle finger off his thumb, as if he were flicking away an insect.

"Get behind me, Meg," Eli commanded. Jake might be bigger, taller, stronger, and the certain victor, but there was no world in which Eli walked away and left Meg alone. *Lord, help us.*

Meg thrust herself between them. "Jake, don't."

Eli gulped as Jake's upper body tensed and stretched his T-shirt across his muscular chest.

"Jake!" Meg gently touched his arm.

Jake spun and lifted his hand in one motion.

Meg hit the ground. The move was so instinctive, so automatic, that bile shot up Eli's throat. "Don't touch her!" Spittle flew from the corners of his mouth.

"Meg? Eli?" A thready voice called from outside.

Mrs. Brisbane.

Meg groaned.

"I called the police." Footsteps padded across the floor. "They're on their way." Mrs. Brisbane's voice rose in volume.

Meg half rose, and Jake shoved her back down. She clipped her head on the edge of the dresser and went still. Eli lurched forward, and Jake swooped his thick arm, catching Eli across the chest. The impact knocked the breath from his lungs. Eli landed next to Meg, gasping for air.

Mrs. Brisbane rounded the corner. "Is everything ok—"

Jake elbowed past the old woman, and she emitted a quiet *oomph* when she landed on her bottom. A door slammed. Jake was gone.

Eli cradled Meg's head in his lap. There was no blood, but the early signs of a bruise colored her forehead. Her eyes stayed closed. "Meg? Meg?"

Three

Meg blinked several times. Eli hovered over her, zooming in and out of focus. Her brain fuzzed around the edges and hummed in its core. She squeezed her eyes shut.

"Are you okay?" Eli's words echoed.

She peeked through narrow slits. His brows puckered together, and concern carved deep grooves across his forehead. His face was so close that she could have counted the flecks of gold near the irises in his brown eyes.

But it hurt too much to focus.

Her lids slid closed again. *Brooding*, she decided. Eli's eyes were brooding, but in a different way than Jake's.

Right. Jake.

Meg pushed herself into a sitting position and rubbed circles over her queasy stomach. "I'm fine." She scrunched her face as a fresh wave of dizziness muddled her brain.

A high-pitched nattering played behind Eli like an annoying soundtrack. Was someone else here? For one crazy second, all Meg could think was how grateful she was that she had made her bed this morning and cleaned up her breakfast dishes. She pushed herself to her feet. A sharp pain pierced her head, and she massaged her temple.

"You're not fine." Eli cupped her elbow as she swayed.

Meg prodded her tender scalp. He wasn't wrong.

"Is everybody okay?" Mrs. Brisbane's head popped into view like a jack-in-the-box. Her nosy neighbor had been angling to get inside her house from the day Meg moved in. She was always asking Meg personal questions, digging for more information, wanting details on Meg's life. But Meg didn't entertain guests, and she didn't need friends. Putting hope in people only set a girl up for disappointment.

As a child, when she finally worked up the nerve to tell a teacher that her dad hurt her mom, her mother denied it, and then looked the other way when her dad taught her a lesson she'd never forget. She learned a long time ago to only count on herself.

"I'm fine," Meg repeated. Maybe if she said it enough, she'd start to believe it.

The elderly woman cupped Meg's other elbow, and Meg relented, allowing Eli and Mrs. Brisbane to lead her to a chair in the kitchen and help her sit.

Clara Brisbane's head swivelled as she gawked at Meg's home. If it had been under any other circumstances, Meg might have laughed. The woman finally got her peek behind the curtain. Yet in a strange way, the presence of the grandmotherly woman uncorked relief inside Meg. Kim had always said the freedom Meg longed for would be found in the light of Christ first and then in the openness of community, not the darkness of being alone. And Jake's arrival had left her no choice but to do the one thing she didn't want to do. Step into the light.

"Who was that guy?" Clara relocated the tissue box from the kitchen counter to the table, nudging it closer to Meg.

Meg twisted her lips to the right. She wouldn't be shedding any tears for Jake. "He's my ex-boyfriend. He was waiting for me when I got home."

"You poor thing," Mrs. Brisbane clucked her tongue. "I'm going to make you some tea."

Because hot tea fixes everything. Meg bit her tongue. Enough negativity. If Jake's reappearance forced her to move again, she'd miss this. Miss them.

It'd been a long time since anyone cared for her. Meg forced a weak smile.

"That's better," Mrs. Brisbane prattled as she moved the kettle that Meg always left on the stovetop to the front burner and turned it on.

"Do you know what Jake wanted?" Eli pulled the curtain back and peered outside in much the same way that Jake had done to watch Eli as he pretended to leave. A guy like Eli didn't need a girl with her kind of baggage.

What did Jake want? To show dominance? To terrorize her? To make good on his threat of destroying her if she ever left him? At least Meg finally knew where he was—she'd been waiting for that shoe to drop for months. "Money."

Jake was a rat, gleefully spreading his filth and taking what wasn't his. He did his best work in the dark. Meg saw it hundreds of times when she was under his thumb. His victims felt his presence, but the only evidence was scattered droppings and lingering bite marks. He always managed to scurry away, squeezing through impossibly small holes in the system to avoid capture.

"I've seen it before." Meg massaged her temples. "He's probably in trouble with some pretty bad guys." She'd never witnessed one of his shakedowns, but desperate moments in the past had sent him collecting inflated debts. And most people paid because they were afraid.

She should have run further than Sycamore Hill. She knew Jake would come back one day. Guys like him always did. Her gaze skipped across the room. He didn't appear to have done too much damage if you didn't count her throbbing temple. Nothing *seemed* out of place, but that didn't guarantee anything. Jake had a knack for ensuring most of the hurt he inflicted remained below the surface.

Mrs. Brisbane pulled a chair close to Meg and sat down, patting Meg's knee. "Do you owe him any money?"

She did and she didn't. She had taken about four hundred dollars when she left, just enough to buy a bus ticket, pay for a hotel, and get a bit of food. But considering the amount she earned waitressing over the year they were together, of which Jake took every penny to keep her dependent on him, he owed her. But that wasn't how Jake saw it.

"He thinks that I do." And he must be in a pretty big bind to try and collect from her.

The kettle shrieked. Steam billowed up under the microwave that doubled as a range hood. Before Meg could move, Mrs. Brisbane bounced to her feet and waddled to the stove. "Where do you keep your tea?"

"Top shelf to the right of the stove."

"Tell me about Jake." Eli claimed the chair Mrs. Brisbane had vacated. His gaze dragged over her, slowly, thoughtfully, as if checking for less obvious injuries then the one throbbing in her skull.

Meg supposed Eli deserved to know after his heroic intervention. That was twice now that he'd stepped in when logic dictated that he shouldn't. First, that winter day with the aggressive dog. Now Jake. She relayed a succinct synopsis of her troubled history with the man. Her cheeks burned. What must Eli think of her? He knew she suffered from some kind of abuse, but Kim was the only person who heard the whole story of what she'd endured growing up and how that cycle of abuse repeated in her relationships.

As if he could read Meg's thoughts, Eli's voice dipped. "Would you prefer to do this somewhere else? We can go to my place." He ticked his head toward Mrs. Brisbane, who was busily pouring tea. He lifted his eyebrows in a question.

The tips of Meg's ears heated. She'd prefer to do this alone, but it was pointless to try and keep this private. Mrs. Brisbane was great and all, but gossip flew through the woman quicker than solids through a flu patient. If she was going to chat about Meg—and she was—the woman might as well spread facts instead of fiction. The irony of her situation made Meg snort. The very article she had wanted the townspeople to notice, think about, and talk about had drawn the attention of a man she'd been hiding from. And as a result, that article was going to draw exactly the kind of attention and gossip about her that she'd been trying to avoid since the day she arrived in Sycamore Hill. "This is fine. It's my own fault for writing that article. It made me easy to find."

Eli leaned in further. He met and held Meg's gaze with such ferociousness that it would have been frightening if it were anyone else holding her attention. "None of this is your fault." When she didn't respond, he repeated it. "None of this."

She gave a tiny nod.

Mrs. Brisbane set a steamy mug, honey pot, and a small jug of milk in front of Meg. "Can I call someone for you?"

"Kim Jansen." Meg didn't hesitate.

"On it." Eli moved a few steps away while tapping buttons on his cell. He spoke quietly into the phone.

Meg wanted to ask why Eli had Kim on speed dial, but she

didn't have the right. There were certainly enough things in her life she'd kept from him.

"Don't you worry about that man." Mrs. Brisbane pulled another chair out from the table, leaving the one closest to her for Eli. Mrs. Brisbane stirred a spoonful of honey into her tea. "We'll get this all sorted out together."

Meg forced a weak smile. She didn't do *together*. Besides, she wasn't about to drag her neighbor into this mess. Clara had no idea what kind of damage Jake could inflict.

Eli returned. "Kim's going to spend the night. She needs a few minutes to pull a bag together and bring Oliver to his uncle's place."

Meg's throat tightened. Kim was a good friend. Her willingness to sacrifice an evening with her son made Meg's insides squirmy. She didn't know where to put the conflicting feelings all this attention and aid stirred in her. Alone was harder, but safer. Alone didn't give people an opportunity to let her down. She controlled alone.

Eli covered Meg's clammy fingers with his. Warmth seeped through her skin and her fidgeting stilled. At some point, Eli had reclaimed his seat. His touch remained gentle. Meg could pull away at any time, but instead, she turned her hand over and threaded her fingers with his.

Mrs. Brisbane's eyes lit with approval.

Meg wished she could focus on Eli, but her interactions with Jake replayed like a looped GIF. It was like driving past a bad car accident. She shouldn't look. No good would come from seeing the wreckage, but something inside wouldn't let her look away.

Eli tightened his grip on her hand. "You don't have to face this by yourself. We're here for you."

Meg inhaled slowly and deeply. The pattering of her heart slowed. It was a sweet offer, and it meant the world to her, but she wouldn't drag him into this mess any more than she would drag in Mrs. Brisbane. Jake was a consequence of her choices. One she had to deal with.

Eli looked at his watch. "Shouldn't the police be here be now?"

Mrs. Brisbane chuckled and waved her hand, "Oh, I didn't really call them. I wasn't running back to my house to make a phone call when you needed me here."

"You pretended?" Meg's eyes stretched impossibly wide. Her feisty neighbor had grit.

The woman winked. "I saw it on a television program. Worked like a charm."

"Once Kim gets here," Eli interjected, "we'll see about contacting the police. I'll patrol the neighborhood and make sure Jake isn't hanging around. Kim's picking up dinner on her way over."

"Dinner!" Mrs. Brisbane leapt to her feet with both palms pressed against her cheeks. "My roast! I have to go." She plunked her mug in the sink.

"Go." Eli shooed her with his hands. "I'll stay until Kim arrives."

Mrs. Brisbane hustled out the back door, and Eli locked it after her. He stood at the door for a few minutes, looking out the window. Meg tucked her hands behind her elbows. What Eli must think of her.

"We should let the cops know what happened tonight." He lifted his phone again as if he was about to call them.

"Stop." She'd been down this road before. She'd report Jake herself. After Eli left. She wasn't prepared to answer the kinds of questions the police were bound to ask in front of Eli. "I'll call after Kim gets here."

When he's gone.

Eli mouth gaped. "You'll get a restraining order?"

She had in the past, and she would again. Once Kim arrived, she'd talk it through it with her. Oliver's Uncle Jackson worked with the Ontario Provincial Police. Sycamore Hill was too small a town for a police force, so the OPP provided a police presence. "Let me handle it, please."

Jake had never obeyed restraining orders in the past, so there was no reason to believe that he would start now. His presence in town, stirring up history, messing with her relationships, it was enough to ruin her life—and it could all be done from a distance. A restraining order wouldn't stop that, but every occurrence report filed added to her case against Jake. She sucked her bottom lip. Would she have to move on and start over again? But her daughter lived here. They had an open adoption. She couldn't leave her.

"Is Sonya Jake's daughter?"

And there it was. The one question that could destroy their friendship. The one that revealed her broken history wasn't all Jake's fault. Before the Lord intervened and set her life on a new path, Meg was an active participant in her sin.

"No." She dropped her gaze to her hands. She wasn't ready to tell Eli about the man she met the first time she tried to leave Jake. The man who positioned himself as savior but only used her. But she wouldn't lie to Eli either. Not after all he had done to help her tonight. Meg forced the worry from her mind. No sense in borrowing tomorrow's trouble. Jesus only ever promised her strength for today.

Instead of asking her more questions, Eli dropped onto the chair Mrs. Brisbane had vacated—not the one closest to her but the one across from her. She tried not to read too much into the potential meaning of his seating choice. "If the problem is money, I can help."

Meg stiffened. A woman didn't escape bondage to one man by becoming beholden to another man. "There isn't enough money in the world to satisfy Jake." Especially when he claimed that the four hundred dollars she took when she left had accumulated enough interest to make it four thousand.

Eli dipped his head to engage Meg's gaze. He placed his hand over hers again. "I have enough."

She snorted. If Eli paid Jake, he might as well announce himself as her new ATM. Jake would never leave. Besides, Eli didn't have that kind of cash. His dad might, but not Eli. Eli lived a simple life. He shared an apartment with Addison, his business partner, and they rented a small room above The Muffin Man as an office space. Eli recently confided that unless he and Addison scored a huge client or developed the next big software tool, they were close to closing up shop. Nothing in his lifestyle indicated he had squirrelled away millions. "What are you, secretly rich or something?"

"Like Richie Rich," he deadpanned.

She pulled away from him. There was no twinkle in his eye, no bowed lips to indicate that he was joking. It sent every conclusion she had drawn about Eli into question. How was it possible that she'd known him for so long and not known *this*? Her midsection squeezed like a wrung-out dish rag. "Why didn't you ever say something?"

He laughed, but cut it off when she glared at him. "What would you have liked? Hi, I'm Eli. Oh, and by the way, I'm loaded."

"That's not what I meant." She folded her arms defensively. "It just feels—" She dropped her hands into her lap.

Eli's eyebrow raised. "Like I was holding back?"

She flinched. She deserved that.

His posture loosened. "It's okay to need people."

No, it's not. If Jake knew what Eli meant to her . . . She couldn't let her thoughts drift there. The only way she could control the outcome was to manage Jake herself. "If you give Jake money, he'll never leave."

Eli reached across the table. He moved slowly, giving her time to pull away. When she didn't, he tentatively stroked her cheek. The move was perfectly chaste but strangely intimate. "You deserve to be happy."

Meg dipped her chin, and he lifted it so he could hold her gaze.

"You are so much more than what Jake thinks. I wish you could see yourself the way I see you instead of through the prism of his ego-driven fixation."

Meg's breath caught. Her heartbeat thundered in her ears. Emotions that she had worked hard to keep stabled broke free. Her insides galloped wildly out of control, and it loosened her anchor. It scared her. Not in the way that Jake scared her. In a way that made her afraid of losing Eli. If he knew who she was—really was—would he stay?

Control.

She needed to get control. Of Jake. Her emotions. Her environment.

Her gaze darted to the window, and Eli's hand dropped from her chin. Meg could just make out the roofline of Mrs. Brisbane's house. The woman was likely telling the story of tonight's adventures right now. Could Meg—for once—be transparent and vulnerable with her friends? Instead of letting them speculate, could she provide facts?

Dread seeped into her bones. She wasn't ready to share the rest of her story with the entire town, how abuse rooted its way all the back to her childhood, shaping and damaging her in more ways than they could imagine. She felt like a bad seed trying to mix in and grow alongside the healthy ones.

She closed her eyes. If she let her thoughts go there, she'd never recover. She needed to think about something else. Anything else. But like water flowing over the falls, she couldn't stop her descent.

If she depended on her neighbors and the people of Sycamore Hill let her down, she'd never recover. She'd be worse off than she was now because she'd *know* she didn't belong rather than just suspect it.

"Meg?" Eli said her name like a question.

A new topic.

A safe topic.

Her mind scrambled. She needed something concrete to hold onto. Something to distract her from worrying about Jake, Eli, and what everyone would think once they knew.

Alfred.

Meg's roots wrapped around the one thing in her life that she could control. Her breathing slowed. She locked eyes with Eli, who watched her with a questioning stare.

"I want to talk about Alfred," she said. "I have an idea."

To Eli's credit, he moved along with the current, letting her direct the conversation. His quiet acceptance slowed her heart rate to an acceptable number of beats per minute.

She might not be able to do much about Jake, but she was going to save her tree.

Four

"I don't know how to describe it." Eli dragged his hands though his hair and fisted his fingers, tugging on his scalp. For some strange reason, the tiny bursts of pain that shot through his skin soothed his raging insides. His business partner, roommate, and friend, Addison, sat across from him, partially hidden behind his computer monitor.

"Meg cowered on the floor and I couldn't do anything to help her." The image of Meg turtled at Jake's feet soured his breakfast. It was the polar opposite of the woman who stood on the platform at the recent Life House gala and shared her story of giving up Sonya for adoption and eventually finding freedom and strength in the Lord. He hated Jake for turning back the clock on all the progress Meg had made.

"I don't know how to help her. She didn't want my money. She wouldn't call the police. At least not with me there. And every time I brought it up, she changed the topic, and we ended up discussing Alfred." Eli drummed his fingers on the desk. The repetitive sound synced with the thudding in his chest.

Addison clicked his mouse a few times and frowned at his computer screen. Or maybe he was frowning at him. His friend's thin lips narrowed until they almost disappeared. He roughed a hand over his unkempt bedhead. "It's probably a coping strategy. Abuse is tricky."

Addison would know. Eli and Addison went way back, all the way to second grade, when the teacher assigned Addison the job of taking the new kid around the school for a tour. Eli's grandparents lived in Sycamore Hill, and his father moved back to the small town after his mom died. The boys shared a love of video games and sports that set them up for hours of fun, but what really glued them together was their status as oddballs. Eli's home lacked a mother, and Addison's home was unstable at best, abusive at worst. His friend's scars might not be black and blue, but they cut real and deep.

"Triggers hit us all differently." Addison's features pinched as he spoke. Was discussing this with Eli a trigger for him? Did Jake remind him of his father?

"And seeing her ex would have been worse than a trigger," he continued. "It's a resurrected nightmare. Focusing on Alfred probably feels like a safe goal. It's something she can do. Something she can control." Addison's dark eyes slammed into Eli's and held. "She needs that right now. If you want to help her, don't take it away."

Eli rolled his friend's advice over in his mind and massaged the tight muscles in his neck. "I want to help. But she won't let me."

"Don't make this about you," Addison warned.

Eli jiggled his computer mouse and woke his computer. A few clicks opened the software that he and Addison had started building for Meg. Building it was Eli's coping strategy. It allowed him to invest in Meg's life without meddling. Of course, Meg knew nothing about *Return to Eden*.

"Keep it about Meg and what she needs." Addison's tone remained absolute. There was no room for discussion or argument.

Return to Eden was a promising piece of coding. Eli had plugged away at it on his own time. He planned to give it to Meg as a birthday gift. It was exactly the sort of program that would set a landscape architect apart from the competition. But if he gave it to her now, it could help her save Alfred. To get it fully functioning, he needed Addison's help. Giving it to Meg early was keeping it about Meg, wasn't it? His hands stilled over the keyboard. Or did it make him more like his father, offering a gift to get his way?

Eli throat thickened. *He was nothing like Morgan Martin.* He gave Addison a curt nod, indicating he'd heard his friend's caution, and Addison returned his attention to his screen.

Eli and Addison spent their days designing, creating, deploying and maintaining software for a specific set of users, functions, and organizations. Their custom programs aimed at a narrow target, and they charged fees accordingly. Getting their custom software development business running viably hadn't been easy, especially since Eli's father opposed them at every turn. But Eli didn't need much to be successful. Just a powerful computer, a small office, and a brilliant partner like his childhood friend. He certainly didn't need his family's money, which was a good thing, since his father froze his trust fund the day Eli dropped out of law school. Now his father dangled it like a prize at the finish line he preferred Eli cross.

If Meg had accepted his offer to pay off Jake, Eli would have enrolled again to make it happen. But she didn't.

Eli mindlessly scrolled through the coding of *Return to Eden*, and an idea hit. "If we run an algorithm in *Return to Eden* that pulled internet history from Alfred's location, we could compare it with population trends and anticipate the social pushback for cutting down Alfred."

Addison straightened in his chair. "Then Meg would be able to gauge how many people in the community would be on her side."

But Meg didn't want Eli's help.

It's not about me.

"We could simplify the process of pitching an environmental, social, and aesthetically pleasing design to the town," Addison murmured, his attention now glued to his screen. He had that look—that furrowed brow, tight muscles, set jaw kind of look that meant he was on the verge of a breakthrough. Eli knew better than to keep talking. When Addison got like this, the fragile threads needed time to connect and solidify or they could be lost. Eli bit his tongue.

It's not about me.

"It can suggest a range of possible designs that utilize the elements of unity, scale, balance—" Addison muttered.

Eli closed the program. There was nothing for him to do but wait. He drummed his fingers on the desktop.

Addison's gaze flicked to his twitchy fingers and then back to his screen. Eli fisted his hand. They had positioned their desks facing each other so they could chat easily. But right now, Eli wished he could hide from his perceptive friend. Addison's ability to read people had probably saved his life in his abusive childhood and definitely helped them in meetings with clients. But right now, being read so easily only ticked Eli off.

"When you get like this, all twitchy and impatient, you remind me of your dad."

Eli harrumphed. He was *nothing* like his dad. His dad railroaded people. His dad had to have things *his way*. His dad pushed and pushed until—

"Hold up." Addison's gaze slammed into Eli's. Eli expected a smile and some smart-mouth comment about Eli needing to save Meg. But instead, he got a scowl. "Jake isn't your biggest problem."

"He's not?"

Addison disconnected his laptop from the power cord and slid it across the desk surface. He jutted his chin toward the screen. "Your dad represents New Horizons."

Eli scraped his hand down his face, smoothing the stubble on his jaw. He could only guess what Meg would think when she learned that his rich father backed the demolition of her favorite tree. It wouldn't matter that Eli had no part in the business. It never did. The Martin name was enough to sink him with the ship.

"She's gonna hate me."

It's not about you.

Or worse, she'd assume he'd kept the information from her, like he'd held back the fact he came from money. But people changed once they knew how many zeros showed up before the decimal on his bank statements. It was the entire reason Eli didn't date women from Sycamore Hill. Too many found financial security more attractive than him. He wanted to be more than just a provider for his future wife. At least, that's how he felt before meeting Meg. Something about her made every protective instinct rise. He'd do anything to give her the security she longed for.

Lord, how do I stop making it about me?

Eli glared at Addison's computer screen. Sure enough, his father's face beamed beside Meg's opposition: Franklin Cooper. The online article gave the rundown of Cooper's plans. On the surface, they sounded great. Sycamore Hill was slowly turning from a small hick town into a quaint touristy destination. The Sycamore family was pushing for any improvements that moved the town further down that road. A condo that reserved some units as week-long rentals, yet maintained the historic and charming look of the town, fit the bill.

A groan swelled in Eli's chest until his lungs pushed against the confines of his ribs. According to the article, work started in the next day or two. The breakfast muffin he'd snagged as he walked through The Muffin Man on his way to the office suddenly wasn't sitting so well. His stomach heaved at the lingering cakey scent that usually stirred pangs of hunger. This was a lose-lose situation. Meg would feel betrayed when she connected the dots, and when Eli supported Meg instead of the family, his father would be furious. Eli was, after all, supposed to be the second Martin in *Martin and Martin Law Firm*. This would land like an act of treason. Family stuck together. Sacrificed for one another. Nothing but death separated them.

Eli heard the story for the first time after his father moved them back to Sycamore Hill. Eli's gramps—Albert—got caught up in a flash flood, and his great-grandpa died saving his son because *that's what a father does.*

"You know you need to call," Addison prompted.

There was no place to hide in their tiny office.

Eli removed his phone from his back pocket. He set it on his desk and sighed. "Call Morgan Martin," he spoke into the voice recognition.

"I meant call Meg," Addison hissed.

Eli swiveled in his chair so his back was to Addison and popped in an earbud.

"Eli," his father boomed. "How are you, Son?" His dad's pleasant tone would surely sour once Eli made his request.

For as long as Eli could remember, his father pushed and pushed and pushed. It was like he was trying to prove they belonged here, which was crazy, since he grew up in Sycamore

Hill. But Morgan Martin had rejected the family mantra and escaped to the city as soon as he could, quite vocal about shaking the dust of this hick town from his feet. Moving back after Mom died humbled his father. His mantra—*family matters more than anything*—returned with more force than that legendary flash flood, because they needed all the help they could get.

Then Grammy and Gramps died, and a switch flipped in Father. It was like he suddenly had to prove to the community they had a right to stay.

It was why he pushed so hard. He was pushing Eli to safety by funnelling him into law when, really, he was pushing Eli away. He'd renamed his law firm Martin and Martin, partly to remind the town of Gramps, who was the high school principal until retirement, and partly to manipulate Eli. His father simply didn't understand Eli's need to make it on his own, to show everyone that he was more than the amount in his bank account.

"I need a favor," Eli said. "Can you stall the developer of the New Horizons project?"

Silence.

Eli shook his phone to relight the screen. They were still connected. "You there?"

All the lightness left his father's voice. "I must not have heard you right, because you know that I'd never do something so unprofessional."

"My friend is working on a plan to save the tree growing in the middle of this new condo plan. She needs a bit more time."

"Your friend is going to be disappointed."

"This is important to her, important to me. And I'm not asking you to do something you've never done in the past." Martin and Martin Law knew every tactic possible for stalling when it benefited the client, but it shouldn't surprise Eli that his father wouldn't budge when it only benefited Eli. So much for the mantra.

"It is unethical for me to get involved in a movement that is in opposition of my client's best interests."

Eli snorted. He had to be joking. The firm never crossed a legal or ethical line, but they had blurred them when it suited their purposes.

"Come on, if we work together, we should be able to get both our clients what they want." Calling Meg his client was a stretch. Technically, he and Addison were building a software that she needed . . . she just didn't know about it.

Now who was blurring the lines?

"Martin and Martin: it's what you always wanted." Phrasing his sales pitch like that felt a little bit like selling his soul.

One problem at a time.

"The plan is to demolish all four houses and clear the land this week. In fact, I'm at the site now, ensuring everything is good to go. I'm not getting involved with your friend's project. If you know what is good for you, neither will you. A good businessman separates his work life from his personal life."

A click sounded in his ear. Eli threw his earbud to the desk. When would he learn? No good ever came from asking his father for help. The man moved in one direction only: his way. Eli shoved his chair back from the desk and snatched his coat from the hook near the door. "I'm heading out."

Addison nodded, wisely not commenting.

His father wouldn't be able to dismiss him so easily in person, and Eli knew where he was. With Alfred.

Five

The Sycamore Hill Museum occupied a tiny, old church. Meg scoured the shadowy corners and bushes for Jake as she approached: an old habit that returned with a vengeance. It wasn't fair. Jake's reappearance coinciding with her need to focus on Alfred was another example of life kicking her while she was down. She shouldn't feel so surprised. The deck had been stacked against her for her entire life. Why should now be any different?

Jackson took her statement and filed an occurrence report. He noted Jake's violation of her restraining order and said he'd discovered a warrant for his arrest. But none of that helped her unless Jackson found Jake, and Jake was good at evading capture.

The sun caught the high windows in the peak of the museum's roof. Meg shielded her eyes and tipped her head back to appreciate the intricate stained-glass design. Something about the stature of the building stirred a sense of reverence within her. Her fingertips trailed along the intricately carved porch railing as she slowly climbed the steps to the double arched wooden doors. The sheer weight of the wood demanded respect as Meg gave it a shove.

Now that Jake had reappeared, Meg needed a distraction. Anything to stop her from obsessing about where he was and what he was doing or saying about her. That was part of his MO. Psychological warfare. He would show up just enough times to toy with his prey and undermine her feelings of safety. He would flash in the background, mix into the crowd like a cameo in a movie, or eat at a nearby restaurant table, over and over until he was all his victim could think about. But Meg wasn't playing his game. She wasn't going to stay at home and cower in fear. She threw her whole being into researching Alfred and the company trying to cut him down. Anything to stop Jake from occupying her mind.

Meg had spent much of yesterday trying to connect with the developer, but he never returned her calls, despite the many messages she left detailing her concerns. After chatting with her teacher about the issue, she decided not to waste another day waiting on someone who clearly had no intention of addressing her questions. Alfred needed her.

And she needed Alfred.

A chime sounded. Church bells. Meg's feet whispered over thick carpet, and the gentle scent of wood polish welcomed her inside what must have once been a grand sanctuary. Arrangements with short framed write-ups filled several display cases in the dome-roofed room. The lack of wooden pews, communion table, and pulpit made the space appear larger than expected. Meg stuffed a ten-dollar bill into the square, black donation box that sat on a small table under a decorative arch and signed her name to the guest book. She dragged her fingertip down the names listed before hers. These were the people who cherished history.

Meg tapped her fingernail on a single entry. Morgan Martin. A relation to Eli? Her heart panged. Eli had called her several times already this morning, but she let it go to voicemail. She couldn't figure out why she resisted his help. Nothing about Eli threw up red flags. He seemed to be exactly what he presented himself to be. Maybe that was the problem. After learning Eli was rich, she realized that he rarely spoke about his family or personal life. She couldn't even be sure that Morgan Martin was his dad, that's how little she knew about the man she'd been dating for six months. She'd been so focused on rebuilding her life that she'd failed to be a good friend and ask him about his life. All she really knew was what she observed, because she'd hardly asked the poor guy a question that dug deeper than topsoil. Meg didn't like the feeling that revelation stirred in her.

An interior door from the back swung open, and a plump woman emerged from what might have once been a rectory. Her dark, spiraled curls bounced with each lively step.

"I'm Valerie Rowe." She extended her hand, and the cuff of her suit jacket rode up, exposing a tiny tattoo on the inside of her wrist. Valerie smiled widely. "I run the museum and volunteer with the Historical Society."

Valerie was a curious contradiction. Her sense of style leaned toward history professor, her demeanor reminded Meg of a preschool teacher, and her tattoo suggested a streak of independence. Valerie's easy smile, full face, and bright eyes welcomed Meg like an old friend, making her instantly comfortable.

"I'm looking for information on the development at the corner of Second Ave and Main Street. I thought the Historical Society might be involved."

Valerie nodded her head and pushed a fistful of curls off her face. They immediately tumbled back over her left eye. "Yes, we know of that project."

Meg sagged and released a breath she hadn't realized she'd

been holding. Finally, something leaned her way. "Are those homes protected by the Historical Society?"

Valerie shook her head. "No, I'm afraid not. Several others in the neighborhood are, but the ones involved in this project were completely demolished and rebuilt in the 1980s when the area flooded. They are too new to be designated as Heritage Homes. In fact, that's why the developer chose to build in that area."

"You were in touch with the developer?" Maybe Meg had given up too easily on connecting with the man.

"No, his lawyer. I can give you his number. He completed his due diligence in ensuring the homes in question were not on our radar." Valerie moved to a nearby computer and opened a file. Her neatly filed, pale pink fingernails clicked against the computer keyboard.

Meg pressed her lips together so tightly they tingled. If the developer had a lawyer who already examined these details, Meg had little hope of finding a loophole that would save Alfred. She rubbed her right hand up and down her left upper arm. Was she fooling herself to think she could stop this?

"The developer is Franklin Cooper. He owns New Horizon Properties. His lawyer," Valerie paused, and the keys clicked some more, "is local. Martin and Martin Law Firm."

Meg's eyes stretched. "As in Morgan Martin?"

"Yes, Morgan Martin."

"Any relation to Eli Martin?" Meg's fingers found her earlobe and played with her earring stud, spinning it. It had to be a coincidence. Eli would have told her if his dad was involved.

"Yes, father and son. But Eli is not a lawyer. He does something in computer software."

Warmth crept over the back of Meg's neck as a quiet buzzing filled her ears. That *was* Eli's dad's name in the book. If he'd already been here, the odds of her finding anything to help her cause were getting slimmer by the second.

She slumped against the nearest display case. Why didn't Eli tell her that he was involved? She had assumed that Eli was on her side because of all his insightful questions, but what if he was just gathering information for his father?

No. She bit the inside of her cheek. She rejected that idea almost as violently as her body rejected Jake's sudden reappearance in her life.

Valerie had continued speaking, and Meg realized that she had missed what she had said. The woman finished with, "There is nothing original to save on those lots."

Nothing original? Meg's mouth slackened and she massaged her throbbing temple. A tingle started in her chest and intensified until it restricted her breathing. "What about the tree? Its sheer girth indicates it's been here longer than most of the homes we protect."

Valerie lightly touched Meg's upper arm. "Are you okay?"

Valerie's thoughtful expression and clumsy attempts to comfort Meg made Meg's face, neck, and ears impossibly hot. Her lower lip trembled. "I think I need to sit down."

Valerie led Meg to a tiny armchair with a pedestal table to its right. She snagged a box of tissues and set them on the table. "Can I get you some water?"

Meg shook her head. Water wouldn't fix what was wrong with her. All the emotional supports she'd put in place since arriving in Sycamore Hill crumbled around her, and there wasn't anything Meg could do to stop the destruction. "I'll be fine. I just need a minute."

"The new structures being erected are going to have the same feel and design of the heritage homes in the neighborhood," she prattled on, as if grasping for anything that might comfort Meg. Valerie tugged at the hem of her suit jacket.

"The tree they're cutting down is older than the town. Would the Historical Society be able to save the tree?"

Valerie tilted her head to the side thoughtfully. "We've never gotten involved over a tree before."

Meg dug through her purse for her phone, encouraged by the fact that Valerie didn't outright refuse her. Thank goodness she'd thought to ask her teacher about Alfred before leaving class. He'd sent her several articles. Meg had compiled quite a collection of stories involving communities taking on the town to save a slice of history. She handed the phone to Valerie. "I've found several examples of other historical societies successfully protecting established trees in their communities."

Valerie pursed her lips as she scanned the headlines, her thumb swiping through the links. The longer she read, the more her body posture perked. Her eyebrows furrowed. "The tree would have to be connected to a specific event in history," she murmured. "Why don't we see what we can dig up on the original owners of the land?"

"You'll help?" Meg's stomach quivered.

Valerie laughed. It was rich, deep, and comforting. "Of course! It's my job. It'll be fun. Small-town museums like ours are a little different from the ones you may have visited in the city. We showcase items that would be overlooked in other places, such as lettermen jackets from the high school, vintage coffee cans, old cameras, baskets, and old photo albums. You never know what we'll find once we start digging."

Meg struggled to keep her expectations in check. "Do you work for the Historical Society full-time?"

"Heavens, no." Valerie waved a hand at the idea. "The Historical Society is run by volunteers, but the town employs me at the museum. I think the items that would most interest you would be in the ancestry display. You stay there," Valerie said when Meg started to get up. "I'll bring it to you."

Valerie moved toward the far wall, and Meg was slammed with the hypocrisy of her actions. She wouldn't accept help from Eli, but she eagerly welcomed Valerie's.

That's different.

But was it?

Valerie leaned over the display, searching. She rattled a keychain on her wrist and unlocked the glass cabinet, withdrawing an album, a small book, and a stack of letters.

Seedlings of hope planted in Meg's heart sprouted. If they could link the plot of land on which Alfred sat to someone prominent in history, they might be able to save him. They didn't need to find someone world famous, just Sycamore Hill famous. That would be enough to convince the community.

Valerie handed Meg the items. "I think the diary could have some information on the land. The tree you're concerned about used to be part of a farm, and this journal is from the daughter of one of the first immigrants to work the land. These letters are dated from the same time."

Meg reverently traced the lettering embossed on the leather cover of the book. "What a treasure." She lifted her face to Valerie's. "Did Mr. Martin look at these items?"

"No, he was more interested in the legal documents. Few people give the personal items we display more than a cursory glance." The phone rang from the back room. "Come and get me when you are finished, and I'll put them back." Valerie hurried away.

This was it. Meg clutched the items to her chest. This was how she was going to save Alfred. She'd tell his story. Sure, it might not carry the legal weight of land transfer paperwork, but the story mattered. It had to. She leafed through the items, devouring the content.

Davina Mhartainn's family farmed the land around Alfred. They emigrated from Scotland after being ejected to make way for sheep grazing. That couldn't be right. Meg opened a web browser on her phone and inputted the question: Did Scotland evict people to make way for sheep grazing?

But it was right. It happened to a lot of families. History referred to it as the Highland Clearances that spanned the mid-to-late 18th century and continued intermittently into the mid-19th century. It was politely referred to as the "depopulation" of the rural areas. Despite most of the Scots settling in Eastern Canada, some came to Ontario. This particular family, the Mhartainn family, settled in Sycamore Hill.

Davina's penmanship was difficult to decipher since she spelled phonetically. Meg snapped images of the diary pages with her phone. She'd need the correct spelling of the family name and the family details. Her insides squirmed at reading the intimate letters Davina exchanged with a friend.

The voyage was difficult, but we finally arrived. I expect things will settle between Mathair and Athair.

From what Meg gathered, those were the Gaelic terms for mother and father. She read slowly, translating the phonetically spelled words as she went.

I take unspeakable comfort that our hearts and souls are in the hands of the Lord. I desired to stay in our beloved country, but I aim to be content with the ordering of a kind God who knows what is best for me. This second chance is a gift from Him.

Davina seemed educated for a farmer's daughter. The page had ripped at the bottom, and Meg couldn't read the signature line. She chewed on her bottom lip. She hadn't met anyone in town with the Mhartainn surname, but with a bit of time on the internet and some luck, she'd be able to figure out what had happened to the Mhartainn clan. She shifted her attention to the photo album. Photos were rare from this period, so there were not many.

A forest of sycamore trees provided a gorgeous backdrop in the earliest photos. Even in the winter months, the trees were beautiful. The largest looked like Alfred with spreading canopies, lobed deciduous leaves, and white bark peeling to reveal darker patches. A journal entry noted the sycamore belonged to the Platanaceae family and originated from Europe. Did the Mhartainn family settle here because the foliage reminded them of home, or did they bring a piece of home with them that grew into this woodland? How would they feel about the depopulation of their forest?

She snapped a picture of one photograph. Using the zoom option, she magnified a tree that appeared to be close to where Alfred was today. She flipped though the album quickly. As the years progressed, more and more pictures were added. She was looking for other photographs taken at a later date from the same angle. Sure enough, there were enough images that she could have compiled a flip book and animated the thinning of the forest until only Alfred remained.

The church door opened and a man stomped his feet on the mat and smeared his boot soles over the word, *Welcome*.

"Can I help you?" Valerie dusted her hands across her thighs as she approached.

He lifted his face, and all the saliva evaporated from Meg's mouth.

"Just browsing." Jake trailed a hand along the edge of a display cabinet. "I'm visiting Sycamore Hill, collecting on a debt."

Meg's midsection cemented. She felt his unsettling stare, but she refused to meet his eyes. It didn't matter that she owed Jake nothing. He'd laid claim to her earnings and wanted his share.

"Someone mentioned the museum as a hidden treasure. I thought I'd check it out."

Valerie blushed, and Meg's soul crumpled as the woman's gaze appreciatively moved over Jake. Meg snorted, quickly covering the noise with a cough. Valerie had no clue that a wolf lurked under that sheepskin.

"It fascinates me how the past impacts our present." Jake's lips peeled back from his teeth with a smile designed to woo the woman.

Meg kept her head ducked, but the weight of Jake's attention settled heavily over her shoulders. Her heart thundered in her ears. Meg flicked her gaze up.

Jake's hardened gaze drilled into hers with the delight of a cat fascinated by a mouse trying to escape. His muscles tensed up, ready to spring, coiled with delightful feline anticipation.

Dread stiffened every joint in Meg's body.

After a few long seconds, he cleared his throat. His unmistakable deep and smooth voice knocked her off-balance. "History always catches up with us."

Six

2:45 p.m. Eli rolled his shoulders to release the tension as he waited in his car for Meg. Students moved about in clusters on the university campus. The half-hour drive from Sycamore Hill afforded him time to draft his confession. He had to tell Meg about his father's role in the Alfred issue before she learned about it from someone else.

My father's law firm is representing the business cutting down Alfred, but I have nothing to do with it.

No. Too cold.

You know Alfred? Yeah, well, my father has his hand on the chain saw.

Too flippant.

I'm on your side, Meg. But I just learned that my father is not. We'll face him together.

Maybe. Eli's leg bounced so quickly that the vehicle shook. He stretched and flexed his hands.

2:47

Eli often functioned as Meg's back-up ride to and from

school, but Meg wasn't expecting him today. His decision to come was so last minute that he hadn't even told Addison. He fired off a text message to his friend. *I'm taking the rest of the day off work.*

Everything okay?

His friend's immediate response made Eli smile. *Yeah. I decided to surprise Meg and pick her up from school.*

Silence.

The more seconds that ticked by, the higher Eli's back went up. Finally, his phone vibrated.

The last thing Meg needs is to feel like another man is stalking her.

Eli typed a reply, then deleted it. He tried again. Nope. Eli powered his phone off. Despite the bravado Meg put forward and Addison's cautions against overstepping, Eli had to speak with Meg. He had to tell her about his father face to face, so she could read the sincerity in his expression. And maybe even more importantly, he couldn't shake the feeling Jake wasn't done yet. Jackson hadn't been able to find the man, and being the only police officer in town meant he couldn't devote all his time to the search. As long as Jake was at large, Eli was stepping up. He wasn't about to watch as some punk terrorized the woman he loved.

Loved?

Eli swallowed and shoved the revelation down deep. She wasn't ready to hear that any more than he was ready to admit it. Because what if she didn't love him back? A long pull from his water bottle failed to quench his thirst. It didn't matter. Eli would do whatever it took to make Meg feel safe again.

He tapped the pads of his fingers against the steering wheel in time with the radio. He still didn't know what he was going to say to Meg when he saw her. It wasn't like he could bring her home and say, *Let me introduce you to my father. He's the one the holding the axe.*

Throngs of people milled about the campus, enjoying the mild spring day. Eli examined every single guy with beefy upper body strength. Guys like Jake never simply walked away. He was here. Somewhere. Eli felt it in his gut.

2:50

Meg spilled out the door with two other students, their heads pressed close together as they walked and talked. She might be one of the older students at Grander University, but in her T-shirt, dark jeans, and youthful energy, she fit right in. Meg held out a piece of paper that the breeze kept folding forward.

Eli opened the window and called out, "Meg!"

The women never looked up.

He waved his arms out the window and shouted again.

The girl next to Meg flicked her attention his way and nudged the others. Meg stiffened and followed her pointed finger. Her elbows pressed into her sides as if she were trying to make her body as small as possible.

Eli flapped his appendages, and Meg wilted as she recognized him.

Great start, Sherlock. Freak her out by showing up unannounced. Addison's warning rang in his ears loudly. The man was wise beyond his years.

The tension in Meg's features softened, and she smiled. His heart hammered in his chest.

Please, don't let her be mad, God.

Meg said something to the others, stuffed her paper in her bag, and jogged to the car. Eli powered down the passenger window.

Meg leaned into the vehicle, resting her forearms on the window frame. "What are you doing here?"

"I, ah—" He couldn't say it. He couldn't tell her that his father would be the reason she lost Alfred. "I wanted to be sure no one bothered you at school. Did everything go well?"

She shrugged. "Yeah, it's all good."

"Can I drive you home?"

"Sure." She slipped into the passenger seat and fired off a text message, probably to her carpool.

"What did your teacher think about your plans for Alfred?" Eli slid his arm around the back of her seat and twisted his torso for a better view behind him.

"My professor thinks I have a shot, but it's a long one. He gave me some material on other successful instances where a community tree was saved."

"Do you have a plan?" If she'd let him help, his program could shoot out several viable options and organize them from most cost effective to the most expensive. Addison was almost done tweaking it.

But Meg had made it clear that she didn't want help. At least, not his help. And Addison insisted that Eli not push.

Eli put on his turn signal to merge with traffic. A red Civic filled his rearview mirror. He tapped his brakes, and the guy backed off.

"I'm working on a plan." Meg pulled out the paper that she'd been showing her friends. She'd sketched a rough design. "If the contractor flips his layout, he can build the apartments where he'd planned the parking lot and build the parking lot around Alfred."

Eli nodded. Solid idea. He merged onto the highway, and the Civic followed suit. Eli slipped into the right lane between a black sedan and a beat-up pick-up truck to let the impatient driver pass him.

He glanced at Meg's design. Running Meg's idea through *Return to Eden* would polish it up, but the program wasn't quite ready. If he only had one shot to sell her on the idea of using his software, he wasn't pitching it until it was one hundred percent finished. "I did a little research for you today."

Meg slid her design into the backpack at her feet and folded her arms across her chest.

"You have to go over the contractor's head to whoever is writing the checks if you want to make changes. He's heavily invested financially, so I doubt he'll just pull out. But you might be able to convince him to change direction." He left out the bit about his father's involvement.

Meg stared straight ahead. She opened her mouth, then she stopped short, snapping it closed again.

"Meg?"

"This is my project. I told you I need to do this myself."

Eli adjusted his grip on the steering wheel, hating how Addison was proving to be the wiser of the two of them by the second. His smile slipped. "What's wrong with a friend helping a friend?"

"Nothing, when that friend *helps* and doesn't *take over*." Meg's complexion reddened.

Eli forced his mouth closed before he said something he'd regret. Addison had been right on every count, so before he stuck his foot further down his throat, Eli needed to sit down with his friend and talk. Really talk. Talk until Eli understood how to be the sort of friend Meg needed. Eli glanced over his shoulder to change lanes and passed the truck.

The red Civic, still trailing them, changed lanes, too.

"I can handle the project. I will save Alfred," she repeated.

Not if his father had anything to do with it. Eli sucked in a breath and held it briefly. It was now or never. "I need to tell you something. It's about my father." He changed lanes again. The Civic followed. Again.

Wait.

Something about that car sent tension tightening down his spine. Eli peered into the side mirror, but he couldn't see the driver's face clearly. "I think we're being followed." He carefully controlled his voice and tone.

Meg cranked her neck to look behind them.

"The red Civic. Two cars back." Eli squinted. The driver wore a ball cap pulled low on his head and reflective sunglasses.

Meg's eyebrows pulled together for a brief second, then her eyes bulged. Her coloring paled. "That's Jake." It came out all raspy and fragile. She clenched her hands in her lap but wasn't able to camouflage their trembling. She got out her phone and called Jackson.

"Isn't this a violation of your restraining order?" Eli let off the gas to see if he'd pass. No luck. Eli floored the gas pedal.

"Yes." Meg braced both hands on the dash and yelped. Her nostrils flared. "Jackson will be here as soon as he can."

The Civic barreled up behind them, revved its engine, and positioned itself parallel to them. The driver pulled his sunglasses down his nose and glared. An evil scowl twisted his mouth.

Meg's sharp intake shored up Eli's resolve to keep showing up for Meg, however and wherever she'd let him in. She was not facing this guy alone. Not if Eli could help it.

Jake revved the engine again, gave them a wicked grin, and fell back.

"Hold on." Eli hit the gas again and shot ahead. His heartbeat thrashed in his ears as the car fishtailed. They crossed lanes, cutting off the pick-up truck to the soundtrack of a blaring horn. They sped up the exit ramp, and the back end slid as they careened onto a side road. Eli cranked the wheel to the right, and gravel shot into the air. He thrust the vehicle into park. The momentum pitched their bodies against their seatbelts and then back into their seats. Deafening silence filled the car interior.

The red Civic missed the exit and disappeared from view.

Meg's chest heaved. Eli's breath shot out like a pressure valve released. He could tell himself all he wanted that he was in control of his feelings for Meg, but the terror carved on her face cracked something inside of him. A simple and striking realization left him feeling vulnerable in a way that had nothing to do with Jake and had everything to do with fear. Meg mattered to him. She mattered more than he was ready to admit to her.

Meg's tongue bumped over her cracked lips.

"Where to?" *Please say the police station. Or home. Or his place. Any place they can sit down and talk about how to fix this mess.*

"The Muffin Man," she croaked. "I have to work." For one endless second their gazes stuck. Her pupils dilated. Eli forgot about Jake, Alfred, and the secret program he was building. He forgot everything except her and how much he cared about her.

Thank you, Lord, for keeping her safe.

Meg's lips parted slightly. The woman should be frazzled, angry, or at the very least, afraid. But her expression softened, and her eyes never left his face. All Eli could think of was how long he had wanted to feel her lips on his. How long he'd waited to see the invitation he saw now in her gaze.

She reached up. Her hand trembled as she trailed the tip of her finger along his jawline. The tension in his body doubled. Eli turned toward her caress as his blood heated. Her eyes dropped to his mouth.

What was he doing? Her ex was stalking her, and instead of doing something, he was sitting here imagining what it would be like to kiss her. She didn't need to be objectified. She needed help. He pulled back.

She blinked, and her brief expression of rejection splashed cold water on the moment. She blinked rapidly, and the cloudiness in her eyes cleared. "I'll update Jackson." She focused on her phone.

Eli bit his tongue.

She sent her message and then stared straight ahead. The stiffness in her neck sucked up the previous intimacy like a vacuum.

Eli put the car in gear and merged back onto the highway. No red Civic. At least something good came from the detour. The tension in his shoulders should have released, but a sideways look at Meg only increased it. He knew nothing about abuse. His closest encounter was dealing with his controlling father, trying to get him to back off when he pushed for Eli to follow his footsteps and get a law degree. As awful as that one horrid year in law school played out, it had nothing on Meg's experience with Jake. Eli had gathered the courage to stand up to his father and follow his dream of custom software development. He knew his decision would impact their relationship. He knew it would make things prickly between them. But he never, not once, feared his father. Not in the physical sense. The man wasn't like Jake. His father wanted good things for Eli; they merely disagreed on what those good things were.

After several more quiet minutes, Eli parked in front of The Muffin Man and cut the engine. They couldn't leave things like this. He opened his mouth, but Meg's slackened jaw, chalky skin, and red-rimmed eyes silenced him. He followed her gaze.

Jake chatted with Pastor Owen near the door to the bakery. Jake's pushed-up shirt sleeves exposed the bottom half of a tattoo, and his voice penetrated the car. "I heard some chick is kicking up a fuss about a tree being cut down. What a waste of time. The last thing this town needs is a divisive issue hitting the news. Am I right? These are the types of things that split churches."

Meg's gaze hardened faster than the candied apples in the window of Ethan's shop. She pinched her mouth, narrowed her eyes, and scowled. "Thanks for the ride," she muttered.

"Wait—" But he was too late. She lifted her chin and entered the bakery, threading between the men without a word. The door slammed shut behind her.

Eli ground his teeth. Jake had stood in that spot, under the arch of the gilded bakery sign, to force Meg to walk past him. Like a cocky chimpanzee, he relished lording his power over potential threats.

Jake sauntered his way. "You Meg's new man?"

Jake oozed a sleazy confidence as he rested his hand on the roof of the car and leaned through the open window. A move of intimidation. Eli might not have finished law school, but he'd been around lawyers all his life, and they were masters at using their body language to tell a story.

"Leave Meg alone," Eli growled.

"I plan to, as soon as she gives me what I want."

"She's doesn't have any money."

"No, but I did some checking. You do."

Seven

The Muffin Man door slammed behind Meg, knocking her backside. She stumbled into the bakery to the jingling tinkle of the bells strung along the top of the door. Every customer in the shop looked up.

She dipped her head and hurried behind the counter, rubbing her heated neck. She fired off another message to Jackson, updating him on Jake's location. But the man had been called to the countryside to investigate an act of vandalism on a nearby farm. By the time he arrived, Jake would be long gone. In fact, she wouldn't be surprised if they learned Jake was behind the farm incident, ensuring Jackson was otherwise occupied when Meg needed him.

Meg's insides churned. She cinched her apron around her waist a little too tightly and tried not to dwell on the stories Jake might be telling Owen.

"Table seven needs wiping down." Ethan poked his head through the kitchen door. "And Kim was looking for you."

"Thanks." Meg nearly sagged with relief. Kim would know

what to do. She'd help her make sense of her raging insides just like she'd helped her make sense of her past. She'd understand how Meg could be so angry at Eli one second and want him to kiss her the next.

Meg snagged a damp cloth and headed for table seven. She loved working for Ethan at the bakery. She'd only been there three months, but so far, it was great. He scheduled Meg's shifts around her school timetable, and he didn't mind her catching up with her friends while she worked, as long as the job got done. Every so often, his girlfriend, Kathryn, would come in and the two love-birds perched at a table in the quiet corner. Their sweet affection for one another filled Meg with hope. Good guys existed.

Too bad her scowling ex, standing on the sidewalk in front of the bakery window with his arms folded across his chest as he boldly defied her restraining order, wasn't one of them.

Meg scrubbed table seven until her fingers cramped.

"Are you cleaning that table or sanding it down?" Kim arched an eyebrow. She lifted a coffee mug to her lips, crossed one leg over the other, and sipped. A plate with two Cranberry Burst muffins sat in front of her.

Before Meg could respond, Ethan swooped by, landing a platter with two oversized muffins between the patrons at table nine.

"Sorry," Meg mumbled. She'd been so distracted by Jake that she didn't see the order waiting.

"Chocolate Burst! Thank you, Daddy!" The little girl clapped her hands in glee.

If only a muffin could make Meg's life better.

Ethan paused briefly and held Meg's gaze. "You okay?"

She nodded.

He made a *hmmm* noise in his throat before pivoting to clear a table behind Meg and Kim and head back to the kitchen.

Meg folded her lips. She needed to get her head in the game. Ethan didn't have time to do her job as well as his. Kim took another sip of coffee, but the rim of the mug failed to hide a bemused smile. She didn't say anything, but somehow, Kim's silence was louder than Mrs. Brisbane's nosey questions about Jake.

"You got a customer, Meg," Ethan called.

Drat. Caught daydreaming again.

Meg spun, and her insides froze. Jake leaned against the counter near the register. His chin jutted out with the cocky tilt of his head. His probing gaze pinned Meg to the spot. Her mouth fell open, but no sounds came out.

Kim hopped to her feet. "I'll take care of it."

Meg turned her back to Jake and stacked two empty plates and a mug from a vacated table. She balanced them in one hand while wiping the wooden surface down with the rag in her other hand. Her hands shook so much the dishes clattered.

"I don't know what's going on"—Ethan tapped her shoulder—"but Kim can't run the cash." He spoke kindly, but pressure shot to Meg's eyes and built behind them.

"Sorry," she said faintly.

Jake's arrogant laugh filled the bakery despite Kim's stony face. She hissed something at him and Jake smirked.

Meg's face burned.

"Is this guy going to be trouble?" Ethan's gaze darted briefly to Jake and Kim.

Meg closed her eyes. If only he knew. "I have a restraining order against him."

Ethan's entire demeanor changed.

Kim handed Jake his order, and he moved like he was about to leave. Meg's mouth dried up. "It'll be fine," she assured Ethan. "I've already notified Jackson. He's coming for my statement as soon as he can." She pivoted, and tripped over Jake. The dishes she'd gathered crashed to the floor. Ceramic shards splayed out in all directions. How did he get here so quickly?

"Sorry!" Jake gripped her upper arm and lifted her to her feet before Ethan could intervene. She looked from Jake's fingers to his face. He glowered, but he released her. "Be careful. I'd hate for you to get hurt."

Weakness hit Meg's knees. Jake blurred. He wasn't supposed to be here. This was her second chance at life. She'd worked too hard. It wasn't fair.

Ethan stepped between them as Kim bolted from behind the counter. Ethan stared at Jake, not moving or flinching. It hit Meg that Ethan wasn't afraid.

Jake leaned in aggressively, not so much that he overtly challenged Ethan, but just enough to make a point. He had the upper hand.

Ethan didn't blink. "If you have your order, it's best that you go."

The men's locked eyes made every fiber in Meg's body tense.

Then, out of nowhere, Jake's posture slackened. He winked at Kim and lifted the take-out bag. "Thanks for the muffin." He swaggered out of the bakery.

Meg dropped to her knees, and the tray rattled onto the floor beside her. As she piled the larger broken pieces into it, her hands trembled so violently that a shard sliced her fingertip open. Slowly, as if in a daze, she popped the wound into her mouth.

Ethan squatted in front of her. "If he comes in again, you come get me."

A swell grew in her chest, and she stuffed it back down. "Thanks," she said thickly.

Kim appeared with the broom and started sweeping.

Meg deposited the dirty dishes on the counter and tucked her cloth into the waist of her apron. She dug a bandage out of the first aid kit, applied it, took the broom and dustpan from Kim, and put them away. She took her place at the till and avoided all eye contact.

Kim claimed the nearest barstool at the counter. "I'd like you to come and stay with me until all this blows over. You shouldn't be alone."

Meg's gaze jerked to Kim's. "And bring the trouble to your house? With Oliver there? I couldn't."

"Jake broke into your house. He knocked over your neighbor. He came in here just to flaunt his power. He is unpredictable and dangerous."

If she brought trouble to Kim's door, she'd never forgive herself.

"My work at the shelter puts me in the middle of volatile situations all the time. It's literally part of my job description. But I'm not offering as a counsellor. I'm offering as a friend."

As a friend. Meg sure could use one right about now. Meg swiped at her eyes with the back of her hand. "Thank you," she whispered. "And just for the record, I did call the police after he broke in. They are up to date on everything except today."

Kim nodded approvingly. "I knew you would. I told Eli you were too smart not to document everything."

Meg wiped the same spot on the counter for what felt like the millionth time.

"His arrival has really messed with you, hasn't it?" Kim's voice remained low enough that Ethan wouldn't be able to overhear from his place in the kitchen.

Meg snapped her gaze to her friend's, but the compassion filling them softened her retort. "Of course, it has."

Kim lifted the edge of her plate and tipped it toward Meg. "I bought one for you."

Meg smiled. A lull in the crowd afforded them a few minutes. Ethan had returned to the kitchen, and Meg fiddled with the wrapper. She peeled a strip of the crinkled paper down the side like a banana peel. Kim followed her movements with a curious expression that tipped down the corners of her lips.

"Have you seen Jake since the night of the break-in?"

"Here and there. He showed up at the Historical Society and at school today." It was pretty clear God had rejected her plea to send the man packing.

"What are you going to do if the restraining order isn't enough?"

Why did Kim always have to do that? Take the issue to the extreme and ask the what if. She frequently employed this tactic in their counselling sessions, but Kim wasn't her counsellor anymore, and Meg didn't feel like playing Kim's game.

Meg pushed the muffin away from her. She tucked her hands in her armpits and sucked in her cheeks. "I'll leave. I'll start over again somewhere new. I've done it before."

"That's certainly an option." Kim paused, as if she considered Meg's words, but she wasn't fooling Meg. "Another option is dealing with Jake once and for all. Ridding your life of his presence and power forever. Stopping him from ever doing this to another woman."

"And how am I supposed to do that?" Meg snapped. What worked in theory often stood in opposition to real life. The man kept turning up like a bad penny.

Instead of responding, Kim took a huge bite of muffin and chewed slowly.

Meg mashed her lips together so tightly that they tingled. She knew what Kim would have said had this been a session. *God equipped his children in the storm. When he wanted a strong tree, He planted it where the storm would batter it, because it is in that battle that the tree develops its strength. After the storm, beauty rises. Blah, blah, blah.* Meg didn't want to face Jake's gale winds. She wouldn't survive a second time.

Kim continued to chew.

Meg huffed, "If I pay Jake off, he'll keep coming back."

"I didn't say pay him off. I said take away his power." The food in Kim's mouth miraculously disappeared at just the right time.

"Whose power?" Ethan had emerged from the kitchen with a rack of warm bagels. "The jerk from earlier?"

Meg stiffened. She wasn't ready to deal with Jake, and she definitely wasn't ready for her boss to get more involved than he already was. She snatched up the muffin, ripped the wrapper the rest of the way off and tossed the paper into the garbage. "Why didn't either of you tell me Eli was rich?"

Kim's eyes widened as Ethan's brow wrinkled.

That's right. We are not discussing Jake.

Ethan ducked back into the kitchen, mumbling something about the oven timer.

Kim wiped at her mouth with a disposable napkin, seamlessly accepting the transition in topic. "It didn't occur to me that you wouldn't know. Besides, it's not like you two were dating exclusively or anything."

Meg's fussy hands stilled, and her gaze slammed into Kim's. "Is Eli dating other women?"

A low, throaty laugh rumbled from Kim. "That's not what I meant, but it's good to know how you feel about him."

How could Kim know how she felt about Eli? Meg didn't even know how she felt about Eli.

Kim rested her hand on top of Meg's and stopped her from obsessively cleaning the counter. "Eli's been waiting for months for you to let him in, but you haven't. Why do you think that is?"

"I thought Eli was different. But if he withheld something this big, what else isn't he telling me?"

Kim leaned in as if she were about to share a secret. "Eli is different. But that's not the reason you're holding back."

Meg pulled her hand out from under Kim's and started to clean the counter. Again.

"Do you want to know what I think?" Kim pressed.

One of the perks of their relationship shifting from counsellor to friend was that Kim would now share her personal opinion. In sessions, she was always turning it back on Meg, asking what Meg thought and what Meg wanted to do.

"This is not about Eli's money," Kim said. "You've been holding the man at arm's length for months. You didn't even know about the money until recently. That's an excuse you've latched onto because it is easy. It gives you an out."

Meg's face warmed.

"I think you are taking your frustrations about Jake out on Eli, and that frustration is exactly what gives Jake power over you."

The words settled around Meg's heart. Was Kim right? Was that what Pastor Owen meant last week when he spoke of people obsessing over what others thought about them? He called it a consuming insecurity. The sin of pride dressed in a humble costume. Had Meg allowed pride to root in her heart? And if so, how did she weed it out? Meg slumped onto her elbows.

Kim's expression softened. "I think you still believe Jake. You believe him when he says there is something deeply wrong with you."

Because there was *something wrong with her.*

The thought jolted her insides like an electric current. When had she accepted that lie? There was nothing wrong with her that Christ's death on the cross hadn't already paid for. His forgiveness threw a cloak of white over her stained body. She knew that intellectually, but her heart still struggled to believe it. The gospel truth not only applied at her moment of salvation, but in every moment since.

"Jake's fixation on you, his rage over you moving on and building a life here, is more about you getting the best of him than anything else. He's enraged by the fact he can't control you anymore." Kim leaned across the table and placed both her hands over Meg's to stop them from twisting.

"And there is nothing wrong with Eli coming from money." Kim squeezed her hands. "Considering the number of women who have dated him solely because of it, I'm not surprised that he hesitated to tell you how much his family is worth."

Did Eli's omission have more to do with his issues than Meg's? The fact she hadn't even considered it only proved that Meg had been too fixated on herself.

Just like the prideful person in Pastor Owen's illustration.

"You're right. Eli has been nothing but kind to me, and I keep shutting him down." A million acts of kindness flitted through her mind. Eli, showing up at her house with flowers just because. Taking time off work to drive her to and from school whenever she needed it. Even his offer to look into the contractor planning to chop down Alfred, as misguided as it was to jump in and take over, came from a place of kindness. It wouldn't be so bad to let Eli help her. She didn't need to do everything all on her own.

Meg bit her lower lip. At some point, she had to tell Eli what she'd uncovered about him. After she left the Historical Society, she continued digging into the Mhartainn name. Considering what she unearthed on the Anglicization of that name, the battle for Alfred could be more Eli's fight than hers.

Eli Martin. Martin, the first Anglicized form of MacMartin—according to her research—came from Mhartainn, an early Scottish emigrant family to Sycamore Hill. Did Eli already know they were relations? If so, did he know the rest of the story? And if he did, why wasn't he speaking up?

"We need a plan." Kim broke through Meg's thoughts. She cupped one elbow with her palm and tapped an index finger to her lips. "A way to get you to my house tonight safely." Kim's face lit up. "And I think I see the answer."

The hairs on Meg's neck bristled. But this time, it was Eli standing at the window, waving. Her shoulders heaved forward with a heavy exhale. Relief emptied her lungs, and she quickly deflected her gaze, lest he see the wreckage of her soul.

Eight

E li circled the block several times. Each loop added a layer of ice to his frozen gut. If he had immediately followed Meg into the bakery, she would have pushed back against him. After what Jake pulled, she needed enough space to feel like she had regained control. He wrinkled his forehead against the throbbing in his skull as he waited for an acceptable amount of time to pass so he could enter and not appear clingy.

He caught Meg's attention through the window. His inner iceberg started to melt, and a pent-up breath shot out. She hadn't smiled, but her posture softened.

The bells above the door jingled as he entered. He passed the cash register, which was flanked by two tall glass cases filled with muffins, doughnuts, and swollen loaves of banana bread. His stomach growled at the aromas wafting from the back kitchen.

Kim lowered her voice and said something he couldn't hear. Meg's cheeks reddened.

"Speaking of Eli . . ." Kim projected her voice and grinned as she stood up, unhooking her purse from the back of the barstool and slinging the strap over her shoulder.

"All good things, I hope." Eli slid into Kim's vacated seat and folded his hands on the stainless steel lunch counter.

Kim caught his eye, and her eyebrow lifted. "Can you give Meg a ride to my place after work? I have to pick up Oliver, and she's decided to stay with me until this mess with Jake is sorted out."

Relief would have weakened his knees had he not been sitting. It had been thirty minutes since Jake moved on. Thirty minutes of Eli stewing and planning and trying to figure out a way to save Meg, and it turned out she didn't need saving at all. She'd made her own plans. Good plans. Smart plans.

"I have some work to do upstairs, but I should be done by seven-thirty or so." The staff schedule posted on the wall said Meg was off work at eight o'clock. Something Jake would have seen as well. "I'll come down and grab dinner for the last half hour of your shift." Eli played it cool. Nonchalant. But the truth was he would have turned his schedule upside down to escort Meg safely to Kim's.

Meg murmured a quiet good-bye to Kim but still hadn't spoken directly to him. He pretended to check his text messages while tracking her in his peripheral vision. Her usual smooth movements were stiff and jerky. Was she thinking about Jake making good on his threats to destroy her life? He wanted to ask, but she'd made it clear the topic of Jake was off-limits. And somehow bringing up his father's involvement with Alfred felt insensitive after everything that just happened. Like kicking her while she was down. So he said nothing.

Meg pulled a berry pie from the pass-through into the kitchen and placed it into the display case. Purple juice oozed through the decorative slits in the crust. Meg never looked his way. She exuded calm. Or, more accurately, she would have exuded calm had her thumbs not begun twiddling away like an out-of-control hamster wheel the minute she set the pie down.

An unwelcome thought hit with the subtlety of a two-by-four. Had he put her on edge? Maybe her twitchiness had nothing to do with Jake and everything to do with him. Had he crossed the line into obsessive territory that Addison always teased him about?

Eli sagged into the seat. He wouldn't be able to help her if she pushed him away. He rubbed the hinge of his jaw where it ached from clenching. There was no point in moaning about it now. He was here. At her workplace. For better or worse. But a little damage control couldn't hurt. "I hope I haven't overstepped by hanging around."

The vulnerability in Meg's face capsized his insides like the Titanic. "Your office is right there." She pointed to the ceiling. "You're here for coffee all the time. You and Addison might be Ethan's best customers." The corners of her lips lifted just enough to toss him a life preserver. She sat a mug of coffee in front of him. A ceramic mug. Not a to-go cup.

Relief loosened his posture. Crisis avoided. "Best coffee in town," he drawled, lifting the cup to his lips.

The slimy residue that followed an encounter with Jake convinced Eli she'd been dealing with this thug for too long. Sycamore Hill's troops needed to rally. One of their own was under attack. But that would only work if she believed she really was one of Sycamore Hill's people, and she belonged here. Meg might have her doubts, seeded by the demons in her past, but Eli knew the town had her back no matter what filth Jake planted.

Meg busied herself with rinsing the crumbs off a stack of plates and loading them into a stainless steel dishwasher. "I saw you waiting outside."

Waiting. Praying. Asking God to show him how to help Meg. "I came up with a plan to get rid of Jake."

The only indication she heard him was her slight delay in closing the dishwasher door.

Wow. Cue the creepy music. "That came out sinister. I mean, I came up with a plan to get him to move on and leave you alone."

Meg's mouth opened, but no words came out.

"You were right. We can't pay him to go away." Now Jake knew Eli had money, they'd never be rid of him. "But there might be another way to send him packing."

Meg's mouth remained slack in a tiny O shape. The chatter from customers and the crackle of wrappings and clatter of cutlery on plates faded into the background. Eli couldn't tell from her posture if she leaned toward hope or annoyance. His words tripped over each other in his effort to get them out before she shut him down. "Ben works for the paper, and he's broken some pretty big stories."

Meg picked up an unused napkin from the counter and folded it into increasingly smaller squares. "Have I met Ben?"

The chime of the door interrupted. Meg moved to the cash register and rang in a sale. She poured a coffee into a paper cup and slid on a cardboard sleeve. She handed it to the customer with a paper bag that had the edge folded down to keep the yeasty bread warm. "Have a nice day."

Before resuming their conversation, she plated a cheese croissant and set it on the counter in front of him. His favorite. A peace offering.

"Ben's been covering the Emergence drug scandal. We could use him." Eli pulled the croissant into two pieces, more to have something to do with his hands than anything else.

"How can he help?" Meg's fingers splayed over her upper chest. She rubbed circles into the notch at the front of her neck.

"He can dig up dirt on Jake."

"You want to blackmail Jake?" Meg finally looked at him, really looked at him with an incredulous stare. She shuffled back a step or two. The knuckles on her hand clenching the napkin whitened.

He'd botched this up good. Eli exhaled hard through his nostrils. "Let me start over. If we can find leverage that forces Jake to choose between you and him, a guy like Jake will always choose himself."

Her lips pressed together with a slight grimace. A soft noise gurgled from her throat, but she didn't say no. She didn't say anything.

"Can I ask Ben to poke around?" Eli needed verbal consent.

Meg rubbed at the middle of her forehead; eyes closed. "You mean, you haven't yet?"

Okay, he deserved that. He reached across the counter and touched her hand. "I think enough people have tried to force their preferences on you. I'd like to help because you don't need to do this alone, but I'm not going to make the decision for you."

His foot jittered against the floor, making his knee bounce. Finally, a smile cracked her unreadable veneer, and he inhaled his first full breath since the conversation started.

"You have my permission." Her attention dropped briefly to the counter before she lifted her gaze to his. Red rimmed her eyes. "Thank you for asking first."

He relaxed against the back of the barstool. They were going to be okay. He picked off a wedge of croissant and popped it into his mouth, speaking around it. "I'll call him as soon as I get into the office."

Meg's forehead knitted. Her eyes narrowed and her fists clenched at her sides. She focused on something over Eli's shoulder, and he turned to follow her gaze to the TV screen mounted in the corner of the bakery. His heartbeat halted. The Titanic was going down and taking him with it.

Someone had muted the sound on the television, but dialogue scrolled across the bottom of the screen that framed his father and Franklin Cooper standing in front of Alfred. *Travelers should avoid the downtown streets of Sycamore Hill tomorrow. Demolition on the corner of Main Street and Second Ave is set to begin earlier than scheduled.* And right behind his dad stood Eli.

Oh no. Sourness filled his mouth. He'd intended to tell her all about his father's involvement, but he never got the chance. "Meg," he croaked.

She swung around, her hair fanning out from the motion. Her blazing eyes uprooted hope, root bulb and all. Pain shot through his chest.

Meg stiffened and blinked hard and fast until the dampness welling up in her eyes cleared. She folded her arms across her stomach and coiled protectively inward. "You're working with your dad?" Her chest rose and fell from her quickened breaths.

"It's not how it looks. I'm sorry." A lump wedged in his throat. He was sorry for so much more than he could put into words.

"Why didn't you tell me?"

It was his turn to avoid eye contact. Heat burned his neck. "Because I'm ashamed. My family is backing the demolition of something you love."

"Why are you there with him? Are you supporting his decision?"

She was entitled to these questions. She deserved answers. But the panic overwhelming his body stole the breath from his voice. He couldn't articulate his complicated relationship with his father to himself, let alone to another person. Desperation pierced like bullet. It didn't matter how hard it was. He had to make her understand. "I went there to ask him to stall and give you time to make a plan. To give you time to save Alfred."

Her gaze swung back to the TV where the broadcast had moved on and then back to him. But the softened lines on her face gave him hope.

"My father makes a big deal about family sticking together, but the one time I asked him for help, he turned me down." Shame landed like shovelfuls of dirt. Eli looked her right in the eyes. If he could communicate clearly, maybe she could see it in him. See the truth. This had wrecked him. "I grew up hearing how my great-grandpa had saved my gramps. A flash flood hit, and the current carried Gramps far from the main house. Just when Gramps thought he'd go under for good, Great-grandpa was there, thrusting him high into the arms of the nearest tree."

Her face paled.

"Great-grandpa was too weak to keep fighting the current, and after Gramps was safely stowed away, the flood waters carried Great-grandpa downstream to where they later found his body."

"That's awful," she croaked.

"It changed Gramps, and in some warped way, it's why my father pushes so hard. It's like he thinks it's his responsibility to save me."

Meg suddenly pushed to her feet and collected the napkins and wrappers strewn on the counter from departed guests. She stacked the plates on the counter and tossed the trash in the garbage. "I have to get to work."

Eli nodded. "I have some work to do upstairs, but you can call me when it's time to go home."

Meg nodded, then bent over her notebook, the soft sounds of her pencil on paper playing her song of determination.

Eli took his coffee with him to his upstairs office. He wanted to hope. He wanted to believe that Meg would succeed. But the truth was that God allowed some people to sail through life without so much of a paper cut and appointed others to suffer and struggle immensely.

Please, Lord. Grant Meg's request.

Nine

"Thanks for seeing me." Meg took the chair across from Morgan Martin and smoothed a hand down the front of her white button-up shirt. A calming inhalation failed to slow her racing heart. He was just a man. He was no better or different than any other person.

But he held the power to save Alfred.

The guest chair sat slightly lower than his desk chair, a subtle tactic of intimidation that matched the dark tones and masculine vibe of his office. The room smelled of upholstery and coffee which stirred the empty sensation in her stomach.

Behind Morgan loomed two massive built-in bookcases filled with thick volumes embossed with book titles she'd never heard of. An open reference book lay on an additional desk-like surface that spanned the two bookcases and offered a fantastic view of Sycamore Hill's park. The space lacked potted plants and greenery or anything that might suggest life and vibrancy. It portrayed exactly what she suspected Mr. Martin wanted: a no-nonsense man who got things done.

Mr. Martin's gaze flicked to Meg's hand as she fiddled with the collar of her shirt. She pushed a stray lock behind her ear before dropping her hand to the folder resting on her lap. It didn't matter that this wasn't the way she had hoped to meet Eli's father. It was what the Lord had ordained.

"It's a pleasure to meet you." Morgan's gaze swept over Meg with a lazy perusal. It was as if the jury were still out deliberating her worthiness. "Eli speaks highly of you."

Funnily, up until last night, he'd rarely spoken of his dad. But sharing that tidbit of information wasn't going to help her cause or heal the rift between the men.

"What can I do for you today, Ms. Gilmore?"

He could stop pressuring his son to conform to his idea of success. He could see how much Eli longed for his father's approval and, for once, tell Eli that he was proud of him. He could counsel his client to save Alfred. But none of those sentences slid off her tongue. Her continued research into the Scottish emigrants and the Sycamore tree kept bringing her back to Morgan. Whether he knew it or not, Alfred mattered to his family, and Alfred might even be the key to him finding his place in the town he once rejected. He just didn't know it yet.

She cleared her throat, which suddenly felt impossibly dry and scratchy. "It's my understanding that you represent New Horizons Properties."

"That is correct." He pressed his fingertips together and peered at her over their tops. He leaned into the back of his chair, oozing confidence and a touch of . . . cockiness? Arrogance?

She shifted in her seat and pulled her bottom lip into her mouth to moisten it. She half expected Jake to burst through the door and interrupt, destroying her opportunity to convince Mr. Martin that what she was about to say was true. Jake seemed to lurk in the background every time she turned around. Addison,

Eli, and Ethan had started taking turns escorting her to work and school. Kim insisted that Jackson was working the case from his end. Jake was going to slip up, and when he did, they'd catch him. But none of that settled her stomach right now. Not when so much was riding on this meeting going well and Jake was still out there thinking of ways to sabotage her.

"I've been collecting research on the properties involved with their latest development project, and I wanted to bring some things to your attention."

Morgan studied her, and she squirmed like a bug under a microscope. His complete attention unnerved her. She shifted in her seat, crossing her legs, trying to find a comfortable spot.

When Morgan remained quiet, she pressed on. "Do you know anything about the history of the large sycamore tree slated to come down?"

"The tree?" His eyebrows lifted.

Ah, he had expected her to discuss the buildings, not the landscape. Being able to surprise him gave Meg a shot of confidence. *Buckle up, big guy, this ride's about to get bumpy.*

"Yes, the tree." Meg opened her folder and removed several papers she'd copied from Davina Mhartainn's diary. *Please, Lord, let this land on a soft heart.* She placed them on the desk and slid them toward Morgan. "If you look at the originals," she pointed to the document on his left, "the author spelled phonetically. For ease, I've written the letters properly." She pointed to the paper on his right. "But you'll see they communicate the same message."

From her brief research on Morgan, and from peppering Eli with questions long into last night, she'd concluded that family mattered to Eli's dad. It mattered even more than Eli realized. It's why he pushed Eli so hard. He wanted good things for his son. It's why he withheld the trust fund when Eli launched his business: not to manipulate Eli, but to make him stand on his own two feet.

Eli was so desperate to prove to the community that he was more than his bank account that he couldn't see that his father was just as desperate to prove they belonged here now his parents had passed.

Morgan Martin wanted Eli to join his law firm, but even more than that, he wanted his son to make the Martin name proud. Meg was playing her last card in this meeting and betting everything on Morgan's claim that family mattered more than anything else. She rubbed her forearms.

Morgan picked up the pages. His polite smile faded as he skimmed the first page. His mouth pinched, and his lips disappeared. He moved the first page to the back of the stack and skimmed the second page. She knew the moment he reached the portion that referenced his family history. His jaw tightened. He got the same muscle twitch near the hinge that Eli got when he was worked up. Morgan's fingers stiffened, and the papers snapped. Little by little, he lost the cocky, confident edge that he wore in the courtroom like a comfortable suit jacket. He flicked his gaze to hers. "Why did you start looking into this?"

"Trees have a history," she said. "And I wanted to learn about this one. If you learn to listen, they will tell you their story."

"You can do that?" The incredulous expression that crossed his face made her feel one seedling short of a forest.

"I can do more than that." Meg dampened her lips with her tongue and leaned forward. Her heart raced as she placed enlarged photographs on the desk. One by one she lined them up, taking her time, making him wait for it. "The more I researched this tree, the more I saw your story running parallel to his."

"His?"

Heat filled her cheeks. She lowered her eyes and bit her lip. Somehow, she doubted Mr. Martin would find the personal pronouns and names she affectionally used appropriate. As much as she wanted to pitch her design idea and appeal to Mr. Martin's business side in order to save Alfred, they had bigger plants to pot. Meg understood the difference between a living person with an eternal soul and a living tree programed to survive. And when push came to shove, she'd focus on the eternal soul over the tree every time.

Meg chose her words carefully. "Trees are a lot like families. The ones that survive have to be strong. They ration their strength and maintain an inner balance that ensures they have enough energy to meet their needs. It's kind of like what a father does for his son."

Encouraged by the glint of interest in his eye, she carried on despite the way her nerves tangled raw. "Much energy goes into growing a tree, but an equal amount must be held in reserve so the tree is able to protect itself from an attack."

Meg could only imagine the inner strength it took for Morgan to regroup after his wife's death. No one was prepared for that kind of loss.

"How are trees attacked?" The way he angled his body away from her warned that she was losing him.

"Not in the same way that people are attacked. We face illness, loss, death." Was he thinking about his wife and the day an unforeseen attack stole her and the future he thought they had?

"Trees face things like wind, storms, drought, insects, humans," she said. "A single mature tree has the potential to produce millions of seeds, but on average, only one survives the dangers of their environment and makes it to adulthood. That seed can lie dormant for years, waiting for just the right time to sprout."

He huffed a sound of exasperation. "This is a great biology lesson, Ms. Gilmore, but I fail to understand how it connects to my client's project or me."

"This tree is the single surviving child of its parent. Its destiny is to grow and take its parent's place in the forest." He had to see the parallels to his life. Eli was his only child.

"You're a perceptive woman, Miss. Gilmore." He patronized her, probably trying to be polite for the sake of Eli.

It was time to drop the metaphors and spell it out. "You had plans for Eli, hopes that he would join you in your business and one day take your place."

He jerked his gaze to hers, and the intensity of it nearly melted her. "What does this have to do with the New Horizon project?"

"If you'll indulge me just a bit longer, you'll see."

He jerked his head affirmatively while working his jaw back and forth. Another habit of Eli's.

"Trees that grow slowly are flexible and resistant to breaking. They have an inner strength that's been cultivated for years. They recover from injuries easily and compartmentalize the wounds. Even though they are smaller in size due to their slow growth, their parent remains connected to them through their roots. The parent feeds their child, ensuring they have all they need to survive."

"Eli doesn't want my help," he said gruffly. Relief rocketed through her. He understood the metaphor.

"Partly because you've nurtured him so well. You've allowed him to find his own way, but like an intricate root system, you are still connected to him. You're ensuring he has all that he needs."

Morgan expelled a tired sigh. "I appreciate your insight into our family, and it's clever how you have connected it to this tree, but how does that impact your case? I know you're trying to save the tree. Eli told me."

"You've been longing for meaning in your life, a connection to the past, a reason for your continued presence in Sycamore Hill. This tree holds the answers you've been searching for."

His body went rigid, and his words came out just as stiffly. "You don't know me. We've never met before today. How can you sit there in such judgment and pretend to know anything about me or my family?"

She placed before him one more sheet of paper. "I know more than you think." Her late night with Eli confirmed a lot of details for Meg, the most important being that Eli loved his dad, but he was too close to be objective about their relationship. Because Meg had distance, she could see that the things Eli's father did that rubbed Eli the wrong way came from a place of parental love. A desire to protect and belong. A need to be needed.

His skin paled. He lifted his face to hers and his bottom lip trembled in a rare sign of weakness. "You've confirmed this?"

She nodded. "I have."

Doubt filled the creases on his face. He dragged a hand over his eyes and sat back in his chair. "How is it possible that you dug this up just in time to benefit your cause when my family lived in Sycamore Hill their whole lives and never heard even a whisper of this?"

"With all due respect, sir, I doubt you were as motivated as me." Meg couldn't tell if her reply angered him or impressed him. He hadn't struck her as the type of man to search his family history. Like most people, he knew what his parents told him and what little he could remember from his grandparents. Most never bothered to look further than that. They were too consumed with the needs of the day. Too invested in the current state of life and too focused on the future to look back. But, like Valerie had said that first time she visited the museum, small-town history was fascinating if you only knew where to look. And looking back at the personal items in the museum, specifically at the items that referenced the flash flood that nearly claimed the life of a small boy, was exactly what Mr. Martin needed. If only she could convince him.

Meg softened her voice. "Trees live in community. The type of community I've never had, and the kind you've tried to give Eli. You, Mr. Martin, belong in Sycamore Hill. Your roots go deeper than you could ever imagine. Alfred might be the final surviving tree in his forest, but you and Eli don't have to be yours. If you'd like, I can help you follow your roots. I can tell you what Alfred is trying to say."

Did she really say that? She sounded like some hippie kook claiming to be a tree whisperer.

He remained focused on the papers in front of him. Finally, he set them down. Then, he slowly examined the images she'd placed on the desk one at a time. He even pulled a magnifying glass from his top desk drawer and used it to study every square inch of the photographs she'd provided.

She waited, her heart thumping a beat that vibrated deep inside her ears. Mr. Martin was a difficult man to read. She had no idea which way this would sway. But at the end of the day, whether she saved Alfred or not, she was proud of what she had uncovered for Eli and his dad. Everybody deserved to know where they came from.

"Since my parents died, I've been afraid that if I dug too deeply, I'd find something that proved the opposite. That we didn't belong." He frowned at the pages and images. "I'm going to need some time to look into this."

Meg lifted her eyebrow in a direct challenge. "Time, Mr. Martin, is exactly what you're running out of."

Ten

Dreams roused Eli from his sleep. After tossing and turning and finally waking from a nightmare, he gave up on the idea of rest altogether. If he was up, he might as well be productive. He pulled on a hoodie and sneakers and walked to the office.

The black curtain of the midnight hour gradually started to lift, and little by little, Sycamore Hill revealed bits and pieces of itself. Still, the cool morning air and his brisk walking pace failed to shake the dream-laced images of Meg cowering under Jake's hand. A sense of helplessness stirred his spirit that a sloping countryside and the distant expanse of a pond couldn't ease. It wasn't fair. Nature slept peacefully with hardly a ripple to disturb it. Dew dropped a kiss on the earth, and trees luminous in the streetlamps failed to ease the earthquake rumbling in his chest. Meg's crumpled expression and Eli's powerless position lingered as clear as the day dawning around him.

And to top it all off, Alfred was coming down despite Meg's

attempts to save him. Eli squeezed his hands into fists and his foot-steps fell heavier on the sidewalk. She deserved better. Even last night, her final night to save her precious tree, she put in more hours asking him about his dad and caring about their broken relationship, because that's the kind of girl Meg was. She didn't deserve to lose. Not like this.

Her eyes had emitted a sad acceptance of the inevitable that carried into his dreams. But in the nightmare, Meg didn't just lose the tree and yield to Jake. No. She strapped herself to Alfred and Jake wielded a chainsaw. And every single time, Eli arrived too late to save them from the bloody massacre.

Eli stuffed his key into the bakery door and slipped inside, locking the door behind him. He arrived so far before sunrise, The Muffin Man remained dark and unoccupied. Considering the early hours the baker kept in order to offer a fresh-from-the-oven breakfast menu, it was quite the accomplishment. The minute hand on an oversized clock ticked. The hum of electricity flowing vibrated deeply in his chest. It was quiet. Too quiet. The kind of quiet that came before something bad happened.

Eli legged it up the narrow staircase leading to his office two steps at a time, unlocked the door, and plunked into his office chair. He stared at his dark computer screen. He needed to think. Pray. If Meg wasn't in the center of the storm, she'd be the first to tell him the suffering and trials blowing in the wind forced roots to deepen. The resistance seen in nature held divine purpose. When a bird flew for pleasure, it would coast on the breeze, but when it sensed danger, it headed straight into the gale to gain quick alti-tude and escape.

It felt more like God was uprooting everything that mattered to him than strengthening the woody system. He couldn't wrap his mind around what divine purpose God could be accom-plishing here. Eli dropped his head in his hands, and his stomach churned. Meg was gonna head straight into the gale. He could feel it in his gut. And there was nothing he could do to stop her.

The need to help Meg warred with his inability to do so. It produced a fidgety tension that couldn't be relieved. Eli folded his arms on the top of his desk and pressed his forehead into his fists. He was running out of ideas. His father's words kept repeating through his mind. *A good businessman separates his work life from his personal life.*

But Eli didn't live like that. He was never able to compartmentalize the different parts of his life. What he felt, believed, it spilled over into every part of him. It was why he knew he'd never make it as a lawyer. One year of law school was enough for him to see that he wasn't wired like the other students. He didn't have that cutthroat edge his classmates wielded easily. When his heart was convinced of the right thing, he couldn't do anything else. Not even for a client.

His greatest fault, according to his law professor. He unclenched his fists.

Believers are supposed to be genuine.

Deep down, Eli feared his genuineness, his inability to separate work from his personal life, might tank his business and take Addison down with him. He was afraid he was hurting Meg more than helping her. It wouldn't matter that his intentions were sincere; all that mattered were results. He rubbed his forearms and the warmth that the friction created shot a shiver down his spine.

Lord, I don't know what to do, yet I am so overwhelmed by a conviction that I am supposed to do something.

He peppered questions at God, who remained quiet. Eli didn't expect an audible answer, but he waited for the familiar prodding of God moving in his heart. The swelling that accompanied His presence. Nothing.

When was the last time he'd opened his Bible?

The watershed question tightened his core. He last opened his Bible the day before Jake arrived, almost ten days ago. Eli had defaulted to his strength and wisdom rather than depending on the Lord's.

I'm sorry, God.

Eli wasn't looking for a new word from the Lord, not when the complete Word was already available and sufficient for everything. He opened his Bible app and navigated to his reading plan.

He inhaled a deep, pained breath and closed his eyes. *Forgive me, Lord.* His greatest responsibility as a friend was to live a life that reflected the image of God. The right image. A life that led others to trust more in the Lord. All this time, Eli had positioned himself as Meg's savior, but the only man who had the right to direct her steps was the One who was both fully man and fully God.

Eli consumed the daily Scripture passage in Exodus 14 like a starving man. Although the Israelites' departure from Egypt was not directly related to the issues he and Meg faced, the overall truth filled him with a peace that settled his heart. God fought for his people.

God fought for Meg, and He was most concerned with securing victory in the battle for her soul. He had used everything in her life to accomplish that. Now that her eternal destination was secure in His hands, He shifted, and now used everything in her life to continue to sanctify her and to make her more and more like Jesus.

And he was doing it in Eli's life as well.

Eli kneaded his shoulder. He straightened, pulled his cordless keyboard toward him, and powered on the computer. Meg was running out of time, and he needed to help her. Alfred was coming down, but God had given Eli the talent and ability to help.

Eli's phone vibrated on the desktop, rattling across the surface. A picture of his father's face lit up the screen. Eli pressed ignore.

The phone vibrated again, notifying him of a new voice message. Wait. His phone. Eli swiped through his pictures. He'd snapped a picture of Meg's sketch, her idea to save Alfred. If Addison made enough headway on *Return to Eden*, he could input Meg's design.

Infused with new energy, his fingers flew over the keys. He didn't even notice Addison arrive until his friend had set a to-go coffee from The Muffin Man in front of him.

"Do we have a new client?" Addison read over his shoulder. He was probably the only other person in Sycamore Hill that was able to translate the code on Eli's screen. "That's interesting." He leaned in and pointed to a line. "What if you changed this part so that the program automatically pulled data from public sources? If we integrated it with public records, it could generate solutions that yield greater productivity?"

"Good idea," Eli murmured.

"Then we could have it organize the data from lowest cost to greatest cost."

Eli nodded along. They were so close.

Addison paused, and Eli could feel his gaze increasing in weight. "Have you told her about it yet?"

"Meg? Meg who didn't want us to butt in? Meg, who said she wanted to do this alone? No, I haven't told her." Eli stopped typing and pinched the bridge of his nose.

"You're way out on a limb here."

"I know." He focused on the data in front of him. "You don't need to help me. In fact, why don't you take the day off? That way, if this blows back, it's all on me, not you."

Addison barked a bitter sound. "Why do you do that?"

"Do what?"

"Push away anyone that doesn't jump immediately on board with your idea."

"I don't." But even before the denial left his mouth, Eli saw the truth of Addison's statement. He did. When his father didn't support him, he pushed him away. When Meg didn't want his help, he pulled back and worked on a solution behind her back. Addison questioned one thing, and he told him to go home.

He stopped typing. His gritty eyes and hardened stomach quivered. The Lord wasn't holding anything back. The Holy Spirit dropped an anvil of conviction. Eli fully met Addison's gaze, and his voice cracked, "You're right. I do. It's wrong. I'm sorry."

Addison's open mouth made Eli laugh. It released the knot in his gut and made him feel lighter than he had in weeks. "I guess I'm more like my father than I want to admit."

Addison's tight smile loosened. "If you're open to collaboration, I have a few ideas."

Eli rotated his screen so Addison could see it from his workstation.

"On line twenty-four, if we can get buy-in from key businesses in town, this issue resolves itself."

"What's in it for them?"

"If a program can automatically sift through the initial stages of city approval and zoning requirements, it's less manhours for staff. This program has the potential to do more than help Meg. A tweaked version could be used by the city as an initial step to applying for permits, to see if the project is viable before manhours are used up only to deny it."

Eli spun the screen back to him. "Brilliant," he murmured. "And if we secured some sponsors to cover the costs of creating the program, we could rig it so appropriate local business ads appear on the sidebar that pertain to the type of project being run through the software."

The men looked at each other, the huge potential of this project settling on them both simultaneously. "This is it," Addison said. "This is the breakthrough project we've been looking for to stabilize our business. You did it."

Eli shook his head. "No, we did it. I hadn't even considered this application before. I was too focused on Meg."

Addison scraped a hand though his hair. "Right. Meg. Why don't you send me what you have already? I'll start laying the groundwork for the larger application while you keep going with her project. She can be our test case."

The irony of what just transpired was not lost on Eli. He'd been telling Meg for months that she didn't need to keep doing everything alone, yet that was exactly the lesson he needed to learn. They lived in community. The people here cared about them. They cared about the things that mattered to them.

Eli's epiphany birthed another one. *The community.* He'd been trying to help Meg all wrong. She didn't need him. She needed the people of Sycamore Hill. Wasn't that what she was always saying about the trees? They're social beings. They help each other out. That alone is not enough to ensure survival in the ecosystem, but it did give the weakest sapling a fighting chance. Just like her beloved tree, Meg lived in an interconnected community, and when one was weak, the others stepped up to provide what they needed. He flicked his wrist and his watch screen lit up. If he hurried, Sycamore Hill might be able to funnel the nourishment the neediest member of their forest needed.

"Any chance you can table the larger application and finish up programming the software to run Meg's design? I need to step out."

"Sure." Addison must have liked whatever he saw on Eli's face because the concerned creases in his expression shifted into smile lines. "Just send me her design. I should have something for you by the end of the day."

Eli checked the time. Perfect. That gave him just enough time to rally the troops.

Eleven

The contractor swatted Meg's hand away, and her design crumpled in her fingers. Tim—that was his name according to the quick web search she completed on the company—wouldn't even look at it. He wouldn't even take the paper from her hands and consider that there might be another way. A tightening started in the center of her chest and shot tentacles through her body until every limb tingled. Her insides quivered, begging for release. She wanted to stamp her feet like a two-year-old and wail until he yielded.

"You need to move, miss." Tim brushed by, his shoulder bumping hers, taking long strides toward a large bulldozer. "I need to clear the land today."

Meg curled her arms over her head to still her fluttery hands. She followed him. "What is he paying you? Maybe I can get you more?" Eli had offered to pay off Jake. Maybe he'd buy her time with the contractor?

Tim's expression tensed and his face reddened.

Okay. Big fail on the bribery attempt. She shifted gears and applied logic. "You won't even consider another way? How is that right? Fair? I deserve to be heard."

With one hand on the bulldozer's safety rails, he punctuated the air with the other in exasperated motions. "I told you, it's not my decision. I'm a hired man, and I have a job to do, and right now," he leaned forward and emphasized each individual word, "you're in my way."

Meg folded her arms across her chest. Her entire body hardened, and she pronounced each word carefully. "Call the man who is in charge. Let me speak with him."

Tim climbed into the cab of the bulldozer, his lips pressed into a white slash. He inserted the keys. "I don't have time for this. I said move."

Meg extended her paper to him one more time. She had to make him listen to her. "Just swap the parking lot and the building. The tree will be the focal point in the parking lot. It'll be a draw to the town and the area. How is that not good for your boss's business? It's free publicity."

His eyes softened a tiny bit. Kind of like how a parent looked at a child who simply couldn't understand or follow their logic. His gaze held pity. Exhaustion. And a hint of compassion. "You just don't understand how much money change and delays costs a project this size. You're fighting a battle you can't win."

The pressure behind her eyes burst and dampness leaked from their corners. "I don't care," she whispered, shaking her head. "Alfred is more than a tree. He is a part of our town history, and I'm not moving." Meg marched to the tree and stood in front of it. She locked eyes with Tim. All the compassion and kindness evaporated. He flicked the ignition, and the rattly bulldozer roared to life. Meg shouted over the engine noise. "If you're taking Alfred down, you are taking me with it."

Tim grimaced and shifted the machine into gear.

Meg braced herself. He wouldn't—

The bulldozer snailed forward. Two birds escaped the branches above her, crying out as if adding their voices to her cause might save their home. Branches rustled above her head. A squirrel moved deeper into Alfred's core. And twenty meters away, a bulldozer crawled straight for her.

Meg's inhalations shortened, and the scene unfolding momentarily blurred. She blinked hard, clearing her vision. Her breath came faster and faster, yet she couldn't seem to get enough oxygen into her lungs. He was calling her bluff. *He wouldn't hit her. He wouldn't actually run her down.* She stared into Tim's eyes. Their crazy game of chicken intensified with each inch of ground covered, and the man didn't blink. He just pressed his lips tighter and tighter until they disappeared entirely.

When the raised scoop interfered with their line of sight, Tim lowered it. It hovered right at Meg's chest, rattling as the caterpillar tracks worked to level the machine on the uneven ground. Tim never broke eye contact. He narrowed his eyes, shifting in his seat, creeping closer and closer.

Meg steadied herself. *Lord, I need you. If you don't do something here, I'm done. I can't—*

"Stop!" A voice screamed from behind the bulldozer. Eli yelled and flapped his arms as he caught up to Tim and started hitting the machine.

Tim's eyes bulged, and he did a double take as Eli darted in between Meg and the scoop. His hands flew over the controls, and he jerked a lever with enough force Meg was surprised it didn't snap. It halted his forward movement. Tim jumped from the cab. "Are you insane?"

Eli's chest heaved, his forehead dampened, and a wild fear filled his eyes. And he had never looked so good.

"You could have been killed." Sweat beaded on Tim's upper lip and his nostrils flared like a bull's. "What's wrong with you?"

Eli bent forward with his hands on his knees, sucking in deep breaths. He held up one finger to indicate that he'd answer as soon as he caught his breath.

Tim's head swivelled from Eli to Meg and then back to Eli again. "Are you with her?"

Eli nodded, still wheezing.

Kathryn Withers' compact vehicle zipped up the road and hugged the curb. She began unloading her recording equipment from the trunk.

Tim threw up his hands. "Doesn't anybody care that I have a job to do?"

Meg's body grew hot. Another car parked close to Kathryn's and a couple got out and headed their way. Meg pressed both hands over her stomach. "What's going on?"

Instead of answering her, Eli spoke to Tim. "I have hundreds of signatures on this petition asking for the owner to reconsider his plans."

Hundreds of signatures? Meg's heart flipped. When did he collect those? He'd been with her at Kim's house every evening. After she finished her proposal and told him her plans for this morning, he left to go home. At least she thought he'd gone home.

Tim snorted and paced in a short span in from of Eli. "What do you people hear when I speak? I already told the lady, I'm just a hired man. It's not my decision."

Kathryn positioned her tripod and camera so it framed Meg and the bulldozer. The scoop was only a few feet from Meg and Alfred. It had been close. Too close. Meg blinked against the pressure behind her eyes.

She'd told Eli to butt out. She said she had wanted to do this alone. But all she felt in this moment was an overwhelming sense of thankfulness for his propensity toward not listening. Tim wouldn't have actually hurt her—at least, she didn't think so—but she couldn't have stopped him by herself.

Kathryn positioned herself in front of the camera and flicked her hair. She clicked the remote in her hand and transformed from Kathryn, Ethan's girlfriend who frequently visited the bakery, to Kathryn Withers from *Sycamore Hill at Sunrise*.

She looked directly into the camera. "I'm Kathryn Withers, coming to you live from the corner of Main Street and Second Ave, where a local woman, Meg Gilmore, is in a standoff with the construction company New Horizon Properties." Kathryn put her microphone in front of Meg's mouth. "Can you tell the viewers why you are here today?"

Emotion clogged Meg's throat. She glanced at Eli, who nodded encouragingly. Eli did this. Eli gathered the troops to stand with Meg.

Meg stared at the camera as if she were looking directly into the eyes of every single resident of Sycamore Hill. She dried her damp palms on her pant legs. If Tim wouldn't read her proposal, then she'd narrate it. "This tree has been here longer than Sycamore Hill. It's thought to have been a sapling on a farm in the mid to late 1800's. The Historical Society claims the town grew up around it. In years past, development had always happened *around* the tree."

"And what's happening here today that concerns you?" Kathryn motioned to the bulldozer.

"An out-of-town investor has purchased four homes on this block. His plan, according to the permits he's filed, is to build condos and provide parking."

Kathryn tilted her head to the side. "And you're trying to stop him?"

"No." Meg's hair swung as she shook her head. "I'm trying to get him to adjust his plans to include Alfred instead of cutting him down."

"Alfred?"

Heat rocketed from Meg's chest to her face. Did she just refer to a tree by name on television?

The fine lines crinkling Kathryn's forehead softened. "Why is Alfred so important to you?"

Meg met Eli's gaze. He stood behind Kathryn, out of the shot. He nodded his head again. Off to the other side, Tim had his phone pressed against his ear. Hopefully he was speaking with the developer and not the police.

Meg cleared her throat. "I know what it is like to live without roots. But the people of Sycamore Hill don't need to live that way. This town has history and that means something. We can't—and we shouldn't—erase the past. Davina Mhartainn's diary and her family's immigration story was nearly lost to the town even while the Mhartainn's belongings were stored in the museum." Meg's voice softened, and the awe she felt every time she looked at Alfred filled her. "The forest that once stood here predated Confederation; did you know that? It was here before Nova Scotia, New Brunswick, Quebec, and Ontario formed the Dominion of Canada. Our country wasn't the result of revolution, or a sweeping outburst of nationalism. Conversations and civil negotiations birthed the Dominion of Canada. We shouldn't have to fight each other for change. Change can come as a result of respectful interactions where all parties strive for the good of the majority."

"Is that what you're doing here?" Kathryn pressed. "Trying to bring about change?"

"I'm trying to have a conversation, but no one will participate. No one cares that this tree is more than twenty-five meters tall and five meters around. It's survived Canadian blizzards, flooding, windstorms, and fire. Its limbs stretch meters in all directions and its roots even further underground. It shaded the Mhartainns' homestead, and its branches gave sanctuary to a child when a flash flood swept the area. It's all in their diaries."

Eli's gaze sharpened at the familiar tale of the flood.

Meg retrieved the copies she'd made of the diary pages from the bag slung over her shoulder. "The Mhartainn family was forced from their home in Scotland, and they rebuilt a life here. They survived what destroyed others, just like this tree. It's the only one left in the forest; it's a survivor." She met and held Eli's gaze. "Like the boy. Grandpa Albert, Morgan Martin's grandfather. Preserving it is a way to recognize and honor the people that lived here before us and the many that will live here after us."

"There you have it." Kathryn looked fully into the camera. "If history means anything to the long-time residents of Sycamore Hill, now is the time to come and stand alongside Meg as she fights to save a piece of our heritage."

Meg's chest swelled, and her breath temporarily bottled up. Would this be enough? Would people come? Did they really care about the things that were important to her? Her gaze darted to Eli, and a jolt of electricity melted her. Even if no one else came, the one who mattered the most was right here with her, in the trenches, standing between her and a bulldozer with nothing but pages of signatures to defend her. He did it all without waiting to be asked. He did it all despite his dad's objections.

Eli approached, slowly, tentatively, as if he was unsure of his welcome. He stopped and left about a foot between them, but his body swayed forward, and his warm breath tickled her earlobe. "I know you wanted to do this alone, but—"

Meg pressed a finger to his lips. "Thank you."

Eli's eyes were bright and glossy. Her index finger slipped off his lips and trailed down his chin. Even with the shadow of a beard, the strong lines of his jaw came through. She loved the way a tiny twitch near the hinge would pulse like it was keeping time with his heartbeat when he was concentrating.

She loved him.

It hit like a thunderbolt. *She loved him!*

Eli leaned forward far enough that if Meg lifted up to her toes their noses would rub. Their lips would be close enough to—

Tim cleared his throat, and Meg jumped back.

Crimson flushed Eli's neck and cheeks. Meg warily eyed the camera that still rolled. Did the camera catch her and Eli? Was Kathryn live streaming? What would Eli's dad think? If any of the same thoughts flickered through Eli's mind, his expression didn't show it. Instead, he laced his fingers through Meg's and pulled her closer to him until their shoulders brushed together.

"The owner's coming," Tim said. "He'll be here in about thirty minutes. Can I look over that design?"

Warmth radiated through Meg as she handed over the paper and exhaled a deep and gratifying sigh. She did it. They did it.

Tim meandered away, studying Meg's notes, looking at the tree, and then looking at the houses slated for destruction.

Please, Lord. Grant us favor.

Twelve

E li tugged Meg to his side. What was she thinking, standing in front of the bulldozer like that? Eli didn't believe that Tim would ever intentionally hurt her, but accidents happen. He tightened his arm around her waist. When she didn't pull away, his heart quickened.

Meg tipped her head back and looked into his eyes. Her gaze moved, slowly examining every inch of his face with glossy eyes. Her cheeks flushed. "You've been busy," she said softly.

His pulse throbbed in his throat. "I collected signatures supporting your design idea." A yawn swelled, and he swallowed it down. Losing a night's rest was a small price to pay for the joy reflected in her expression.

Her misty eyes darted over the continuously growing crowd.

Eli instinctively looked for Jake's face in the crowd, getting a taste of how Meg had been living since she'd left him. Constantly waiting for the other shoe to drop. If Jake was still in town, he was bound to show up eventually because this is where the action was. Where Meg was.

"But that was just a sketch," she said. "Hardly enough to warrant this kind of response."

"It started with your sketch. But once Addison and I put it through our software, we saw it had real potential. Swapping the locations doesn't just save the tree, it makes more sense from a design standpoint. Preserving a bit of space around Alfred really only costs them a couple of parking spaces, but adding Alfred to the historical tours and the potential draw to the area will give all the small businesses a boost."

She pulled back. His arm slid from encircling her waist to cupping her elbow. Her eyebrows squished together. "Your program? What program?"

Heat crawled up his neck. He still hadn't told her about *Return to Eden*. He folded his lips inward to dampen them. "It was supposed to be a birthday gift."

She angled her head. "What was?"

"*Return to Eden* is a piece of software that Addison and I designed to help you once you graduated. We used this," he gestured to the tree, "as a test run." Disbelief welled up inside of him. "It works, Meg. It not only works, but the basic design has unlimited applications. Our business is going to make it."

She wrapped her arms around his waist and laid her head on his chest. "You added to my idea?"

His heart plummeted. That was her takeaway? He handed her the clipboard with a printout of the design. His breath bottled up as she studied the image. She had to love it as much as he did, but would she see it as him taking over, or would she see it for it what it really was, a gift from someone who loved her?

"This is amazing." She handed the sketch back. "You've been telling me for so long this place is special, but I've been hesitant to believe it. I didn't want to be let down." She swiped the back of her hand across her eyes.

Was she crying? Sympathy pressure grew behind his eyes. "You don't have to keep thinking that you're in this alone." His words came out thickly. "I'm here. I'm standing with you. And the signatures prove that so will Sycamore Hill."

Meg's eyes shifted. They locked onto something behind him and spread wide. If not for the light in her gaze he might have thought she felt fear. But that wasn't fear. It was amazement. "I'm finally starting to believe you."

Eli turned. About a half dozen more vehicles were inching their way down the small side road and threading into tight parking spaces. As Kim unbuckled Oliver from his car seat, she pulled a handmade sign from her backseat. She handed a smaller version to her son, and they walked hand in hand toward Alfred.

Oliver waved his sign. *Save Sycamore Hill Trees.*

The others removed signs from their trunks and headed their way. Kathryn repositioned her camera and recorded their arrivals. Pride in his town made Eli want to burst, making it hard for him to inhale a full breath. Sycamore Hill wasn't a perfect place, not by a long shot, but it was a good place. It was place to belong.

"Save our trees. Save our trees." The chant picked up and rose in volume as people multiplied. But all that warm and fuzzy goodness thickened like cement as a black sedan with tinted windows glided into a vacant spot.

His father climbed out and looked over the growing crowd, and for one second their gazes collided. Eli instantly built a defense against whatever argument the man might bring. It was going to take more than smooth words and a practiced smile to sway his father toward Meg's cause. But he halted drafting his mental speech when Dad pulled out a sign from his trunk that said *Save Sycamore's History*. Eli's breath hitched in his throat. Dad was on their side? What happened to the client comes first? Stay neutral?

Meg watched him. She stepped closer to him as if he was the one that needed support. As if this was his moment.

Maybe it was.

"Sycamore Hill isn't a perfect place. But it is filled with people who care about us. You've taught me that. These people also care about you." She turned his words on him with such softness and love that it stole his breath. He didn't think he'd inhaled once in the entire time it took his dad to walk over from his car.

"You came." Eli hated the way his voice cracked. His dad would hear it as a weakness.

Dad flicked a smiled toward Meg, and she stepped away, giving him a final nod of encouragement. "After talking with your girl here," Dad jutted his chin toward Meg, "I started to see your point of view."

Your girl?

It felt like his eyes had bugged out of his head. He didn't know what surprised him more, his dad coming around or Meg not correcting his phrasing of *your girl*. He reached for Meg instinctively, and she came without hesitation. "You spoke with my dad?"

Meg shrugged her shoulders. "We chatted for a bit."

"After hearing her concerns for the community, and benefiting from her insight and wisdom, I decided it was in my company's best interests to have an arborist look over the tree. It's healthy and poses no developmental issues to the project, I don't see why we can't find a solution where everyone wins." Eli's dad looked him right in the eyes. "It'll be a reminder of how communities and families are better when they listen to each other, better when they work together instead of against each other."

What was happening? Eli scrubbed his face. Sleep deprivation had to be playing with his mind. That was it. Eli was asleep. His dad wasn't really compromising. But— he shifted his gaze to Meg. If he was asleep that meant that their almost-kiss didn't happen either. That meant the joy he saw in her eyes was really a figment of his imagination.

Please, Lord, let this be real.

His dad's hand landed on his shoulder and squeezed. "You did something good here, son."

Eli's mouth slackened further.

"I know you think all I ever wanted was for you to be some hotshot lawyer, but that's not true. I wanted you to reach the potential that I saw in you. I wanted you to be part of this community, working for the interests of the people. Lawyers are goal-oriented, resilient, logical, detail-oriented advocates. You excel in all those areas, as today proves. You are using your gifts, and I'm proud of you."

Eli wiped his eyes.

One by one, the crowd continued to swell until it seemed like the entire town had gathered around Alfred. Before Eli knew what was happening, they surged around Meg and looked to her for direction. He squeezed her hand and stepped back. "This is your moment. Go for it."

At his word, Meg stepped forward. "This area was once travelled by the Martin family's ancestors and the trail they took brought them right by this very spot. I've studied the history and mapped the trails, and I'm proposing the town marks this place as part of a new historical tour that visitors can travel that will honor those who have come before us and forged the way."

Someone cheered from the back, and a smatter of clapping followed. "Where we are planted matters," Meg said.

Meg then launched into such an unexpected message that Eli's jaw loosened. He expected her to keep the attention on Alfred and her, but when given an audience, she did what he'd seen her do a thousand times before. She shone the light on Jesus.

"This tree has survived seasons of drought and intense heat for one reason and one reason only. Its roots are connected to water. It's done the work of making its way through hardened soil, and when the elements hit hard, this tree thrived because of the work it did under the surface."

Meg locked her eyes on his, and just when he thought he couldn't be prouder, she continued. "Hard times, drought, the heat, they come for all of us. And these trials don't change us as much as they expose whether our hearts are connected to the Living Water of Jesus. You gathering here today, picking up a sign and standing with me shows me that in seasons of great drought, this community is connected in such a way that it still produces fruit in a drought."

Her eyes grew shiny. Meg blinked faster, and the lump in Eli's throat doubled in size. "In a way that I don't fully understand, God led me to this town. He led me to Life House. He led me to the community church. He led me to this battle for a sycamore tree to help me face my past and battle my demons. God is growing me into someone that I would have never become without that victory."

A stirring started in the back. Like a widening ripple, a short pudgy man elbowed his way toward Meg. "I'm Franklin Cooper, and this is my land. You need to leave, or I'll call the police."

The chant started up again. "Save our trees. Save our trees."

Mr. Cooper locked eyes with Eli's dad. "This is all great, but my contractor has a job to do. I'm building these apartments, and if you have a problem with that, you can talk with my lawyer."

Eli's dad approached Mr. Cooper, who lifted his chin. "My lawyer has a few words to say."

As the sign hung slack by his dad's side, Eli's hopes fell.

Dad whispered in Franklin's ear and the man's face reddened. A short exchange of furious whispers resulted, and finally, Franklin threw up his hands. "Fine."

Dad turned to the crowd. "The building slated for this area will be completely redesigned to accommodate the tree." Dad lifted the sign, and a cheer swept through the crowd. "As some of you know, Meg has turned in plans to swap the locations of the parking lot and the building. The new design features the tree, and there will be benches and green space worked into the parking lot."

As Dad outlined the new plans to the community, Meg's warm breath heated his ear. "What do you think that your dad whispered to him?"

"Probably something about us having enough signatures on the petition to force the issue to court, a delay that will cost Mr. Cooper far more than changing the plans."

Her gaze rested on him. The milling crowd faded into the background. All he could see was Meg's shining face. "You did it," she whispered.

"We did it."

"It'll take a few weeks to ensure the presented plan is sound, but the residents of Sycamore Hill can rest assured that the tree will remain," Dad said.

A furious whisper exchanged between Dad and Mr. Cooper occurred. Dad's straight spine, lifted chin, and intense gaze all communicated an unwillingness to shift from this position. Mr. Cooper grunted and pushed his way through the crowd.

Before the multitude could absorb him, Meg dropped Eli's arm and reached for Mr. Cooper. She pulled him back to center stage. "I'd like to thank Mr. Cooper for considering a plan that is not only profitable for him and the town, but also meaningful to us all."

Mr. Cooper's complexion colored to an even deeper shade of red no longer fueled by anger. Meg linked arms with the man who only a few minutes before had been her opponent. "Together, we will build a better Sycamore Hill."

The crowd applauded.

A rumble sounded at the edge of the crowd, and Eli followed it to the source. Jake. He elbowed his way toward Meg.

Her complexion paled.

"Well, well, well, what do we have here?"

Thirteen

The familiar timbre of Jake's voice slithered around Meg's heart and squeezed with the relentless pressure of a boa constrictor. She swallowed against bile and fisted her hands at her sides.

The throng surrounding Meg and the tree parted, and Jake cast his greasy smile at people even as he nudged them out of the way. "Little Meggie rallied the troops?"

Meg's stomach knotted at the way Eli eyed Jake. He moved between them, but she placed a palm on his arm. As much as she loved him for the gesture, this was her fight, and she needed to do this.

His muscles rippled under the pressure of her hand, but he seemed to understand. His head jerked in a curt nod, and his arms dropped to his side. But they remained tight and ready. Jake had a short leash.

"Jake." Meg puckered against the bitter-tasting name. It was poetic, in a way, that he showed up today. Her public article on preservation exposed her and drew him to Sycamore Hill, and today, her public stand for Alfred did it again, bookending the last ten days. The tension throbbing at the back of her skull and neck slid down to join the relentless pressure in her chest. The confrontation she'd prayed to avoid stood before her. Strength she didn't have yesterday, God offered today. *I will strengthen you; I will help you; I will uphold you with my righteous right hand.*

Jake's jawline moved like he was grounding his molars. His mouth bowed down. He was stirring for a fight. The realization saturated deeply into her bones and sparred with her faith and the Lord's promise to never leave or forsake her.

God, I need you.

A sudden, gusty breeze blew in like His answer. It pulled strands of her hair from the loose elastic at her neck. Alfred's crown swayed, cheering her on. Dark tendrils danced around her face like the leaves waltzing around his trunk. God was here. With her. In her. Using her tree and the crowd protesting the development to stake her fragile trunk. If Jake expected her to wither like a shrub in salt land, he was in for a surprise. Meg's roots tapped Living Water, and God made her a fighter. A survivor. And she didn't fear the drought or the heat Jake threatened. Not anymore.

"Do your *friends* know who they are following? What you've done? Who you are?" he sneered.

She winced under the verbal blows. Her eyes squeezed shut. A tremble rocked through her fiercely. Knowing Jake didn't deserve any more real estate in her mind didn't stop the cutting comments from leaving their mark.

Something amazing rippled through the crowd. It was as if Meg's response released a chemical scent into the air like a tree registering pain. It signaled a threat to her community. Like mother trees in a forest, they surrounded her, determined to nourish her through their roots, refusing to let her die without a battle. They stood with her. They felt her pain.

Her friends straightened and fell in behind her. Gloria, Pastor Owen's out-of-town girlfriend, tucked into Owen's side. Kathryn kept rolling. Ethan stood by Eli. Kim scooped up Oliver and held him close. A smile loosened the tension in Meg's jaw. She unclenched her teeth and rolled her shoulders back. Meg studied the man who ruled her nightmares for far too long, and a surprising feeling of empowerment mixed with calm acceptance descended. Kim had been right. Meg had given Jake far too much power over her.

And if Meg gave it to him, then Meg could take it away.

Her community displayed varying responses to Jake's taunting and aggressive posture. Some held curiosity. Others disdain. And others still, like Eli, distrust. Someone would have called Jackson by now. All she had to do was keep Jake here until the police officer arrived. This was a thought that would have terrified her a few days again, but today, a sense of calm and belonging filled her. There was nothing that Jake could do to truly hurt her. He might try to harm her body, but he couldn't touch her soul.

Meg lifted her chin. "I've spent my life treating my past with you like a liability, like it was a weakness. I've hidden it, denied it, and at times refused to learn from it. But there's another way." She drilled her gaze into Jake's. He arched a brow.

"God can take my past and make it a strength."

His eyes widened, exposing more white and an unexpected vulnerability, infusing Meg with courage.

"God's fortified me, given me wisdom, and shown me His power. I've learned from you, Jake. I've learned that my life is valuable. My voice is needed. I matter."

Jake scoffed, but his ever-confident smirk faltered. He shifted his gaze away from her and flicked the same handsome smile that once weakened Meg's knees toward the nearest woman and gestured as if to ask if she believed this. She tucked into the side of the person beside her. Jake's shiny charm had dulled. His nostrils flared, and like a villain making a final desperate stand, he thrust out his chest. "You owe me, Meg. After all I did for you, you owe me."

She shook her head. "You don't define me or decide what I owe. I am not who you say or think that I am, and these people know it."

"Do they?" His jeer bared his teeth. "I betcha I could tell them a few stories that would curl their toes."

Meg slashed her arm through the air. "Enough!" She didn't know who was more shocked at her response. "The people that matter know me, and nothing you can say will change that."

Meg sought Eli and read no judgment in his gaze. No shock. Only love. Her chest swelled with increasing confidence.

She found Kim, and she gave an encouraging nod. Kim was right again. There was freedom in letting the past come to light. Darkness fled light, but living in the light didn't obligate her to spotlight every sinful choice or painful event. Meg got to decide when the details of her childhood were shared. It was her decision, her story, and no one, not even Jake, could bully her into telling it prematurely. Today, the spotlight shone on Christ and the redemptive work He had done in her life. She would not mar it with some tale of her former partying days. Those details were not necessary to showcase the power of God.

The only way to stop Jake was to take away his power. She raised her chin. It only trembled a little, wobbling her voice in a way undermined her projected confidence. *Lord, please. Go before me.*

"My name is Meg Gilmore. I am a sinner, born again by the power of the Holy Spirit alive in me. This man," she gestured at Jake, refusing to let his flinty eyes frighten her, "might waste his breath sharing the details of my sinful past, but another man—God in the flesh—is the One who truly defines me."

A few quiet *amens* rippled from the back, bolstering her courage. Eli and Kim nodded along, and the wave of encouragement swelled.

"I've made mistakes. No." Meg gave her head a shake and pounded her fisted hand against her thigh. "Mistake is too kind of a word. I've sinned against God, and those sins nailed Jesus to the cross. But when God saved me, he didn't give the old me a makeover, He replaced the old me with Christ, making me new. The me that lived in the stories Jake might tell is dead. Those sins no longer hold power over me. I'm forgiven, and where there is forgiveness, there is no shame or condemnation. Christ's blood makes me clean."

Pastor Owen was the first to start clapping. Like dominoes falling, the people joined in, and emotion swelled against the back of Meg's throat. Her eyes struggled to control a rush of moisture and pressure. "I used to be afraid that I'd be an outcast." New lightness filled her chest. "But I'm not afraid anymore. I can't change my past, but God has changed my future and secured my eternity. No one can snatch me from His hand."

She levelled a look at Jake. "Not even you."

Eli, who'd stood behind her this whole time, stepped beside her. He threaded his fingers through hers, and the heat of his grasp flowed through her arm and core, reaching her heart. All her pent-up tension released, and a comfortable warmth replaced it.

Jake's attention darted around as if looking for the easiest and quickest exit. His jaw jutted out. His jerky movements and clear discomfort flooded Meg with unexpected compassion. Jake represented everything she once was, and if God could change her, then God could change Jake.

She squeezed Eli's hand and let it go. She took a step in Jake's direction and reached out. Her hand trembled, and she hated the weakness that it revealed. She stopped just short of touching his arm. The back of her throat ached. "Choices have consequences. Yours will find you. And when they finally catch up with you, I hope the Lord uses them to open your ears to the good news of Jesus. But you won't get a single cent from me. You no longer hold that kind of power over me."

Jake's gaze tripped over the people filling in around her. Kim gripped Oliver's hand. Lydia bounced Sonya on her hip. Pastor Owen and Gloria made their way closer to Eli, standing in solidarity with him. Kathryn pointed her camera lens at Meg, and Ethan stood beside Kathryn, his arms folded across his chest like a defensive football player. Emma, a nurse practitioner, lugged her medical bag from her car.

Please, Lord, don't let us need the medical supplies.

"You might want to consider moving on." Ben Sawyer pushed toward them.

Jake ticked up his chin. "Who are you?"

"I'm the guy that pulled up your public records. I visited an old address on file and had an interesting discussion with some men who've been looking for you."

A crack appeared in Jake's cockiness.

"You've gotten in with some tough guys. They were really curious to learn where you've been the last few weeks. Seems you skipped out on a debt." Ben made a tsking noise and wagged his finger. "I was happy to tell them all about your appearance in Sycamore Hill."

The crack widened. Jake's bravado gave way to fear like a burst dam. But he quickly recovered and schooled his features. He threw up an irritated hand. "Whatever. I'm outta here."

"Not too fast," Jackson McGregor called out.

Meg nearly collapsed from relief.

Jake's gaze hit the man's provincial police badge, and he spun on his heel, only making it two short strides before the crowd boxed him in. Jake diverted and landed nose to nose with Eli.

"What's your hurry?" Eli asked. "The officer wants to speak with you."

Jake motioned like he was going to shove Eli out of the way, but Jackson caught his arm. "That's not a good idea."

Jake's jaw moved back and forth in a motion all too familiar to Meg. He was close to losing control, but Jackson was having none of it. He spun Jake around and slapped cuffs on his wrists. "Jake Holt, you're under arrest for breaching a restraining order and for criminal harassment. You're coming with me."

Meg's hand fell over her heart, and she sought Eli. *Was it over?*

"There's a warrant out for you in the city," Jackson said. He caught Meg's eyes. "He won't be able to bother you for a very long time."

Jackson read Jake his rights and led him away.

Ben gave a two-fingered salute from just behind Eli. "Sorry I was a bit late getting to the party."

Meg laughed. It was the first time in a long time that she laughed from that deep place in her soul. The crowd dispersed now that the excitement was over. Their chattering played like background music.

"Where's your save the trees sign?" Eli shoved Ben's shoulder good-naturedly.

"A journalist always stays neutral." Ben winked at Meg.

"Thank you." Meg said it so quietly that only Ben heard.

He dipped his head. "It was nothing. All in a day's work."

Wrong. It was everything, and Ben only found the men scary enough to send Jake packing because Eli kept pushing her until she allowed him to do something to help. She sought Eli like a magnet seeking steel. His expression softened as their gazes met. "Thank you," she whispered again.

Eli bent. His breath caressed her earlobe, sending shivers to her toes. "You're welcome." In the gentlest movement, he turned her, and his lips brushed against hers. It was the sweetest, most innocent kiss she'd ever known.

A cheer ripped through the remaining crowd, and Kathryn turned the camera on herself, "You saw it here first. The people of Sycamore Hill stand together."

Meg pressed her cheek against Eli's chest. The rhythmic thumping of his heart rooted her. His arms dropped down to her waist tugged her closer. She felt his lips against the top of her head. "I can't believe that you did all this."

"You did this." He whispered the words into her hair.

Her heart felt full.

Off to the side, Eli's dad watched them. When he gave a crisp nod and tipped an imaginary hat to her, a deep and gratifying sigh slipped from her. He returned to his vehicle in an unhurried and relaxed pace and put his protest sign in the trunk.

Today was more than her victory. Eli and his dad had won something precious, too. She inhaled Eli's scent and let her eyes drift shut. She pressed her smiling lips together. God was good.

Fall

Fourteen

M eg stood on the sidewalk in front of her home, an early wedding gift purchased by Eli's father. Not that they needed such an extravagant gift now that Eli's dad had released Eli's trust fund, but it was the gesture that mattered. When Meg opened the meticulously wrapped present and the deed to the house fell onto her lap, she could not speak. Her throat had seemed to suddenly contract. The house was Mr. Martin's way of showing Meg that she belonged to the family. Some days she still had to pinch herself to prove that she wasn't dreaming. Sure, it was the smallest home on the street, but she loved it.

And it was hers.

Theirs.

Still, something wasn't right. She held her breath, inclining her ear as she tilted her head to the side and studied the cedar-sided historical beauty. All fell silent. The Canadian flag mounted to the right of the front door failed to ripple in the stillness. The shaded porch allowed just enough light to illuminate the empty, darkened corners. The vintage mailbox remained closed. Pansies and black-eyed Susans stood erect like the queen's guards in their sunny spot in the front garden. Nothing was trampled. Nothing appeared out of place. Everything appeared just as she'd left it this morning.

But *something* was different. The front door sidelights distorted the interior in a hazy blur. A fluttering rooted deep in her belly spread through her insides with delicious thoroughness. *What had Eli done now?*

Eli wasn't moving in until after the wedding, but he'd been at the house nearly every day making improvements. Not a single creaky floorboard or stiff window in need of repair remained.

Meg rushed up the porch stairs two at a time and pushed open the front door. She didn't bother with the key. She knew it would be open and he was waiting for her. The hinges on the front door no longer creaked. "Honey, I'm home," she called out.

Eli turned from the kitchen sink and smiled. "I like the sound of that." He lifted his filthy hands in front of him. "I'd hug you, but, well, you're too clean for me right now."

Meg's grin stretched wider and wider as she approached him and angled her cheek for a kiss.

Eli's breath fanned against her earlobe as he feathered his lips over her skin. Shivers streaked all the way down to her toes. He rinsed his dirty hands under the kitchen faucet. "How did you know I was here?"

She lifted a shoulder. "I didn't. Just had a hunch."

He dried his hands on a blue and white checkered towel hanging over the handle of the stove's oven door. "The wedding isn't for a few more months, but I have a surprise for you. I couldn't wait any longer."

Just the mention of their upcoming nuptials warmed her middle. It still astounded her that a guy like Eli Martin had bought her a ring. On one balmy night under Alfred's canopy and near a smattering of people walking the historical trail that Valerie put together, Eli's knee hit the damp ground.

She arched an eyebrow. "What kind of surprise?"

"I didn't really plan it; it's more like I planted it." He winked as he opened his arms and beckoned her.

Meg stepped into his embrace and wrapped her arms around his waist. She relaxed into him as she tucked herself into the hug. She'd never felt safer than when she was in his arms. "You're full of surprises."

Eli pulled back and lowered his chin to look down at her. He dropped a kiss on the tip of her nose. "I've been hunting for the perfect wedding gift, and I finally found it."

"The house was enough." She rested her cheek on his shoulder. "More than enough."

"That's from my dad. This is from me. I took a trip down the river and dug up your gift."

Meg crinkled her nose. The river?

The corners of Eli's eyes wrinkled with his easy smile, and emotion filled his eyes. This must be some gift. She stepped out of his embrace and moved closer to the kitchen window. Based on the breadcrumb trail of dirt that arced from the backdoor to the sink, he'd come from the backyard. Whatever he was up to, it started out there.

Eli moved behind her. He wrapped his arms around her middle and pulled her against his chest. His heart thudded against her back. He was so confident in his gift it was almost irritating that she couldn't guess what it was. Everything near the house looked the same. Her hammock strung between two trees was still. Her plastic patio set with four chairs remained undisturbed near the back door, just a few feet from the closed barbecue. But further back, where the yard dipped into the ravine, was harder to see. She squinted.

"Alfred is wind pollinated." Eli's words tickled her ear. "That means the fertilized seeds can travel."

She poked her tongue into the side of her cheek. She could write a book on sycamore trees. There wasn't anything he could tell her that she didn't already know, but since he knew that already, she sensed he was leading up to something. Something big, judging from the way his muscles flexed against her.

He spun her around, scooping up her hands. A laugh trickled from her lips and filled the small space. This was her future. Love, laughter, and Eli. God had been so good to her.

"Let me show you." Eli led Meg to the back door, but before he would let her step outside, he covered both her eyes with one hand. The coolness of his damp palm soothed her hot skin. "Watch your step." He guided her onto the patio just as the wind stirred to gently kiss her cheeks and dance with the collar of her shirt. Wisps of hair frolicked playfully, tickling as they grazed her neck and cheek while the warmth of his hand and the security of his arms around her waist anchored her.

The ground beneath her feet softened. Damp blades of the grass nibbled at her ankles. "Where are we going?" she laughed.

"Shhh," he admonished her. "Or Mrs. Brisbane will hear."

Mrs. Brisbane visited frequently now. She and Meg had passed many pleasant hours at Meg's kitchen table, praying and talking about the Lord and His plans for Meg and Eli. The older woman had happily stepped into the role of surrogate-mother-of-the-bride.

"Almost there." Eli positioned her. The thumping of Meg's heart played the soundtrack of their love. Exciting. Unpredictable. Fun.

Eli removed his hand from her eyes. Coolness swept over her face, and she squinted against the sudden light.

He had walked her to the very back of the yard. They had no

rear neighbors. The homes on this side of the street had yards that dipped into a deep ravine owned by the town. One of Meg's favorite jogging trails wound through the wooded area behind her neighborhood.

A hardy sapling staked in the moist soil swayed like a metronome at her feet. Its slender neck bent as if its heavy head was slightly bowed in exhaustion from transplant shock. It would perk up after a few days of care. She glanced curiously at Eli. He practically burst with barely contained joy. "Alfred's a dad!"

Her breath shuddered. Meg fell to her knees. It didn't matter that the grass slowly soaked though her jeans. She didn't care. She gingerly ran her fingertips over the green. "How?"

"I went on a bit of a research trip. Addison and I trekked the riverbanks looking for a sycamore like Alfred small enough but strong enough to transplant." Eli squatted beside Meg. His hands slid down her arms until he folded her fingers in his. "It's my wedding gift to you."

Meg pulled in a gulp of air and shrieked. She launched herself at the best man who ever lived.

Eli fell onto his bottom, and he turned her so her back leaned against his chest. It didn't matter that Mrs. Brisbane might have heard her shriek of delight or their ridiculous laughing as they righted themselves. All that mattered was the man God had given her to love and cherish for the rest of her life. She couldn't drag her eyes from the tiny plant and all it represented.

"I planted him here so that the roots won't interfere with the water and sewer lines in our house or the neighbors," Eli said. "He's going to be a big boy."

"What should we call him?"

"What do you think of Theodore? It means divine gift."

Meg nodded. She liked that. Divine gift. "It's perfect."

His chin pressed against the top of her head. "Just think, as our family tree grows, so will Theo. As we put down roots and add limbs, so will he."

She twisted her torso to wrap her arms around him. She pushed her face into his shoulder, welcoming the pressure that pushed back against her tears as she absorbed the depth of his commitment to their future. He knew her. He loved her. He understood her. Enough to welcome the chaos of construction and add rooms to her tiny house so it could grow alongside their family needs. She spoke into the muscle tensing under her cheek. "Best. Gift. Ever."

Eli's lips pressed into her hair. "We'll all grow old together."

Moisture stung her eyes, and peace descended despite her tears. Her erratic heartbeat and jumbled thoughts added to the growing pool of wet spreading over Eli's T-shirt. She couldn't believe it. Eli had found Alfred's sapling. Alfred was no longer alone in this world.

And neither was she.

His Sycamore Sweetheart

SHE WANTS ACCEPTANCE. HE WANTS APPROVAL.
THEY GET A CATASTROPHIC WARDROBE
MALFUNCTION, CONFUSION, AND A DISASTROUS
CHURCH SCANDAL.

Gloria Sycamore returns to Sycamore Hill and takes on the ultimate challenge: regaining the town's trust while navigating the chaotic pleasure of dating their beloved minister. Under the watchful eyes of the public, privacy is a luxury, and every decision she makes is open for debate.

Pastor Owen finds himself stuck between a rock and a hard pew when rumors of biblical proportions divide him and Gloria. Eyebrows shoot higher than the church steeple and whispers reverberate through the hallowed halls. Owen struggles to balance his flock's demands with his heart's desires. Will he rise to the occasion, or will he find himself delivering sermons in an empty sanctuary?

Despite Gloria's illustrious family name and Owen's honourable character, the couple is caught in the throes of a scandal. As the community questions Gloria's commitment to her faith, the town, and their pastor, the pews become a battleground for a holy war as Gloria and Owen fumble their way to true love.

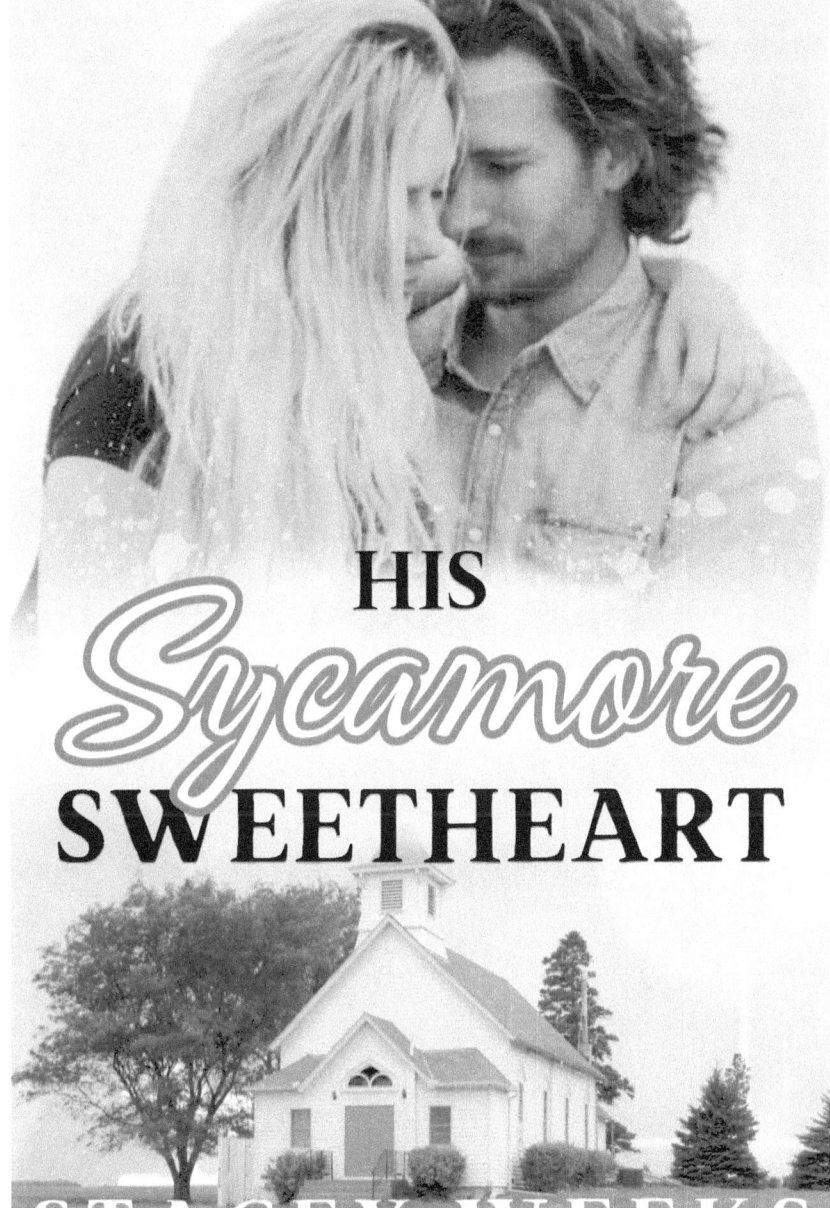

HIS
Sycamore
SWEETHEART

STACEY WEEKS

One

I t could be worse.

Illuminated only by the light of the moon and several strategically-placed motion sensor lights, Gloria Sycamore fisted her hands on her hips. The toe of her three-inch-heeled boot tapped on the asphalt as she surveyed the jam-packed storage unit. Correction—overflowing storage unit. The contents of her life spilled out of the orange, garage-style door. Gloria righted a toaster tipped on its side, and her stomach lurched, just as it always did at the sight of her independence packed neatly into cardboard boxes with the top flaps folded over.

Just folded, not taped.

And neatly was a stretch.

A dot of sweat dribbled down her neck, between her shoulder blades, and over each bump in her spine in its descent. Her long-sleeved T-shirt stuck to her body like shrink wrap, and tendrils of frizzy, blonde hair had loosened from her ponytail, growing fatter and fatter with each passing, clammy second. The post-sunset coolness of the late September evening did little to moderate her inner, raging furnace. Acrylic fingernails one through eight dug into her palms, and nine and ten lay somewhere on the ground underneath her sea of belongings. She stepped around the box erupting with scarves and shoes she'd never wear in a small town as far behind in fashion trends as Sycamore Hill. In three long strides, she reached the open trunk of her car, pivoted, and paced back.

The top half of the storage unit had lots of space, but Gloria didn't have the upper body strength to stack the boxes any higher. She should have waited for Owen. Correction. She had waited for Owen. She'd waited a whole hour. Sixty minutes. Three thousand, six hundred seconds. Now, ninety minutes later, she'd done the best she could, and it still wasn't good enough. It was the tagline of her life. All twenty-four years. Eight thousand, seven hundred and sixty-some-odd days of not being good enough. Her armpits dampened. She'd blame the growing stains on the physical labor. Not her perceived failure.

Owen was the one who'd picked a Wednesday night for her to move her belongings home. When Gloria announced that she'd given up her apartment in the city, Owen assured her parents that he'd help her, and there was no need for her dad to risk twinging his back again. Okay. Giving up her apartment was a stretch, too. Lost was a bit more accurate. Unable-to-pay-the-rent-when-she-didn't-have-a-job hit even closer to the truth. Evicted, if she was being totally honest. But this wasn't about her failure. It was about Owen's. He said that church meetings happened on Tuesday nights. Wednesday was clear. Wednesday was free. On Wednesday, he'd be all hers.

And in a nanosecond of terrible clarity, she understood what she'd been trying their entire relationship to not think about. Owen would never be wholly hers. Not as long as he was a pastor. He belonged to the church—the only acceptable mistress.

She puffed out a breath that failed to loosen the tension squeezing her chest. If Owen had come, he would have stacked the boxes. Then, she'd have a bit more room and all ten fingernails. But instead of enjoying Owen's dry banter and benefitting from his upper body strength, she paced in front of unit twenty-one, the one that spewed waves of stuff into view of anyone who happened to drive by the fenced-off self-storage business on the outskirts of town. She pressed her lips together until they tingled. What to do, what to do.

The little piggy that went to market jammed against the edge of a box with the word *books* scrawled in black permanent marker on the side. As her toe painfully compressed, Gloria threw her hands out to the sides for balance and knocked over a coat rack. She hopped on one foot and shook out the other, her jerky movements knocking the flap of the closest box open because, of course, she didn't tape that one shut, either. The rhyme scheme from the familiar storybook sitting on top mocked her. *When life pours you lemons, think lemonade. When the sun gets too hot, be thankful for shade.*

She could use a cool drink of lemonade right about now. Her inability to secure a job after her co-op placement at Grander Nursery School ended had necessitated her move back home. Gloria didn't want to feel thankful things weren't worse, because right now, as she wondered who watched her from the vehicle that crawled down the road at a snail's pace, life felt pretty bad. Unfair. Rip-roaringly frustrating. Still, she automatically followed the directions she gave her precious kiddos. Find the good.

Worse would be not having a place to store her things while she temporarily moved back into her parents' home. Worse would be *needing* to live in her childhood home, when instead, she'd chosen to. Sure, the alternative was going into debt and living on credit, but it was still a choice—big difference. Worse would be losing eight more fingernails and adding a headache. Worse would be— She caught her reflection in a mirror leaning against the corner. Frizzy, blonde curls. Skin flushed to the point of blotchiness. Dark circles under her armpits. Worse would be Owen showing up and seeing her like this and deciding that maybe she wasn't the girl for him after all. *No matter how awful or ugly it gets, you can be thankful for something, I'd bet—*

"Need a hand?" Owen Mason's question interrupted the catchy rhyme.

Worse had found her again. And instead of offering her lemonade, she sucked the juices from plain, old, sour lemons. Her mouth puckered.

Despite just thinking—literally three seconds ago—that it was good Owen wasn't here, her body responded positively to his familiar timbre. His words wrapped around her like a hug that she needed to shrug out of. She didn't turn around. She wasn't in a forgiving mood any more than she was in a thankful one.

"I know what you're thinking." She spoke to the wall.

"Do you?"

She heard his smile, and it sanded a tiny bit of the edge off her annoyance. She drummed her fingers on her hips. "You're probably thinking, 'How did such a young and successful woman like Gloria Sycamore end up back in Sycamore Hill, living with her parents?'"

He chuckled. It started low and rumbled like the trolley carts the storage unit provided customers for hauling stuff from the trunk of their cars to the units. Carts she wouldn't have used had Owen shown up on time. The comfort building in her chest cooled a bit. His footsteps dragged along the pavement with a scuffing sound. She could feel him moving closer. It had always been that way with them.

"What else am I thinking?" His quiet question caressed the

back of her neck, and she shivered from the warmth of his breath. She tried to hang onto her frustration, but she couldn't stay mad at him. She never could. She leaned into him and further into their game.

"You're wondering if the only reason she came back is because she couldn't get a job."

"Try again."

"You're wondering if she came back because her family lives here."

"Wrong." He loosely wrapped his arms around her middle and tugged her until her back pressed against his chest. If her sweaty dampness bothered him, he didn't show it.

"You're wondering if she is ready for all the changes coming her way."

He dropped a kiss on her temple.

"Because she's thinking those things," Gloria muttered.

"Are those the only reasons she came back?"

This time, steamy warmth tickled her earlobe, deliciously toasting her insides like marshmallows over a campfire. Gloria melted like s'mores. "You're wondering if any other reason drew her back to Sycamore Hill."

"I am." He cinched his arms tighter and rested his chin on the top of her head. They fit perfectly like that. She stood one head shorter, even with heels. She always felt safe tucked into his arms.

"Maybe," she murmured, not voicing the remaining questions that flitted through her mind.

He's wondering if she's pastor-wife material.

He's wondering if his congregation will accept her.

He's wondering if she'll find a new job in Sycamore Hill and stay for good.

He's wondering if they have a future.

He's wondering if she's wondering about those things.

Because she was.

Gloria twisted in Owen's arms and rested her cheek against his chest. The solid throbbing of his heart steadied her. Sure, it was simpler when she lived in the city, but long distance only worked for so long. Still, no one in the city cared who Pastor Owen of Sycamore Hill Community Church dated. Everyone in Sycamore Hill cared. They not only cared, but they held strong opinions. Strong enough that, up until this point, Owen set most of their dates in the city. He came to her. He insisted.

Was that because he shared her unspoken questions?

She inhaled his spicy aftershave until her lungs felt like they'd burst. She briefly held onto his scent before slowly letting the air escape between her tight lips. Regardless of what anyone else thought about her return to Sycamore Hill or her growing romance with Owen, Gloria was home. For better or worse. Gloria had to get some distance from the controversial trial and the hounding journalists that dubbed her *Gloria the whistleblower*. She'd exposed a falsified drug trial connected to Sycamore Hill nine months ago and had to testify at trial as a result. Now that her name had been cleared—finally—she could come home and hold her head high. The only questions that remained were how the courts would punish her former classmate and roommate for her deception and whether the big company, Emergence Pharmaceuticals, would survive the scandal.

"You're trembling." Owen rubbed his hands up and down her back, adding a delightful friction to her stirred-up insides. "Are you okay?"

"Just tired." Tired of interviews. Tired of depositions. Tired of lawyers. Tired of her hero-move mucking up her life. All she ever wanted was a peaceful, quiet existence. But leaving university under headlines that accused her of cheating, starting and finishing her education after a career change to early childhood education, preparing to testify in court, and now dating the well-loved, small-town pastor was anything but peaceful and quiet.

Another forceful exhale lifted most of Gloria's bangs off her forehead. A few sweaty strands stuck like glue. Gloria's parents had raised her to do the right thing, no matter what it cost. And despite being the black sheep of her over-achieving family, that lesson stuck. Better to complicate her life than let the residents of Life House, the vulnerable clients on which Emergence had slated to begin human drug trials, suffer. The women trying to rebuild their life deserved better. Her gaze found the nursery rhyme book cover again.

The rain hits the dirt, and the dirt turns to mud, and it slips, and it slides, and it spreads like a flood.

Her involvement with the case did bring her together with Owen again, spreading a little sugar on the oozy-doozy mud pie that was her life. She lifted her face to his.

But Owen's gaze wasn't on her. It was tripping over the twenty or so boxes still looking for a spot in her unit. "I thought I told you to wait for me and that I would help you unload?" There was only the tiniest amount of admonishment in Owen's tone, but it was enough to annoy like a fingernail on a chalkboard.

Two broken fingernails, to be more precise.

"I thought you'd be here at seven o'clock."

He chuckled again. Was everything funny to him? "I had a small church emergency. One of the deacons called as I was heading out the door."

The church. By tomorrow, the church would know she was back, and someone was bound to speculate on what it meant for her, Owen, and the congregation. If Gloria's friends were right, the people would pull out their scorecards and begin tracking tally marks. Was she worthy of their pastor's affections? Was quitting the sciences and trading beakers and test tubes for preschool rhymes an acceptable decision? They'd rank her reliability as a witness in the biggest scandal to impact the town, score her clothing choices, and decide on her overall suitability as a small-town ministry wife. Tonight, the match was tied at zero, but tomorrow? That was anyone's game.

Oozy-doozy, indeed.

Gloria pulled out of Owen's arms. Coolness hit her sweaty skin, and her flesh prickled. She yanked a sweater out of a nearby box, snagging the cuff and pulling loose a thread. Great. Just great. Was this her future if things worked out for them? Her waiting for him, him prioritizing the church, her making do on her own, sacrificing fingernails, mental health, and her favorite sweater? Was his delay the result of a preemptive strike from Sycamore Hill Community Church? Were they letting her know where she ranked on the scale of priorities? If they were, it was mighty passive-aggressive of them. But passive-aggressive was the weapon of choice for most church-goers.

She lifted her shoulder in a shrug as if it was no big deal. Really, she couldn't complain about the church needing him. "I managed."

"Did you?" Owen cocked an eyebrow. He twisted his lips to the right, strolled over to the largest box, labelled off-season clothes, and peeked inside. "You have a lot of stuff."

I've not seen a mess that I cannot wrangle, 'till I met this web that I cannot untangle!

There was no way to know if the quirky rhyme applied more to her storage unit or life. "Was it anything serious with the church emergency?" She lobbed out a lame question. A filler. A way to deflect from the things they should have been talking about.

"Only if you call a leaky roof serious, but Jason had to go through it point by point right then. It couldn't wait." Owen made the kind of noise that told Gloria being a pastor wasn't all sunshine and roses. Her compassion spiked a notch until she did the math.

The things that ranked higher in importance than her were phone calls from the deacons, a leaky roof, church business, and some annoyed guy named Jason. Good to know. Her gaze found her book again.

Be true to what's you, be you all the way. They can't take from you what you won't give away.

Two

Owen and Gloria sat side by side in two worn armchairs that Owen had scored in a second-hand store. He'd purchased the set shortly after Sycamore Hill Community Church had hired him. Somehow, visiting side by side with a coffee in hand put parishioners at ease in a way sitting across from him at his desk didn't. But he wasn't chatting with a parishioner. This was Gloria. The woman he planned to marry. Back in town, Lord willing, for good. Owen wiped his palms on his pant legs.

His head hurt. He'd been up half the night trying to put his finger on what went wrong between them at the storage unit. Gloria never said anything. She wouldn't. She was great that way. But somehow, between her short answers, sideways glances, and tight features, he heard what she wasn't saying. He'd messed up.

They didn't argue or anything. She still gave him a chaste kiss goodnight on her parents' front porch. But who was he kidding? That rogue woodpecker in sixth grade had pecked him harder than Gloria had less than a dozen hours before. She was unhappy.

Or maybe disappointed was a better word. And he didn't like how that knowledge settled over his heart.

Gloria was the last person he wanted to join the disappointed-in-Owen club.

When he woke hours before his alarm, his gut told him to prioritize damage control and take his girl on an early breakfast date at The Muffin Man. After lingering in the café as long as he dared, he ordered their coffee to-go and moved the date to his office. He made a point to be the first to arrive at the church every morning. He wanted people to drive by, see his car out front, and know he was hard at work.

Last night, Owen might have screwed up, but tonight would be different. Tonight, Owen had plans. Dinner. And not just any dinner. "I booked us a table at that fancy hotel restaurant in Grander City that's famous for its desserts, Queen's Court."

Gloria's eyes lit up. "What a treat!"

The reservation alone guaranteed that Owen would be eating soup from a can for the next two weeks, but the delight on her face made the sacrifice worth it.

Gloria's gaze moved over his small office and eventually settled on his messy desk. Her nose crinkled adorably. He'd swiped his sticky notes, stapler, pad of paper and pencil into the top drawer when they arrived, and he relocated a stack of files to a small round table off to his side. There wasn't anything he could do about the musty carpet smell except open a window and pray to the God of heaven that she didn't think the scent leaked from him. Not the most romantic setting in the world. Even he could see that.

"Have things around here improved much?"

He couldn't stop his gaze from bouncing to the door to ensure no one heard Gloria's question. In a lot of ways, it was easier to confide in Gloria about the difficulties of small-town ministry when she lived in the city. The distance gave her perspective. But now that she was back— His stomach churned, ratcheting up his tension.

Don't come off desperate.

"It's been tough, but God is good."

She angled her head to the side in a way that indicated she wasn't fully convinced. But what was he supposed to say? The employment-honeymoon-period had passed, and no one in seminary prepared him for how hard it would be to keep the peace in a church filled with opinionated people. Whenever the majority of the congregation was happy with him, a small segment remained that wasn't, and that segment was usually the loudest. Love thy neighbor didn't breach the church walls as often as he had expected. At least not during congregational meetings like the one last week.

Heat flushed his skin. Two meetings ago, Hank Sinclair, one of the church's charter members, complained that Owen spent too much time in his office preparing his sermons and not enough time with the people of Sycamore Hill. This last meeting, Hank complained that Owen spent too much time with the people of Sycamore Hill and not enough time in his office preparing his sermons. Ethan, a church member and the owner of The Muffin Man, told Owen not to take Hank too seriously, saying that Hank was so old he probably had a picture of Moses in his yearbook. Still, the criticism burned a hole in Owen's vulnerable psyche. But he couldn't tell Gloria that. He was trying to reel in the girl, not catch and release.

The pressure from Gloria's hand on his knee snapped him back to the present moment. She smiled. "It's okay to admit that it's hard."

Owen peeled his mind off Hank Sinclair. Gloria leaned into him the way she used to when they studied for their grade twelve finals together. Ready to encourage. Ready with a word of hope.

It sent a surge through his veins. This was why it wasn't good for man to be alone. Like Adam needed Eve, like his recently engaged friend, Eli, needed Meg, Owen needed Gloria.

Because Sunday was coming. It hurtled toward him every seven days, like an asteroid that never missed its target.

"Knock, knock." Suzy Chalkey, Jason's wife, waddled into his office like a duck under the influence.

Without actually knocking.

Again.

Gloria snatched her hand off his knee and entwined her fingers in her lap.

This had to stop. Owen would ask Janet to start work earlier so she could filter his visitors. Suzy was becoming a problem. Scratch that. Suzy *was* a problem.

"Pastor, can you help me unload the pumpkins from the back of Jason's truck? Clara needs them for the kids this Sunday." Suzy pressed her fingers into the small of her arched back. The movement thrust out her very large, pregnant belly. She stretched as wide as she did tall, and as she overextended her body, she looked Gloria up and down with a combination of open curiosity and self-righteous doubt. She sucked in her cheeks until two deep hollows appeared.

"Sure thing." Owen hopped to his feet. He noted the time of his and Gloria's dinner reservation on the notepad on the desk and underlined the words Queen's Court. He gestured for Gloria to join him as he followed Suzy into the tiny church hallway and toward the arched exterior doors.

"Suzy, have you met Gloria Sycamore? She just moved back to town. We went to high school together."

Suzy tossed an interested look over her shoulder. "We haven't met yet, but I saw her at the storage unit last night when I was driving back to the farm."

Did he hear a subtle correction in Suzy's tone?

"Your car was just pulling into the storage unit. Kind of an isolated spot to meet up, don't you think?"

Yup. Correction. One hundred percent. Owen stretched his forefinger and thumb across his forehead to avoid answering.

Suzy pushed through the doors to the outside, sending the branches of two overgrown bushes rustling. She fingered the tip of a stray branch as she passed, tugging on it just hard enough that it snapped forcibly back into place.

Right. Suzy had pointed them out last Sunday, claiming those eye-level, lower branches were a hazard to children. "Gloria, can you remind me to come back and trim the hedges on Saturday?"

Gloria's eyes widened, but he gave his head a quick shake. Small enough that Suzy missed it but big enough that Gloria got the message. Her mouth slackened. He'd tell her later why his preaching duties included work as the church grounds keepers, janitor, and repairman. Some days, that job description also included keeping Suzy Chalky happy, but he had yet to success-fully cross that item off his to-do list.

Their footsteps crunched on the gravel pebbles they called a parking lot. A couple of shingles lay strewn about from the high winds that ripped through the area overnight. Maybe now Gloria would understand why Jason felt the need to detain him and discuss the roof last night. Unfortunately, Owen wasn't a roofer any more than he was a groundskeeper or maintenance man. And since their fundraising efforts had stalled at about three thousand dollars, he foresaw several shingling-for-newbies videos in his future.

A third vehicle had parked beside Jason and Suzy's truck. Owen squinted. Nathan Clarke.

"Morning, Pastor." Nathan tugged a ball cap lower over his head as the threesome approached.

"Nathan, it's good to see you." Owen clapped the young, widowed father on his back. Would it ever feel natural to say and do pastoral things for people years ahead of him in life experience?

Nathan stuffed his hands into his front denim pockets. "Do you know the children's schedule for the fall programs yet? I called yesterday, and Janet said you hadn't finished the calendar. I need to firm up my childcare by the end of today, and it would really help me out to know the church's plans."

Nathan had stopped attending services when his wife died, but he still sent his four children to every program they offered. They even showed up for Sunday school most weekends. Owen suspected that necessity drove that decision more than faith. The man was barely staying afloat and took advantage of all the programs that included child-minding that the community offered.

"I don't yet, but as soon as I help Suzy haul these pumpkins into the Sunday school room, I'll finalize the details and give you a call. Your kids are in the musical, right?" Owen mentally added finalizing the fall schedule to the growing list of things detracting from what he wanted to do (spend time with Gloria) and from what he needed to do (write his sermon).

"Yes, they are." Nathan's eyes drifted over Suzy's extended belly, and a softness eased the lines on his face. "Let me help."

"Who has the children now?" Suzy massaged her belly in a circular motion. Even while accepting help, the tiniest bit of superiority came out in her tone.

Owen winced.

Nathan's movements hitched for a beat as he rounded the back of the truck and opened the tailgate, hoisting several pumpkins in his arms.

"That's none of our business, Suzy," Owen gently cut in.

"I disagree," she countered. "The safety of children is everyone's responsibility. Breanna is hardly old enough to handle all the kids on her own."

Nathan's jaw clenched, but he held his tongue.

Owen followed his lead. If it didn't bother Nathan enough to address, Owen wasn't about to overreact. Unless Nathan was waiting or hoping that Owen would speak up. He couldn't tell.

Suzy reached through the open driver's side window door and retrieved her water bottle from the cup holder. She took a long drink before turning her attention to Gloria. "Did I hear right? Do you have a reservation at Queen's Court in Grander?"

Owen sucked in a breath so quickly it whistled. Everyone looked at him. He grabbed two of the larger pumpkins. How long had Suzy stood at his office door and listened before announcing herself? "In which Sunday school room would you like the pumpkins?"

"Clara's room, please."

Owen headed for the side door that opened directly into the corridor of Sunday school rooms. Nathan followed suit. When Gloria picked up a pumpkin and hitched to their train, his chest swelled.

Suzy caboosed empty-handed. "Is it a special occasion reservation?"

"Not really." Owen answered, still steaming over her intrusion. Suzy and her husband had only been in Sycamore Hill three years, but that was enough time for them to put down roots in the church, pump out two kids, and feel comfortable enough to ask nosey questions.

"What's Clara doing with the pumpkins?" Gloria slowed her pace until she walked side-by-side with Suzy.

Suzy hands flapped in front of her. "Oh, you know Clara. She has some sort of lesson on how scooping out the guts is like Jesus taking away our sin and carving a face is like the new creation God makes us." Suzy wrinkled her nose like she was about to sneeze out the devil.

Funny. When Gloria crinkled her nose earlier, Owen had found it to be sweet and attractive. When Suzy did it, he felt nothing but irritation. Or maybe it was her disgust over touching pumpkin innards that soured his gut, unless her expression reflected how she really felt about their Lord and Savior's miraculous work in the heart of a sinner?

But Owen didn't say any of that. He never said half of the comments and questions that raced through his mind. If he did, he'd be looking for a new job within twenty-four hours. Instead, he said, "Brilliant."

Although it wasn't really brilliant. It was cute, but it'd been done before. Every fall that he could remember. But he'd say almost anything to steer the conversation away from Gloria and their date. "Why don't you grab a coffee in the kitchen and put your feet up? Jason told me you've been tired this pregnancy. Nathan, Gloria, and I can finish up out here."

Suzy opened her mouth, but he kept talking. "We bought that decaf coffee you suggested. There's a fresh pot ready. You were right. It's good."

Suzy couldn't camouflage her disappointment at Owen shutting her down, but without a gracious way to refuse, she was bested at her own bossy game.

"I'll come get you when we're done," Owen called as she waddled away.

Nathan forcibly exhaled the minute Suzy rounded the corner.

Gloria outright laughed.

Yeah. He felt it, too. It just wasn't very pastoral to express it.

Three

Gloria didn't remember the last time she'd laughed so hard, and after spending a long afternoon in court testifying, she needed to laugh.

Owen's impersonation of Suzy on a mission to uncover their plans was spot on. Sure, Gloria didn't know the woman, but the few seconds spent in her company were enough to paint a picture. She pinched the bridge of her nose to squeeze off the exit route her carbonated water sought. It fizzed and threatened to spew like a scotch mint in a bottle of shaken diet soda.

Oh, man. She pinched her side—the scotch mint rocket. She'd wowed her preschoolers that day, shooting herself into the realm of hero-teacher-status and prompting a few phone calls from parents looking for clarification regarding the *explosion* at school.

The tension around Owen's eyes had eased, finally lifting around the same time as their dessert arrived. Their laughter had helped loosen the lines that seemed permanently carved on his forehead, which was the only reason she shoved down the twinge of guilt regarding their banter. For the first time since Gloria moved back to Sycamore Hill, things between Owen and her felt normal. But that could be because they were back in the city having dinner far from his observant town, nosey Suzys, and bossy Jasons. Insecurity jellified her insides, and it squeezed off her gaiety. "Why do you think Suzy wanted to know our plans so badly?"

Owen shrugged. A tiny vertical frown line returned to his forehead. It was just one wrinkle. A single fold to indicate that the smoothness of Owen's youth was puckering toward adulthood on a track parallel to Gloria's. Only Owen's train led to a town named *distinguished* and *respectable*. Gloria's rocketed toward *undesirable* and *old* faster than her famous scotch mint.

The corners of his icy blue eyes crinkled. "The ladies in church, especially the ones who befriended my last girlfriend, are quite—" He lifted his gaze to the ceiling while he searched for the right word "—motherly," he concluded. "I'm still earning back their trust."

Gloria felt her eyes bulge as she emitted a bark of disbelief. It wasn't Owen's fault the Jezebel he previously dated duped the congregation. "You didn't do anything wrong."

He shrugged. "Except show poor judgment, which throws all my decisions into question."

Gloria's confidence buckled. She tried to remember everything Owen had told her about Jillian, a cheat dressed in dignified clothing. She'd hoodwinked him and the congregation, charming her way into their lives, laughing at all the jokes and hitting all the right notes, enticing them with her smooth words. All the while, she viewed this town as a stepping-stone to bigger things.

Jillian made plans for Owen. She had envisioned a large megachurch future where she filled the role of First Lady. The woman came from an urban setting that was far more city mouse than country mouse and planned to return there with her celebrity pastor on her arm.

Gloria forced her clenched hands to relax. Hot pink nail polish reflected the light from the massive restaurant chandelier—a light that was very much city mouse, hanging over the repaired fingernails of a city mouse that wore a very city mouse outfit while on a date with a one-hundred-percent country mouse man.

Which begged a question. Why did her country mouse constantly plan dates in the city? Gloria swallowed her insecurities. As the similarities between Jillian and her stacked up, she pressed her pink painted fingernails to lips smeared in a complimentary hue of gloss. With cheeks growing hotter by the second, Gloria talked herself down from the ledge. Having the last name *Sycamore* should help the people accept her. Her parents practically founded the town. It almost guaranteed that no one would be outright mean. At least not to her face.

Gloria tugged at the billowy scarf wound casually around her neck. She and Emma Powles had debated the scarf. Gloria had hit it off with the nurse practitioner months ago when the woman snuck into the hospital to find important documents that turned the tide of the Emergence trial. As the prosecuting attorneys prepped them to testify, they'd grown close. They shared common interests, including an appreciation for the occasional impractical item just because it looked stylish. But the loose folds of the draping fabric they'd previously admired now choked off Gloria's oxygen supply. The women of Sycamore Hill Community Church had a stranglehold on Owen, and an exceptional talent for communicating cutting remarks through smiles and pleasantry.

Stop it, she scolded her snowballing thoughts. But she couldn't stop her catastrophizing fears any more than she could stop a snow boulder rolling downhill. Just who did his congregation think they were? They had no right to impose their insecurities about

Jillian upon her. No right! And making their pastor pay for the sins of his ex? Totally unacceptable. The bigger the snowball got, the more it riled her up. But instead of expressing her fears and engaging in the kind of open and honest communication two people considering marriage should be able to have, she pasted on the type of insane smile she imagined a suitable pastor's wife would wear, cleared her throat, and said, "Tell me more about the children's programming at the church."

Owen prattled on about the annual fall musical spearheaded by Clara Brisbane. Meg Gilmore, Clara's neighbor and Gloria's friend, had told Gloria about Clara, her sweet grandmotherly neighbor that came to her aid during a break-and-enter a few months back. Gloria looked forward to getting to know the feisty woman that stepped into a motherly role for Meg. Meg and Eli and Owen and Gloria hit it off, and they often double-dated in Grander. They had spent many pleasant evenings together playing board games and watching movies at Gloria's apartment in the city.

"The musical is the only church program that starts in August, before the fall program kick-off, doubling as a late vacation Bible school," Owen said. "They'll perform the musical at the Fall Festival in a few weeks."

Gloria made supportive sounds as she spooned the last bit of her creamy dessert into her mouth. She hadn't eaten all day in anticipation of this evening. The second Owen had mentioned Queen's Court, she started a fast. Not a fast to fit into her new dress, although the dress was totally fabulous, and somehow, putting it on while her empty stomach growled made her feel like it hung a bit more loosely than before. The entire purpose of Gloria's fast was to better appreciate the creamy chocolate mousse currently melting on her tongue with delicious satisfaction. More delightful than waking on Christmas morning to an overstuffed stocking at the foot of the bed. "Did you make arrangements to fix the roof?"

Owen's expression tightened some more. "The roof's going to cost more than I expected. We'll either have to fundraise some more first, or I'll learn how to lay shingles. The fund is about a thousand shy of what we need. It's tarped for now. As long as we don't get another driving rain, it'll be enough."

Gloria had never tasted a dessert so creamy. She tried to keep her attention on Owen, but it was so hard with such delicious goodness overwhelming her taste buds.

Owen.

The roof.

The church.

Right.

"You'll fix it? Don't you already do more to maintain the property than the average pastor?" Owen had never been a handy guy. A pair of unruly bushes that needed trimming on Saturday came to mind. "You know, there was a time when Sycamore Hill Community Church rotated volunteers to maintain the church's exterior property. I remember the weeks the responsibility fell on my family. Dad would trim the hedges while Jessica and I would weed the garden. Mom dusted and vacuumed."

Did Owen remember how he'd join them? He and Gloria would sneak off past the tree line and pick wild raspberries. They'd only been kids, but a tiny clearing hidden from view became their secret spot.

A faint pink washed Owen's cheeks as his attention drifted to the tree line. Oh yeah. He remembered all right. The taste of their first awkward kiss was raspberries and sunshine. "Things changed after they caught my predecessor stealing from the offering."

Her spoon clattered against the side of the bowl, and the couple at the neighboring table stared at them. She gave a little shrug and mouthed, *oops*. "Between your ex and the former pastor, the past casts a pretty big shadow over your present."

"Hank says that hard, physical labor keeps a man honest." Owen's tone held no humor, contradicting his smile.

The waiter brought the bill. Gloria hated to wrap up the evening, but everything about this relationship needed to be above reproach. She needed to get home at a reasonable hour. She was dating the pastor, after all.

After paying for their meal, Owen held out her jacket. She slipped her arms into the sleeves, and he slung an arm around her shoulders. Gloria leaned into his side. The evening had been everything she had hoped it would be. But as Owen pushed open the exit door, Gloria's heel turned. It caught in the crevice on the cobblestone sidewalk. She teetered into Owen with a gasp and a giggle.

The entire block in this portion of the city had that old-town feel. Gloria adored the cobblestone walks and the Victorian-style buildings with various elements from Italianate and Second Empire. Old town riches in a modern city setting.

Owen steadied her, catching her at the elbows and pulling her to his chest. She lifted her face, her gaze lingering on his lips.

Against such a charming background, the moment turned swoon-worthy. Movie-like. Better than she could have ever hoped. She leaned in closer, and Owen's arms moved from her elbows to her waist. She rolled her bottom lip into her mouth. Then somebody cleared their throat.

Right. They blocked the door.

Owen shuffled them off to the side. "Sorry, I didn't mean—"

"Good evening, Pastor." Suzy's clipped greeting threw cold water on the moment.

Gloria froze. She suddenly saw them as Suzy must. Her fingers splayed across Owen's chest. His arms at her waist. Her giggling and flirting. All the delicious goodness of their three-course dinner solidified into an iceberg in her gut.

"Did you enjoy your *meal*?"

Owen appeared to be temporarily struck mute.

"It was wonderful," Gloria answered.

"At least, I hope you're only here for dinner."

Gloria's smile slipped from her face. She glanced back at the hotel. Suzy couldn't possibly mean . . . The women locked eyes. Suzy knew exactly what she was saying.

Gloria stood there for several seconds, stunned into silence at the tawdry insinuation. The hotel with its intricate design, decorative features, and Victorian influence certainly created the ambiance of a romantic getaway, but Suzy knew Owen. He was always a gentleman, always aware of the image he projected. The gall of her to accuse—

"I assure you that we only had a meal here tonight." Owen finally found his tongue, although his words came out all gravelly and rough. "I hadn't considered how this might look, coming out of a hotel. It's good that you saw us and approached us immediately to clarify things. Another woman might have simply speculated and gossiped. Thank you for your directness."

Thank you? He was thanking the woman for practically accusing them of having some torrid affair? Gloria's face grew hot —hotter than it should be on a cool fall night. Owen dropped one arm to his side and pressed his other hand against the small of her back in a warning. Gloria shored up her tenuous grip on her last shred of self-control.

"Rookie mistake, Pastor." Suzy's smugness and Owen's passivity hurled a few unchristian thoughts through Gloria's mind.

"Now you have the facts. Do you remember Gloria from this morning?" Owen straightened to his full height. "She's Teresa and

David Sycamore's daughter. Gloria, you must remember Suzy Chalkey, from church? We helped her with the pumpkins. She moved to Sycamore Hill after you left for university." Owen swayed, and it shifted his upper body even closer to Gloria, making it clear where he'd land if Suzy forced him to pick sides.

That tiny movement almost made up for the polite dance he and Suzy waltzed. Owen might want to pretend their meeting was happenstance, but Gloria wouldn't. She'd spent much of her childhood cowering before alpha-females. The Suzys of her high school had looked down their noses at Gloria. Always judging her. Always finding her lacking because she refused to yield to their whims. It carved a hollow in her soul. Never fitting in. Never being accepted. Suzy's knife twisting reopened the vulnerability.

But she wasn't that little girl with frizzy hair anymore. And she'd known Suzy was trouble the second the woman waltzed into Owen's office without knocking and posed her nosy questions. However random Suzy tried to make this encounter, Gloria knew it had been planned and expertly executed.

"Yes, I remember Gloria." Suzy flicked her gaze to Gloria for the briefest second before locking it back on Owen.

Gloria's gaze trailed over the vehicles parked on the side of the busy street in front of the hotel. Bingo. Parked right across from the window that had framed Gloria and Owen while they ate sat a pick-up truck that looked suspiciously like the one that carted pumpkins to the church this morning. From that vantage point, the woman knew they'd only had dinner, but she felt the need to play out this . . . this . . . Gloria fumbled for clarity. This passive-aggressive power play.

"What brings you to town, Suzy?" Owen's eyes iced over, and Suzy must have felt the temperature dip, because her posture wilted just a bit. "Such a drive at eight months pregnant couldn't have been comfortable in a truck. Is Jason with you? I remember him mentioning his concern for your comfort this close to the end of your pregnancy."

"No, no, I'm here alone." Suzy shifted from offensive to defensive. "I better get going." She shuffled a few steps away and gave a little wave. "See you Sunday, Pastor."

"We'll see you Sunday, Suzy." Gloria answered for Owen and threaded her arm through his.

Owen's breath rushed out as Suzy blended into the crowd and disappeared. "I know we didn't do anything wrong, but somehow I feel like a boy caught with my hand in the cookie jar."

Gloria stared at the spot in the crowd that swallowed Suzy. This was going to be harder than she thought.

Four

Owen dragged his index finger over his left eyebrow. The slow, methodical action of stretching the skin did little to relieve the churning in his stomach. Gloria sat across from him with such hope in her eyes. Such certainty.

His gaze flicked behind her to the wall where an inspirational Scripture passage painted on white-washed barn board hung.

Philippians 4:6-9, "Do not be anxious about anything, but in everything by prayer and supplication with thanksgiving let your requests be made known to God. And the peace of God, which surpasses all understanding, will guard your hearts and your minds in Christ Jesus. Finally, brothers, whatever is true, whatever is honorable, whatever is just, whatever is pure, whatever is lovely, whatever is commendable, if there is any excellence, if there is anything worthy of praise, think about these things. What you have learned and received and heard and seen in me—practice these things, and the God of peace will be with you."

Despite his internal upheaval, he smiled like he always did whenever he looked at the tableau. After he accepted the role as pastor, he'd looked up old Mrs. Canmore. She had a storied career as an artist and liked to fill her time with odd jobs. A few people warned Owen against hiring her, because the older Mrs. Canmore got, the more mischief she stirred, and she'd never set foot in a church in all her days. But Owen commissioned her anyway to style these verses. He laughed out loud when he came into the office one day to find the old gal hanging a board on the wall that said the peace of God would guard his heart and mind *in Christ's cheeses*. Later, Mrs. Canmore would claim it was an honest mistake, but Owen wasn't so sure.

The twisted memory failed to lighten his mood. God had heard his list of requests, all right. It frequently held names like Suzy, Jason, and Hank. But where was his promised peace? Why did his insides feel like a roller coaster about to shoot off the tracks?

Because I have as much of God's peace as I let myself have. Words from his most recent sermon bit back. This wasn't the first time the difficulty of applying the abstract theology he proclaimed from the pulpit resonated. He understood the message, but what had to change in his life for that truth to bring peace? That bit remained foggy, making him the worst pastor ever.

He rubbed his palm over his gut. If it churned any harder, he'd be producing butter.

What would Gloria think if she knew how difficult it was for him to apply the truth he preached? The question lingered like a bad dream where someone swung open a door to a bank vault and told him to take as much as he wanted, and he left with only a couple of pennies because all he had on was a pair of underwear with no pockets to haul the cash.

This all flashed through his mind in a millisecond while he maintained a pasted smile and fixed his attention on his newest source of turmoil: Gloria.

"Well?" She leaned forward, eyes wide and eager, certain her request wouldn't be a problem.

Except it was.

And therein lay the reason for his discomfort. The woman he loved needed something within his power to provide, but he couldn't. That's right. *He loved her.* He loved Gloria Sycamore, but she was going to struggle to believe it when he said no. He didn't like how the negative word tasted.

Janet's soft movements from the volunteer secretary desk just outside his door trickled through the open doorway, left ajar for accountability. There was no way Owen was giving his congregation the opportunity to gossip about him having a young woman in his office alone. Despite the noises of opening and closing filing cabinets and the clicking of computer keys, he was pretty sure Janet listened to every word. She maybe even kept a loop of women updated as he and Gloria battled it out. She seemed to make a lot of passes across the door while texting on her phone, and she'd offered them coffee three times in twenty minutes. An adolescent temptation to feed her fake intel just to see what she would do with it shot through him.

"It's not ethical for me to write a personal reference for someone I am in a romantic relationship with," Owen explained again.

Gloria blew out a *harumph*.

"What about your teacher from the ECE program? Or the preschool where you completed your co-op placement?"

"She wrote me a referral letter. I picked it up after my appointment with the lawyers wrapped up. But Cathy wants a reference from someone in town, a non-relative that has experience with kids. That's the only way she'll consider me."

Owen knew Cathy Whitmore. Her wire-rimmed glasses and sharp eyes missed nothing. Children liked her plump cheeks and a turned-up nose. There was something wonderfully *grandmoth-erish* about her, despite her young age. Cathy carried the faint scent of mothballs with her wherever she went. As friendly as Cathy was, she'd always reminded Owen of some twisted version of the movie Freaky Friday, except in this case, Cathy was an eighty-year-old woman forever trapped in a thirty-year-old body. She seemed like the type of person who had always been old even when she was young, but they didn't interact much. She didn't attend his church, and when their paths crossed, she seemed a tad uncomfortable around him. But that was often the way it was once people learned he was a pastor. Suddenly their posture straightened, their language cleaned up, and they felt compelled to justify their spiritual choices.

Gloria's voice dropped as if she was onto Janet's ploys. Owen envisioned Janet holding a paper funnel to her cocked ear. "If I can't get a job, I can't stay."

That hit below the belt. If God wanted them together, God would make a way. But it was easier for him to say that. He had a secure job. "Don't make this about our future. That's not fair. I can't manipulate circumstances to get my way."

Janet walked by the door again. The paper funnel must not be working.

Was that a *tsking* sound from Janet?

Gloria's eyebrows lifted, and the right side of her lip shot up like it'd been hooked and someone had yanked the line. "Ah, you run a Sunday school program."

He shook his head. "That falls under Clara Brisbane's domain. She's been running the Sunday school classes for years. Have you seen her since you've returned?"

It was Gloria's turn to shake her head no. "Meg told me about how important she's become to her, and I remember Mrs. Brisbane from when I was young, but that's it."

"A recommendation from me is a conflict of interest," Owen repeated, more to convince himself than her. "You have to see that."

An *uh hum* rounded the corner. The woman might as well be amening Owen. Verbal affirmations lifted his heart on Sunday mornings but had the opposite effect right now.

Gloria slumped back into her chair. All the joy and excitement drained from her. "It's not. Not really."

His insides cramped. He hated this, but he had to care about appearances, especially since the fiasco at Queen's Court. It came with the job. He was held to a higher ethical standard. But he also wanted to be supportive and encouraging to Gloria, and therein lay the conundrum.

"I suspect Mrs. Brisbane would welcome help in the kid's department," he started gently. "In fact, the musical has turned into a far bigger production than she expected. Why don't I reintroduce you, and if you work with her for a few weeks, she can provide the reference."

A harumph covered by a cough came from outside the office. At least Janet tried to cover her eavesdropping.

Gloria glowered at the open door.

Owen was half-tempted to shout that Janet should take the rest of the day off and go to the doctor to get her throat checked. Anything to let the woman know that he was onto her—but he forced himself to focus on Gloria. One problem at a time. "Volunteering isn't as quick or as neat as getting me to write the reference, but it does serve both our needs."

Gloria drummed her fingers on her thighs.

"Is something else going on?"

She rubbed the back of her neck. "Cathy asked about the trial and why I changed career tracks."

"Isn't it normal to ask questions in a job interview?"

Gloria scrunched her eyes and pinched the bridge of her nose. "That's what Emma said when I told her. But they're gateway questions into the trial against Emergence. I don't know why it surprised me, and I don't know why it bugs me."

Owen's tongue pressed against the roof of his mouth. Of course, Gloria had spoken with Emma about the trial. Emma played a key role in securing the proof Gloria needed to expose the dangerous plan. Owen tried not to look too deeply into why Gloria hadn't confided in him.

When Gloria was accused of falsifying results from her experiments, the university forced her out. Ben, a local reporter Owen had looped in to help Gloria, exposed the truth. Gloria's roommate, Tiff, had framed her. Tiff had been working for the drug company as a student and had been promptly promoted after she graduated. When Emergence was about to begin drug trials on residents of Life House, Gloria came back to town armed with enough evidence to set Ben on the right trail and to clear her name.

But that's where his involvement ended. Gloria hated talking about the ongoing trial. She hated everything to do with that period of her life, proved by the way one innocent question in a job interview burned her chops.

"Did you explain the entire experience is what set you on this new career path to work with children?"

"I did, but she's concerned that once the trial wraps up, I'll head back to the city, and she needs someone long term. Committed."

A part of Owen shared Cathy's concern, but he shoved it back down his dry throat. But no matter how deeply he buried his doubts, one question still managed to push its way to the surface.

Was he enough reason for Gloria to stay? He wasn't before.

He shoved away the memory of the *Dear John* letter she'd left him. When the drug scandal hit the news, Gloria disappeared. She left her family, the town, and him with nothing more than a written good-bye. Who's to say she wouldn't do that again? If things heated up at church, would she have what it took to stay and fight for them?

Owen turned his hands palms up. "Honestly, I don't know what to do. All I can say is that I am trying to make the best decisions I can with the information I have on hand. And right now, a reference from me won't be good for the ministry here and won't be as good for you as an unbiased reference."

"Then Clara it is." Gloria conceded, but it didn't it feel like a victory.

Gloria pulled her phone from her purse and called Cathy. "Is it possible for me to put in some volunteer hours at the church and then hand in a recommendation? It'll take longer, but it appears to be the only way." Gloria's expression hardened as she listened to whatever Cathy said, and her grip on the phone tightened. "Thank you." She hung up and folded her arms across her middle. "She won't hold the position for me, but if it is still available when I have everything in place, she'll consider me."

Owen eyes went heavenward. *Thank you, Lord!*

"It'll work out. You'll see." He inhaled sharply, but the inside of his chest pinched in a way that undermined his confident declaration.

It didn't feel worked out. Not even close.

Five

Janet walked by Owen's office door again, and twitchiness pulsed in Gloria's extremities. She rubbed a fingertip along the seam of her jeans, distracting herself with the warmth the friction created. She and Owen couldn't dance around it forever. At some point, they had to talk about the church and its impact on Owen's personal life.

At least she thought they did. She didn't know. She'd never dated a guy in ministry before. Yet somehow, she knew today wasn't that day. Today, they'd pretend everything was fine when it wasn't, talking *around* the issue instead of discussing the issue.

A shiver swept over Gloria as if the room temperature suddenly dropped a full ten degrees. She glanced at the window to see if it was hanging open so she could blame her inner freeze on the weather. But no luck. She had no one to blame but herself.

Not Owen.

Not Janet.

It was her. It was always her.

Suddenly, she was a child again. Not quite fitting in. Standing on the outside of the group. Smiling as a teacher commented on having her sister in his class a few years prior. Then, reading disappointment in her teacher when Gloria failed to perform as well as Jessica. Clapping while Jessica accepted another honors award, and indulging her parents while they assured her that her best effort was all they required.

But it wasn't true. There was no award for best effort. There was no honors certificate for a solid B average. Teachers didn't remember average students. And girls with frizzy blonde hair and braces weren't invited to pool parties.

Gloria ran a hand over her hair. The braces eventually came off and she learned to control the frizz, but she still wasn't enough. Suzy made that clear. Janet didn't approve of her. Gloria couldn't remember when the shame of not measuring up wasn't a part of her, making her dirty. Contaminated. Unclean.

Gloria bit the inside of her cheek and tasted blood. There was something about how she felt that asked for blood.

If she had to move for work, her future with Owen would crumble like the remnants of a shack after seismic activity hit a ten on the Richter scale. Yet, he sat there with a goofy grin on his face that implied she was overreacting. Here she was, fighting to save her future, *their future*, and he had the nerve—*the nerve*—to sit there and smile.

Okay, not really smile. But the corners of his lips twitched in that annoying way that meant he was trying *not* to smile, which was just as bad. Maybe even worse. He was *handling* her. Trying to manage her response like she was Janet, or worse, Suzy.

"The job posting has been up for some time." Owen pushed his chair back from the desk and retrieved a light jacket from a nearby hook. "I don't think anyone will swoop in to steal it from you in the next few weeks." He motioned to the office door for her to lead the way out.

Gloria snorted again. Where did he get off saying that with such confidence? It wasn't his career hanging in the balance. She lifted her chin a millimeter and sailed past him and out the door.

Janet called out cheerily, "Heading out?"

Gloria snorted. Janet had probably already called Mrs. Brisbane to report that Gloria was trying to corrupt their dear pastor by asking him to go against his conscience. A slight tinge of disapproval shone in the woman's perky eyes.

First Suzy. Now Janet.

She was oh for two.

This was not how Gloria envisioned meeting Owen's congregation. She'd written an entire Sunday morning scenario in her mind that had the congregation anticipating her arrival like the guests at a wedding. Meg had laughed at her vision. Emma said she was out of her mind. But Gloria imagined that she'd come in on her father's arm, and they'd collectively inhale, convinced that she was the missing piece to Owen's puzzle. Not once in her little dream did she tick off a nosey secretary or deacon's wife. Nevertheless, here she was. Down by two.

Not that any of this would matter if she didn't get the job.

Without a job, Gloria would be forced to move wherever she could find employment. She'd work all week. He'd work every weekend. They'd drift apart, neither of them wanting to terminate the relationship but unable to stop the trajectory of them hurtling toward breaking up. She'd be alone—again. And every time she returned to Sycamore Hill to visit her parents, she'd be forced to make polite small talk with whatever woman Owen eventually settled down with—a woman the congregation wholeheartedly approved of because she didn't wear high heels, or paint her nails bright colors, or ask their pastor to do something he didn't want to do.

Gloria pressed a palm to her heaving belly. It was suddenly

difficult to inhale. How could Owen just move on like that? How could he replace her so easily? How could—

"I'm walking Gloria to Mrs. Brisbane's to introduce them. I won't be long," Owen said.

Gloria snapped back into the present. She couldn't be sure, but she would have sworn that she heard Janet *tsk*.

Again.

Gloria smiled at Janet anyway.

This was why she worked with kids. Working with kids was a million times better than working with adults. Children were one hundred percent honest. Sure, that brutal honesty might hurt. Preschoolers had yet to develop an inner editor. They just spoke.

The small volcano on your chin just popped.
Your belly is nice and soft, just like a pillow.
I can smell what you ate for breakfast.

Brutal, yes. Honest? Always. She'd take that over spun truth and manipulation any day.

For a moment, Owen studied her, looking as though he could read her mind and was considering whether her catastrophizing was worth addressing. Gloria held his gaze until he blinked. He turned to Janet, whose mouth hung slightly ajar as if she was fluent in subtext. "Can you please find me a book about roofing? I want to look into the project a little bit more."

"Yes sir," Janet snapped into action, her fingers clicking away on her keypad as if Owen had just asked her to decipher the final clue in a search for the Ark of the Covenant. "It was nice to see you again, Gloria." Janet didn't look up from her screen. A subtle snub. Like Gloria wasn't worth the time it would take to glance her way. "I hope to see you on Sunday."

And there it was again. *A tone.* A facial tick. Subtext that almost dared Gloria to try and prematurely claim a spot beside their pastor.

"Oh, I'll be there." Gloria gave a little wave of her hand. "My family never misses a Sunday." But Gloria wasn't stupid. She wouldn't be sitting with Owen. She'd claim her old place in the Sycamore family pew, and that's where she'd stay. The sacred spot beside the pastor was only hers after a ring circled her fourth finger on her left hand. Claiming it prematurely was suicide.

Fifteen minutes later, Gloria and Owen strolled down the street, nearing Clara's house. Gloria tucked her hand into the crook of Owen's elbow. Leaves in various shades scraped along the sidewalk. Maple, ash, and oak mixed and danced in the breeze. All except the sycamore. The sycamore trees hung onto most of their leaves throughout the winter unless a harsh wind of heavy snow blew them free. They didn't usually shed their dead until early spring, until the swelling buds completed the separation. Was Gloria too much like her namesake, holding onto Owen and the hope of a future together, refusing to release him to the ministry until something outside of her control forced her to let go?

Owen squeezed her hand between his elbow and side, tugging her a bit closer.

She gave him a sideways glance. He nodded and smiled at everyone they passed.

"Do you ever get tired of it?"

"Of what?"

She overlapped her long cardigan around her body and cinched the belt. "Being the pastor. Of everyone having an opinion on your decisions?"

Owen reached for her hand and threaded their fingers. His shoulders lifted and released. "It comes from love."

Her facial muscles tightened. Did it? Or did it come from a need to control?

"After high school, when you left for the city, things in my life got complicated."

The cramping in her face spread to her chest. If complicated scared him, she was in trouble. So far, nothing about her return to Sycamore Hill had been easy, simple, or straightforward. She bled complicated. "How?"

His eyes found hers. "Jillian."

Right. Jillian. The woman they all loved until they didn't.

"Everyone assumed we'd marry."

Unexpected pain stabbed, and agony shot from the point of impact, electrifying every nerve ending in her body. Owen had loved another woman. Owen had proposed. The congregation loved her. Welcomed her. Accepted her. And all Gloria got was a refusal to provide a reference and a stalker named Suzy.

"Jillian wasn't genuine." Owen's attention followed the erratic path of a bird. Was he that taken by the species or was he still grieving Jillian and therefore couldn't bear to meet Gloria's gaze? Was Gloria just—she gasped internally—a rebound romance? Did Owen still have feelings for Jillian? This woman who was, what? An international spy? A narcotics dealer? Secretly married with children? What could have been *so bad* that Owen felt *so grateful* for this second chance from the community that he forfeited his privacy and personal life, granting access to anyone who demanded it?

"Jillian said and did all the right things, but Janet saw her one night at a restaurant in the city. As she approached the table to say hi, she overheard Jillian mocking Sycamore Hill, our country way of life, and boasting about her plans for me."

"And?" Gloria leaned in closer.

"And after welcoming her and showing her kindness, it hurt."

That hardly seemed like a big enough crime to scar the congregation for life.

"She went on for some time about our backward ways and hokey fashion."

Fashion? The clicking of Gloria's heeled boots against the sidewalk grew in volume until they were all Gloria heard. She had agonized over her outfit today. She must have tried on a dozen ensembles, looking up outfits on Pinterest for that perfect combination that said educated and professional but willing to get dirty and play with the kids. She fingered the high collar of the red knitted sweater she layered under a long cardigan. Her painted fingernails perfectly matched. No wonder Suzy and Janet acted as they did. She reminded them of *her*.

Someone should have warned her.

Before Gloria could respond, a howl shouted from behind, "Look out!"

In a blink, Owen yanked her to the side, and Gloria stumbled out of the path of a scooter zipping past them that gravity pulled downhill.

"Sorry!" the girl called as she blurred by them. A girl wearing —Gloria squinted—pajamas?

"Be careful, Breanna!" Owen shouted at her rapidly-disappearing form.

He tightened his hold around Gloria. "You okay?"

A hum of contentment vibrated deep in her chest. She was more than okay.

His arms relaxed around her waist, but he didn't remove them.

She lifted her face to his. She could almost see her reflection in his eyes. Owen was a good man. A kind man. He wasn't letting the church walk all over him. He was being gracious. Showing them mercy because of all they'd endured before him. His gentle nature was one of the reasons she loved him.

The air between them charged. If she leaned in just a little bit more . . . Her gaze dropped to his lips.

Owen cleared his throat.

Just like that, the spell was broken.

"Breanna's probably late for school because she was helping her dad with the twins."

Twins? Gloria's midsection hiccupped. There were only one set of twins in Sycamore Hill. "She's Nathan's daughter?"

"His oldest. Here we are." Owen pushed open a waist-high gate that fenced in Mrs. Brisbane's front yard and motioned for Gloria to go first. A white picket fence gave the property a cozy feel. The homes in this historical part of the town were smaller than Gloria's parents', but they had just as much character.

Owen used the brass knocker on the front door, and Gloria shifted her weight from side to side.

"Pastor Owen! What a pleasant surprise." Mrs. Brisbane opened the door wide.

Yeah, right. As if Janet hadn't called already and prepped her.

"This is my girlfriend, Gloria."

Girlfriend. All her cynicism fled. It was the first time Owen had introduced her that way, and she had to admit it; it sent a thrill tingling from her head to her toes. After all the subtle put-downs, Gloria practically glowed. Owen had claimed her publicly.

"Gloria needs a reference for her application at the preschool, and I suggested she volunteer with you in the children's ministry. Afterward, if you feel it appropriate, you could write her a recommendation."

As Clara Brisbane's gaze moved up and down Gloria, Gloria couldn't help but straighten. Then, the woman did something so completely unexpected that Gloria wasn't sure if she was serious or not.

"Hallelujah!" Clara threw her hands into the air. "Meg and I were just praying the Lord would provide, and here you are. His provision standing at my front door, hand-delivered by God."

God? More like hand-delivered by Owen.

"Come on in, dear," Mrs. Brisbane opened the door even

wider and gestured for Gloria to enter. "I have the perfect job for you. My doctor was just telling me that I need to cut back and get control of my diabetes. But how was I supposed to say no to all those kids? They've been working all month on the play. I couldn't just up and walk away."

Gloria stepped over the threshold into Mrs. Brisbane's house as Owen simultaneously stepped back. Her gaze locked on his. He wasn't coming?

"I'll wait out here. I have a few emails to answer." He wiggled his phone, indicating that he could work from it. "Thanks, Clara. I knew I could count on you."

Gloria didn't know why, but she'd just assumed that Owen would come, sit beside her the whole time, and be the buffer between her and, well, everyone. But he withdrew to the porch, and Gloria's heart thudded with each step of his retreat.

Six

O wen really did have emails to answer, but he also needed a minute. He couldn't help but feel like he'd fed Gloria to the lions. Their church had yet to pull off a musical without a disaster. At best, little Tommy emerged shirtless. At worst, the background came tumbling down. It had felt like a good idea when it first struck him, but now he felt like he might chuck.

Owen could almost hear Clara's deceased husband reminding him to breathe. His catch phrase was, *The good Lord didn't bring you this far just to abandon you, so don't you go abandoning Him.*

Clara's husband of forty-five years, Frank Brisbane, had been gone two years, having only lived for nine months after Owen accepted the call of lead pastor at Sycamore Hill Community Church. Frank faithfully mentored Owen for those nine months, meeting with him weekly to pray for the ministry and for him.

Frank encouraged Owen to be open and honest, and to resist stirrings of pride, which, according to Frank, made a man unwilling to hear constructive feedback or answer honest questions. Pride made a leader unapproachable and defensive and birthed an unhealthy focus on self. After the last pastor, the church needed a humble and approachable man at the helm of the ship.

Owen tried to imagine how Frank would counsel him right now. If they could sit on the porch's wicker furniture one more time, what would he say about Gloria? About the church? About the way Suzy and Janet were nosing about, certain they knew what Owen needed better than Owen did?

But to be fair, if Janet hadn't overheard Jillian at the restaurant, Owen might have never known of her grand scheme. He might have married the woman and been stuck for life on the hamster wheel of her insatiable ambition. He owed the church a debt of gratitude for saving him a lifetime of misery.

But he didn't owe them his life.

The thought came out of nowhere. Suddenly, Frank's wisdom, poured out over dozens and dozens of cups of coffee on this very porch, came rushing back.

Your vows are to God and your wife, not the church. A healthy marriage keeps Christ central, not ministry.

Sure, Frank thought his counsel would apply to Owen and Jillian, not Owen and Gloria, but it didn't make it any less right.

Trust the Lord to care for his church, and trust that He will care for you as you prioritize Him.

Owen wanted to emulate Clara and Frank's marriage. It thrived for forty-five years, keeping Christ central. That was what Owen wanted. Longevity in life, marriage, and ministry.

Lord, if You could put it on Clara's heart to be to Gloria what Frank was to me, I'd be so grateful. Owen eased his way across the porch, avoiding the creaky wooden slats, and claimed the rocker next to the window. He hadn't intended on listening. Not consciously. But just enough sound trickled out from inside the house to assure him the Lord answered his prayer.

"It's been two years since the good Lord took my Frank home," Mrs. Brisbane said to Gloria. "I thought it would get easier with time, but it hasn't."

"I'm sorry. I can't imagine the pain of such a loss." Gloria's reply was partially muffled by a clattering of ceramic dishes.

Owen's palms moistened at the clink of ceramic cups on saucers. The first time Clara had served Owen hot tea, he fumbled the tiny china like a monkey wearing mittens. Every visit since, she served his beverage in a fat mug, regardless of its contents.

"I saw the way Owen looked at you," Clara said. "The Lord is entrusting you with a great honor."

Owen peeked through the window.

Gloria's forehead crinkled. "How so?"

"The Lord's assigned this ministry to Owen. If I read things right, by extension, that ministry is also being entrusted to you."

Gloria shook her head, loosening her hair so it fell forward and covered her profile. "Owen and I are not even engaged."

"Yet." Clara smiled in that way that drove Owen mad. It was the smile of a mom who knew which child stole the cookies despite posing the question. It was the smile of experience and indulgence. "There are good people here. This is a good church. It's not perfect, but it's good. You'll do just fine."

Clara shifted, and Owen ducked, his heart throbbing. He opened his email on his phone. *Focus!*

But the scraping sound of tissues being pulled from a box made Owen's heart skip. Was Gloria crying?

"I don't know if I'll make it." Her stifled words nearly flattened Owen.

Clara made motherly, supportive noises. "I understand you're applying for a job at the preschool. You've worked in a preschool before, haven't you?"

Owen dared another peek.

Gloria nodded and accepted a tissue from Clara. "But I am not applying for the job of Owen's wife. This is not something the church gets to vote on"—her voice dipped—"is it?"

Owen didn't hear much after that. Gloria wasn't applying for the job of his wife. The minute those words hit his ears, a roar filled his head. Each breath in hurt and each breath out sent pain to every nerve ending in his body.

Frank had warned Owen that ministry wives were sponges. They absorbed hit after hit over things like personal style, employment choices, and their involvement in the ministry. And every sponge has a saturation point. It's a point where it can absorb no more. But Owen couldn't believe it would happen here. Not to Gloria. Not even before they were married.

"Tiffany ruined my reputation in college." The resoluteness in Gloria's tone caught his ear. "I've been fighting all year to bring the truth to the light. The last thing I need is someone new dragging what's left of my name through the mud." A whimper escaped with her last word, and her intonation went from indignant to defeated.

"Oh honey, you have nothing to be ashamed of. I've followed the Emergence trial in the news. From what I can tell, speaking up took a lot of courage. The town should be grateful."

"Then why do I feel so ashamed?"

Owen's insides hardened. Gloria was the hero in the Emergence scandal.

"There was a time when shame didn't exist on earth," Clara said. "It was back in the garden. Adam and Eve were naked, and they were not ashamed."

Gloria snorted. "How does that help me now?"

"It shows us that when God makes right all that is wrong in this world, one of the things He'll eradicate is shame."

"What do I do until then?"

"You remember your God. He didn't just take away your sin, He gave you His holiness. That's what defines you."

Owen practically *amened* before he remembered he was eavesdropping.

"Now." Clara's tone changed to all business. "About your need for a reference. I've been praying for someone to take the musical off my hands."

"You can hear better if you tip your head to the side."

Owen's entire body jerked, and he found himself eyeball to eyeball with Breanna Clarke. The rims of Owen's ears burned hot, and he pulled at the collar of his shirt. Busted.

Breanna's features perked, and she pressed her ear against the exterior siding and tilted her head. "Like this," she whispered, overly exaggerating a head tilt. Her eyebrows puckered. "Who we listening to?"

"Shouldn't you be in school?" Nice redirect, *Pastor*.

A chair scraped across the hardwood in the house. It took all of Owen's self-control to remain focused on Breanna and not peek into the house.

Breanna wrinkled her nose. "I'm going. Dad sent me to the drug store to pick up some milk. I just dropped it off."

"Afternoon, Pastor."

Owen's head whipped toward the sidewalk so fast he tweaked a muscle. "Hey, Eli." Was the entire town taking the day off responsible work and school attendance?

"Nice day, isn't it?" One of Eli's eyebrows lifted with his real, unasked question.

Owen looked from Breanna, still listening through the wall, and back to Eli. They did make an odd pair.

"Yes, yes, it is." Owen straightened.

Owen's shoes slapped the stair boards loudly as he descended. Should he extend his hand? Fist bump? Do the one-armed hug with a double back slap? What was the proper greeting between men after getting caught eavesdropping? He went with stuffing both hands in his front pockets and hunching his shoulders. "How are the wedding plans coming along?"

"Great." Eli's gaze flicked momentarily to Meg's house, which stood next door to Clara's. "Meg has it all organized."

Eli and Meg didn't have a typical courtship by far, but Owen couldn't deny they were great together. He knew them as friends, but since he'd begun working through pre-marital counselling with them, he'd also found them to be solid, mature believers, committed to the Lord and each other. And even more, the four of them, Gloria, Owen, Meg, and Eli, really got on well together. What more could a man ask for? Owen glanced at Mrs. Brisbane's front door.

Approval from the masses?

"How are things with Gloria?" Eli probably knew Owen better than anyone else in town. They met weekly for Bible study and accountability.

"Good. Things are good."

Breanna, still with her ear pressed against the wall, gave him a thumbs up. Owen winced. What was that rhyme Gloria was always spouting? *I've not seen a mess that I cannot wrangle, 'till I met this web that I cannot untangle!*

It was a mess, all right. As evidenced by the truant girl with her ear pressed to the wall.

The front door opened, and Clara saw him immediately.

And then Breanna.

And finally, Eli.

Like an experienced mother, she created a hierarchy of importance in a millisecond with minimal information and clucked her tongue. "What are you doing here during school hours, young lady?"

Mrs. Brisbane didn't need to speak twice. Breanna leapt from the porch to her scooter, lifting it from where she had dropped it in the grass and swinging it under her feet in one smooth motion. "See ya later, Pastor Owen!"

The seasoned woman turned her perceptive gaze to Owen, who instinctively ran a hand down the front of his shirt and smoothed his hair. "I thought you had emails to answer, Pastor?" Mrs. Brisbane raised her eyebrows until they disappeared under her hair. Even Eli straightened at her tone.

Owen's flesh prickled under a cold sweat. What was it about Clara that made him revert to boyhood insecurities? He restuffed his hands in his pockets and clamped his elbows to his side. "I was, but then Eli and I got chatting."

"Ah, I better go. Meg's waiting for me." Eli scampered away. *Chicken.*

"Thanks again, Clara. I can't tell you how much this visit has meant to me."

Mrs. Brisbane's steely gaze softened as it landed on Gloria. "Come again. We'll visit longer next time."

Owen laced his fingers with Gloria's, and they started back to the church. The way her lower lip continued to tremble birthed an ache in his bones. It was a whole-body ache like the kind that accompanied the flu.

Owen stopped walking. It was so sudden that Gloria stumbled a bit. He steadied her and then reached to tip Gloria's chin with his fingers, waiting until she met his eyes. The minute their gazes collided, her eyes filled with tears. He didn't care who might see them. He didn't care if he spent the rest of the day answering phone calls about an inappropriate public display of affection. All he cared about was the hurting woman standing in front of him. He'd seen the same vulnerability in her gaze when they were young, back when he'd naively believed that his certainty of her innocence would be enough. But only the Lord could fill the voids inside of her.

He swayed closer until only inches separated them. He tipped his head forward, and their foreheads touched.

"I'm sorry this hasn't gone the way you thought it would. I want you to know that I see your sacrifices. I see everything you are doing for us and for others. It makes me love you even more." Why had he waited so long to acknowledge her efforts?

Her eyes drifted shut. A single tear rolled down her cheek. "It's so much harder than I thought it would be."

Frank's warning returned. How much hurt could one person absorb?

Seven

So far, so good.

The morning was going well. *She* was doing well. Gloria had made it through introductions, smiling and nodding until she felt like her face would crack. This was harder than taking the stand in court to testify. Her insides flipped as she walked down the aisle to take her seat in the family pew. Like the eyes of the jurors interpreting her every hand gesture and facial expression, the congregation followed her movements. They released a collective sigh of approval when she joined the rest of the Sycamores. Owen had invited her to sit with him in the front of the church, but she kiboshed that idea before he'd even finished extending the invitation.

Gloria didn't actually breathe until she slid into the pew beside her family a few seconds before the first song, but that could have less to do with anxiety and more to do with how tightly her dress nipped in at her waist.

Her older sister, Jessica, scooched over to make room for Gloria beside her and her husband, Tate.

Emma and Meg snickered from the other side of the room, probably whispering about Gloria's crazy expectations for this morning.

Perfect. It was perfect. It is perfect. It will be perfect.

No pressure.

"What are you wearing?" Jessica whispered from the side of her mouth.

"Shhh," Gloria hissed. She straightened the skirt of her very conservative, beige, button-down-the-back dress that she bought yesterday from a clearance rack in the city. It felt a big snug in some spots, but the way the fabric gathered and draped hid that flaw well. A morning with an uncomfortable cinch at her waist was worth it to dress exactly how she imagined an acceptable pastor's wife would. Simple. Colorless. Boring.

Jessica's mouth puckered in the same way that Emma's had when Gloria had shown her the dress. "I don't think I've ever seen you in that color."

Was beige even a color? Wasn't it more of an absence of color?

"I'm trying to blend in." Which would work a lot better if Jessica stopped talking to her.

"With what? The walls?" Jessica stood as Owen invited the congregation to join him in song.

Gloria pushed to her feet only a half beat after everyone else. She'd already blown her first impression with Suzy and Janet; she was not blowing her chance with the entire congregation. Sure, they already knew her. But that was as the Sycamores' youngest child, the one that left school under a cloud of suspicion and scandal. Now she was Gloria Sycamore, the pastor's girlfriend and potential future wife. It changed the rules.

Gloria spent the last few days looking for a way to regain some sense of control over her move back home. Hitting those wrong notes with two key women was her fault. If she hadn't been so bold in her clothing choices, so made-up in cosmetics and hair, so certain that Owen should give her a reference, they might have seen her differently. So, from now on, she was playing it safe. Neutral. Flat. Opinionless.

She raised her eyes to the stained-glass window. *Help me, Lord*. Gloria tracked a water droplet building in size on the ceiling joist. It burst free and landed right on the microphone with an amplified splat. A wild storm had ripped through the community last night and peeled a few more shingles off the church. Owen ignored the intrusion and continued. Her chest swelled. What a pro.

The service moved along quickly. Owen's faithful proclamation from the Word made him even more irresistible to her. As she stole a glance around the room, an inner warmth intensified. Finding the pastor attractive had to be some sort of sin.

He wrapped up his message, and the tension inside her inflamed but for an entirely different reason. She didn't hear a word of Owen's final prayer. Instead, she mapped out her exit. So far, nothing outright disastrous had occurred. She just had to get out with her dignity intact.

"Amen."

Gloria eyes snapped open. *It's go time.*

"I'll see you at home," she whispered to Jessica. Gloria wiggled out of the pew and hightailed it to the back door. Ten feet. She smiled wildly. Six feet. Her cheeks hurt. Three feet.

"Gloria!"

Busted.

A family brushed past her and exited out the front double doors, giving her a glimpse of the parking lot before they swung shut again. So close.

Gloria forced a big smile as she turned. "Happy Sunday."

"Yes, yes." The woman flapped her hands as if she had no time for pleasantries. She leaned in, and with a colluding tone, whispered, "I'm Nettie Fry, and the first thing you need to know about me is that I'm not one for gossip, so when *someone*, and I won't say who, because I'm not a gossip, started flapping her gums, I said, 'Hold up. I won't have any part of that. I'm just going to ask her myself.'"

Gloria gulped. The back door might as well be a million miles away.

"What's this I hear about you and Pastor Owen at the hotel in the city? We can't have our pastor at the center of a scandal."

Pressure rushed to Gloria's head at the same time the muscles in her body slackened. Had Suzy said something to this Nettie woman? And after Owen clarified everything? Gloria opened her mouth, but before a word came out, she felt a popping up her back. It rippled from her waist all the way to the nape of her neck like a row of dominos falling. Coolness hit her spine.

Gloria clutched at the back of her dress as the fabric around her hips sprung free and moved up toward the waistline. She backed away from Nettie. With each step, she felt a bit more of the fabric give. She didn't dare turn around. She retreated toward the side hall that led into the restrooms. *Please, Lord, let the hallway be empty!*

Gloria burst into the restroom and crashed into the furthest stall as the entire back of her dress gave way. This was it. This was how she was going to die.

Gloria slammed the stall door closed and twisted the lock. She pressed her forehead against the back of it. She should have never let her insecurities get to her. She should have worn an old favorite outfit, a tried-and-true combo that made her feel like a million bucks. Instead, she let all the comments about Jillian mess with her, prompting her to spend money she didn't have on a dress that malfunctioned *at church!*

A cool breeze tickled her back end. Her *exposed* back end. Her dress had split from top to bottom.

She twisted at the waist to try and see if any buttons remained. She yanked on edges. If it would just wrap around her . . . Did skin swell under stress? Maybe her anxiety about this morning caused her to retain water. There just wasn't enough fabric to cover her body.

"Gloria, are you okay?" Owen called through the outer restroom door. "Mrs. Fry said you'd rushed off."

Ha! That was putting it mildly. "I'm fine," she called out in a too-cheery voice. "Be out in a minute."

She slipped her arms out of the dress to assess the damage. She must have left a trail of buttons from the foyer to the restroom, because not a single one remained. She put the dress on backward and tried to wrap it around herself. No luck. She couldn't very well waltz out of the church with the front of her dress open with only her bra and granny panties underneath.

She wasn't sure if her constricted lungs were from the seemingly ever-shrinking bathroom stall or the onset of a panic attack. Her breaths came harder and faster. She couldn't breathe. No, that wasn't right. She *was* breathing. Panting, actually. Like a racehorse after a win.

Calm down. Nobody knows. You're in here alone. Just leave the stall, go to the sink, and use the mirror to figure out how to cover yourself.

She gulped. She pressed both palms against the door. *But what if somebody came in?* She flashed back to elementary school. She had hidden in a restroom stall while her best friend asked the popular kids what they *really* thought of Gloria Sycamore. She should have known better. Eavesdroppers never heard kind words. But she had hoped—had longed—to hear they admired her. Liked her. Wanted to be her friend. Instead, Gloria perched on the toilet seat with her knees pulled into her chest and buried her face. Never-good-enough Gloria. Geeky Gloria.

Her hands grappled for anything fabric to hold onto, and she heaved on the dress again. If she could just stretch the material— She couldn't leave the safety of the stall. She couldn't.

Her heart throbbed. The heat from her body must have made the dress shrink. She couldn't cover herself. It was some sort of malfunctioning fabric, and that was why it had been on sale.

She contorted her limbs like an acrobat, trying everything to force the fabric to cover the most intimate parts of her body. But however she twisted, something hung out.

"Gloria?" Owen rapped on the door.

"In a minute," she repeated.

What exactly was she going to do in a minute? Waltz through the church half naked? Nope. Call Owen in to help? That wasn't an option. Her mother? *Her mother!*

"Owen," she called sweetly, "Could you grab my mom for me? I need a hand."

"Sure." His footsteps faded.

Now, if only no one else entered the restroom. *God, if you can hear me, please—*

The outer door burst open, and giggling girls bounded in. *Forget it.*

"Breanna banana." More giggling was followed by what sounded like a little bit of shoving.

"Leave me alone."

"Breanna banana wears smelly pajamas."

Pajamas. The school must have had a P.J. day on Friday. That's why she was dressed in them.

"Get lost," Breanna growled.

The high-pitched laugher of preadolescent girls mixed with quiet sniffs.

"What's going on out there?" Gloria used her sternest teacher-voice.

Silence.

Dead air.

A pregnant pause.

There was one more loud sniff, and the sound of the door opening and closing again, and more footsteps. Had someone planned a party in the restroom after church? For crying out loud, there were more people gathering here than in the church foyer.

"Gloria?" Her mother called. "Are you in here? I thought you'd gone home."

The tears that pooled in Gloria's eyes were second in volume to the moisture that pooled under her armpits. "In here," she hissed.

"Where?" Her mother's heels clicked as they tapped the floor.

"The last stall. Help."

The girls giggled some more. A few hushed, unintelligible words, then more giggles. Then the door swooshing open and closed.

Silence.

Gloria cracked the stall door. "My dress ripped."

Her mom's chuckles were not helping. Gloria opened the stall door completely and folded her arms around her middle. "The buttons are somewhere in the foyer."

"Oh, dear." Mom pressed a hand to her mouth.

The bathroom stall blurred in and out of focus. She was going to die in the Sycamore Hill Community Church restroom. Those girls would be telling this story at youth retreats for years to come. No one would remember her name; she would be the crazy woman who thought she'd marry the pastor but met her Maker after being bested by a faulty dress. *An ugly, faulty dress.* The kind of dress Gloria would have never bought had she not already been feeling insecure. The story embellishments would make her a legend. She'd have to leave town again, and this time, she'd never come back.

"Can you wrap it around like a housecoat?" Mom tugged on the material.

Tears squirted from Gloria's eyes. "I tried."

"I know! I'll get my jacket. It's long enough to cover you. Don't go anywhere." Her mother winked and hurried off.

Gloria couldn't bear another minute stuck in this stall, stuck in this bathroom, stuck in this church, in this humiliation. But where was she going to go? She backed into the tiny cubicle and closed it again, twisting the lock for good measure. She perched on the toilet seat and gnawed on a fingernail. This was not how today was supposed to play out. Today, she'd planned to win over Owen's congregation. She was going to prove to them that she belonged at his side, in this church, and in the community. But she'd only been here one Sunday, and she was already a cautionary tale.

The door opened again. Gloria shot to her feet. "Mo—"

"Can you believe it? She just up and left me. Mid-sentence. I was hopeful, but now I'm not so sure about that girl."

Gloria recognized Nettie's voice. *Oh God, I know I haven't prayed as much as I should. But please, please, please, let me get out of here without them seeing me.*

"I saw them myself, sneaking out of that hotel in the city. A hotel!"

It had to be Suzy.

"We can't let our pastor be taken in," Suzy continued. "He'll come to his senses and see that the type of woman he needs by his side is *not* Gloria Sycamore."

It was the elementary school humiliation all over again.

"I read an article in the paper that said they might discount her testimony at the trial because she's . . ."

Gloria stiffened and knocked the garbage container. Conversation stopped. *She's what? Why didn't the woman finish her sentence? Was she spinning her index finger near the temple, implying Gloria was mentally unstable?*

Disbelief shot through her until she looked down at her dress gaping like a poorly tied hospital gown. She returned to her perch on the toilet in the church bathroom with her feet pulled up. Not exactly the actions of a sane woman.

"Someone needs to speak with Pastor Owen. Dating a parishioner is like a doctor dating a patient. It's just wrong."

Gloria nearly snorted. These two gossips were going to talk about ethics? She should just waltz out there and join the conversation. That would cork their mouths.

And prove she was no longer the same insecure girl she once was.

"It's like a professor dating a student."

"It does seem to be an imbalanced relationship."

"Imbalanced is right. I never pegged Pastor Owen as the controlling type, but this makes me wonder about his character. What do we really know about him? Who dates a person they have authority over unless they like control?"

"I got my jacke—" Gloria's mom clipped her words short. Her strides shortened as if she'd skidded to a stop. "Oh, sorry. I didn't know anyone else was in here. Gloria, are you still here?"

Like she'd be anywhere else.

"Gloria's here?" Their voices hit the same notes as the preteen bullies.

Good. They should feel bad. Still, the pressure that pinched Gloria's chest was worse than the dress. What if they were right? What if her presence brought more harm to Owen's ministry than good? She squeezed her eyes closed. *Lord, if you're ever coming back for your people, now would be a good time.*

She waited.

She cracked open one eye.

Nothing.

She swallowed. "I'm back here, Mom."

The gossip girls inhaled audibly and exited without another word.

Gloria opened the door. *Just when you think it's the worst it can get, your problems grow troubles and worsen with fret.*

Her mom held out her jacket. "Can you put this over it?"

Gloria slipped her arms through the jacket sleeves. Her mom stood in front of her and buttoned the jacket like a mother dressing her toddler. "Come on, love," she gently prodded. "You need to laugh. It's laugh or cry."

Gloria sucked her bottom lip into her mouth and bit down hard enough to draw blood. She was not going to cry. If she did, she'd have to face the congregation not only as a streaker in a trench coat but also with the blotchy skin that came from bawling.

Gloria lifted her chin and forced her stiff face into a plastic smile quickly becoming all too familiar.

Eight

Owen looked at his watch for what felt like the millionth time. How long did it take to put on a new dress? The church doors yawned open behind him, providing people with easy access to second helpings of food. Two long tables positioned end-to-end filled the church lobby, and the rest of the party had spilled outside despite the crisp fall day.

"Gloria will be back soon," Owen repeated to Nettie for what felt like the millionth time. After Gloria's disappearing act following the service, he'd been fielding questions about her from everyone. He'd done what he could to deflect from her clothing mishap, but word had spread. His girl had a cringe-worthy wardrobe malfunction in the back of the church sanctuary.

Fantastic.

Owen smiled and waved at several people. He stuffed his hands into his pant pockets and tried to focus on Nettie, still talking away at him. Talking at him, not with him, because that was the way it usually was. In the crowd but not part of the crowd. Participating in the conversation as a listener, not a contributor.

Off to the right, Hank Sinclair bent down on one knee and was showing Tommy how to properly fold a paper airplane from the papers they handed out for sermon notes. Eli and Meg chatted with Kathryn and Ethan. Meg worked at Ethan's bakery, and she'd brought some of his famous muffins to the potluck. They were the first to go. Kim Jansen gripped her son's hand as Oliver tried to pull her toward the buffet table for what would be his third helping. Officer Jackson, Oliver's uncle, picked the boy up and swung him around like he was weightless, which, at less than three years old, he practically was, despite his robust appetite.

Nettie flapped her hands like a concerned mother hen ruffling her feathers and clucked to regain Owen's attention. She actually clucked, and Owen had to clamp his teeth together to hold back a laugh.

"Oh, Pastor, it was awful, just awful. You don't know what it is like to be a woman and have something like that happen. Her dress ripped." She leaned in, hushed. "And at church!"

True. He didn't know. But to be fair, neither did Nettie. And for all her showy compassion, Nettie was the one standing here still talking about it.

"She must be devastated. Humiliated. I'm mean, to show your"—Nettie lowered her voice— "backside—"

"I think I'm needed in the . . . the . . ." He didn't have an end to that sentence. He simply needed to stop the conversation. He headed for the buffet table under the guise of a second helping. Dozens of empty casserole dishes, serving spoons, and ladles were scattered across the surface. Picked-over leftovers and Gloria's contribution were all that remained. A white, square, ceramic tray filled with hand-rolled cucumber sushi sat mostly untouched beside a cup of single-use chopsticks that Gloria insisted the kids would enjoy. He'd been the only person to take some. Owen piled four more tightly-rolled seaweed and rice discs onto his plate.

"Are we still on for this week?" Eli perused the leftovers. At Owen's blank look, he added, "For pre-marriage counselling."

Right. Owen clicked his chopsticks. "Yes, we'll discuss chapter four in our book." As Owen reminded Eli of his assigned reading on becoming the kind of husband Meg needed, he realized that he'd failed to apply the material to himself personally. It wasn't enough for Gloria to know that he loved God; she needed to know that he loved her. The church could always get another pastor if things went south, but Gloria couldn't get another husband after they married.

If they married.

Technically, they weren't even engaged. But that wasn't the point. The point was that if he planned to marry her, he needed to start acting like the man God had called him to be.

"There you are!" As Clara Brisbane hustled toward him, Eli wandered away. "Is Gloria okay?"

"I haven't seen her since she left. Hopefully, she'll be back soon." They chatted a bit longer before parting ways. Before another person could descend, Owen slid into the corridor outside his office. He leaned against the wall, tipped his head back, and closed his eyes.

"Pastor?"

His eyes snapped open.

Suzy sat at Janet's desk just outside his office door. She folded her hands over her swollen belly and smiled up from her seat. "Are you all right?"

Owen couldn't remember the last time he walked around a corner and Suzy wasn't there.

"I was just going to check my calendar. I can't remember if I have a meeting Monday afternoon or not."

"Oh, let me do that for you." Suzy opened the shared calendar on the desktop. "Schedule's all clear. Would you like me to insert something?"

What he'd like is to know what Suzy was doing at the desk opening the church calendar as if she was the church secretary, but his mental exhaustion wouldn't let him pull on that thread.

"I'm going to pop into the musical practice. Can you block off a few hours, please?"

His breath bottled as he waited for Suzy's typical nosy follow-up question, but it never came.

"All done."

"Thanks." Owen didn't want to return to the potluck and socialize. He couldn't hide in his office with Suzy just outside the door, so he retreated to the sanctuary. He slipped into the back pew and cradled his head in his hands. *Lord, help Gloria find her footing here. Help me help her.*

He felt her presence beside him.

"Did anyone notice?" Gloria's attention alternated between Owen and the exterior doors. On the other side of the open doors, small clusters of people milled about with coffee and baked goods. The occasional shriek of pleasure from one of the kids cut through the crisp air.

"Yes, they noticed, but I covered for you." At least he hoped he did.

He knew the moment her gaze landed on the buffet table, which was just visible from their position. She sagged, features, countenance, and body. She tried so hard. Why couldn't the church just embrace her? Or at the very least, indulge her.

"The sushi was a flop?" She meandered toward the foyer.

He caught up to her in two short strides.

She dragged a fingertip along the edge of the large square platter holding her offering. The muscles in her jaw clenched and released. With a fire he'd never felt before, Owen's insides burned.

He wanted to take it all away. The disappointment. The rejection. The judgment. But he couldn't. Those feelings were intrinsically connected to ministry. To all of life.

A profound disappointment in his people settled over his heart. God had called him to serve these people. They were an imperfect lot that needed the Lord just as much as anybody else. The expectation or hope that they'd function differently was both right and wrong. As born-again believers, they should live differently. They should be filled with love, joy, peace, patience, kindness, goodness, gentleness, faithfulness, and self-control. But they were still people wrapped in sinful flesh that sometimes responded to circumstances with hate, sorrow, disruption, hurt, sinfulness, abrasiveness, unfaithfulness, and impatience. Sanctification was a journey. Yet, however they may have disappointed him, they were still blood-bought children of God, and therefore deserved his tender affection. He and they were sinners that struggled with sin, and that was normal.

But it didn't feel good.

And it didn't feel normal or right for Gloria to absorb the hits.

"I had the sushi." He lifted his plate. "It was great. I'm on seconds."

Her lips tipped up in a tiny, sad smile.

Owen had never eaten sushi before meeting Gloria. He'd wrongly assumed it was always filled with raw fish. Turned out there were several kinds of sushi. Avocado. Cucumber. Sweet potato. It had quickly become a favorite treat, but he couldn't convince anyone else to try it.

When Gloria lifted her head, her expression of defeat stole his breath. "What are we doing?"

The muscle in his cheek began to twitch. He didn't like her tone or the look in her eyes. It reminded him of a younger Gloria, freshly accused of cheating and expelled from school. "We're having lunch."

She wrapped her arms around her middle and hugged herself. If half the town wasn't watching, Owen would have folded his arms around her and kissed away her sadness.

But they were.

So, he didn't.

"Us." She gestured between them. "What are we doing? I'll never fit in. They'll never accept me." She blinked rapidly, and when they made eye contact, she quickly looked away.

"Don't say that." Owen pressed a finger against her lips. "They'll love you when they get to know you."

Gloria snorted. Her gaze trailed longingly over the crowd. Owen followed the path her eyes took. Groups of women laughed together. Children ran. Despite all the questions he had fielded about Gloria, no one approached her to invite her in. Outside of her family, Meg, and Emma, Gloria was pretty much left on her own. The church should be a safe space where everyone felt welcome, but too often it functioned like a social club. "Give them time."

"There is not enough time in the world."

"Are you ready for tomorrow, dear?" Mrs. Brisbane hurried over. She looked Gloria up and down. "I see you've changed your clothes."

Owen stiffened, but before he could speak, Clara continued with a wave of her hands. "This suits you much better than that old frock that ripped," she tutted. "You're far too young for that fuddy-duddy style."

Owen's mouth fell open. Had he not been shocked into silence, he would have let out a wallop of a cheer. Thank the Lord for Clara Brisbane.

"Are you ready?" Clara repeated her question and cocked an eyebrow so high it tucked itself under the log curl on her forehead.

Gloria blinked but remained silent.

"The musical? Have you got everything you need? I told the children that your rehearsals start tomorrow."

"Right, right, the musical." Gloria smiled. This was a real smile. Not the kind she pasted on earlier as she mingled with parishioners. Not the frightened one she wore as she escaped wrapped in a jacket. But a real one. The kind that only emerged when she spoke about her kids, as she called them. "I love the play. Where did you find it?" Gloria turned to Owen. "It's called Buzz Off. It's super cute. It's all about bees."

Mrs. Brisbane patted Gloria's hand. "I can't wait to see what you do with those kids. You have complete freedom to take it in whatever direction you want. I'm just so thankful for your help."

Complete freedom. That could be good.

Or, if the church community continued to resist her, very, very bad.

Nine

The church multipurpose room smelled more than a little damp, but it was the scent of wiggly bodies that triggered some sort of dopamine release in Gloria. Like a timed-release shot of maternal instinct, her biological clock kicked into high gear. She couldn't get enough. About twenty children of various ages clamored around her, and she hadn't felt this good—this needed—since her last day in the preschool.

"Who is excited about our play?" Gloria sat down on a chair and motioned for the kids to follow suit. She kept her voice low, refusing to raise it above the chatter. Experience had already taught her the value of a soft word. Proverbs 15:1 not only defused an angry child effectively, but noisy ones as well.

Quiet rolled over the room, and the kids dropped to their bottoms.

Clara Brisbane's head nod injected a shot of confidence into Gloria. She could do this. She would do this. If she wanted any chance of scoring that job and staying in Sycamore Hill, she not only had to do this, but she had to do it well.

Instead of nervousness, excitement powered her pulse. It was the same kind of feverish thrill that hit her parents' dog when guests arrived and made him leave a puddle on the floor. It was the perfect case of I-can't-hold-back-the-wiggles kind of eagerness, but-I-have-to-because-I'm-the-teacher dilemma. Gloria stretched her eyes as wide as she could, playing up the moment. She leaned forward, sitting on the edge of her chair as if she were about to share the most delicious secret. "Our play is called Buzz Off. You've all been working on it for weeks, but I've just learned about it. Can someone tell me what the play is about?"

Silence.

"Is it," Gloria tapped a fingertip to her lips, "an angry big sister telling her brother to," she mouthed the words *buzz off*.

A child in the front row giggled.

"Is it about a bully?"

"No," a younger voice called out.

"Is it about someone who is mean?"

Laughter peppered out from the kids.

"Hmmmm. Such a puzzle."

"The main characters are *bees*," a preadolescent voice called from the back row. It sounded slightly bored with Gloria's game.

"Like bumble bees? Honeybees?"

"I don't like bees." One of the smallest in the group pulled back so far that he was almost sitting in the lap of the kid behind him. He popped his thumb into his mouth and started twirling a chunk of hair that was about four weeks late for a haircut. His twin sister, Bethann, slung an arm around his shoulder, looking every bit the part of a fierce defender.

Gloria melted. "It's Brock, right?"

He nodded.

"Bees are in the story, but it's also about two boys. Can you tell me about the boys?"

Brock looked to his sister for insight despite the fact she could only be older than him by mere minutes. The girl nodded. It was a curt, tight nod that told Gloria the poor thing had done far more mothering than any four-year-old should ever have to do.

Nathan's twins.

Even if Clara hadn't pointed them out when they arrived, Gloria would have guessed. All four siblings had the same heart-shaped face and wild, brown hair. It sprung in all directions, but the twins' hair retained the downy softness of babyhood.

Clara tapped a few pre-teens on the shoulder and slipped out the back door with them as the rest of the children waited on Gloria. Clara was working with the actors, running lines and reviewing stage direction. Gloria had the daunting task of managing the choir. A dozen kids of various ages on risers, instructed to stand still, be quiet, and not fidget. Possible? Of course. Fun? Hardly.

That was all about to change because she had *complete freedom*.

Clara had given Gloria the run-down of how she usually taught the kids their songs. Those who could read were given the lyrics, and those that couldn't, listened as they sang the songs over and over. This was how it had been done for years. Decades. *Centuries,* maybe. Clara didn't buy into the new student-driven, need-based theories in education. What she'd been doing for years had worked just fine. It wasn't broke, so there was no need to fix it.

That might have been true, but it didn't mean they couldn't improve upon it. Gloria pulled from the students a summary of the musical, outlining the roles of two boys struggling to get along, the bee colony facing division, and the theme of forgiveness. She wanted to hear what part of the story resonated with the kids and got them excited. She followed along in the script Clara had pressed into her hands. "So, the worker bees are trying to run out the drones, who, according to them, don't contribute anything to the colony. Is that right?"

Luke shoved Breanna. "Sounds like you. Useless."

Breanna stomped on her brother's foot. Hard.

There was a gigantic pause like those few moments of calm before a storm ripped through the neighborhood and tore roofs off houses. Luke sucked in a breath—the kind you take before plunging into the lake— and then, he howled. Not just any kind of howl. He howled like a caged dog. He clasped one foot in his hands and hopped on the other, glaring at his sister with such loathing that if looks could kill, Breanna would be face to face with her Maker.

Brian and Sarah, whose gaga eyes for each other hadn't escaped Gloria's attention, used the distraction to drift to the back of the group and erase the space between them like a north magnetic pole finding the south.

"Oh, no you don't." Gloria wagged her finger at the pair who were not-quite-old-enough-to-be-a-couple but plenty old-enough-to-feel-the-early-pangs-of-attraction.

Bethann's finger found Brock's ear, which she poked in, withdrew, examined, and then popped in her mouth.

Gloria gagged.

This was a million times worse than her preschoolers. Wasn't it supposed to get easier as children aged? Shouldn't they be more responsible? What would Clara think—

And it hit her.

It hit her like a baseball bat to the gut. The kind of impact that forces the breath from your body and leaves you gasping.

Clara knew.

She *knew* these kids. She'd run the musical for years. Years! This wasn't a test run for Gloria's referral. This was flat-out sabotage.

Gloria swiveled to the back of the room and stared at the door through which Clara and her handpicked students had vanished. She was probably on the other side drumming her fingertips together in front of her face and barely holding back maniacal laughter. She'd set Gloria up to fail.

Not if Gloria had anything to say about it. "Everybody up."

The kids jolted at her abrupt shift in tone and stood. In her periphery, she caught a flicker of surprise in Breanna's eyes. Maybe even a twinge of respect. If the kids expected a pushover, they had another thing coming.

"Get into a line right here." Gloria extended her hand in front of her. When nobody moved, she scooped up Bethann, swung her around, and deposited her first in line. "Behind Bethann, please."

They fell into a messy row that her preschoolers could have put to shame.

"Worker bees are hardly ever still, so I think," Gloria cupped one elbow with her hand and twisted her lips. She circled the kids slowly. "This choir needs to move."

"We aren't allowed to move," Luke piped up.

"We haffa stay still." Brock spoke around two slobbery fingers. Bethann's head bobbed generously. They were the youngest in the crew—only four years old. Old enough to know how the annual musical played out.

Quiet.

Still.

No fun.

But Gloria had too much riding on this musical to bank on Clara's word that her instructions were best. Sitting still clearly wasn't working for the squirmy litter. Some adults might see their energy as a weakness, but Gloria would make it a strength.

"I get to decide how the musical part of the play works, and I think that we are going to need"—she tapped her lips for a few more beats— "two ribbon dancers and a ballet dancer."

A few of the girls in the back perked up. Sarah actually ripped her eyes off Brian for a few seconds.

"I see a conga line and, of course, we need the usual choir. We don't want to disappoint our parents who are looking forward to that. But this choir will not stand still or be quiet. This choir will dance." Gloria swayed with exaggerated movements. "It needs to dance. And costumes!" She clapped her hands. "We'll need lots of costumes."

Her declarations landed like pebbles in the water that rippled joy across the faces of the children.

"We never get costumes."

"This'll be fun."

"I hope I get picked for ballet."

Only Breanna remained quiet.

"Why don't we spend the rest of our time making flower masks? The opening song happens in a garden, so we should all look like flowers."

Happy chatter and fresh energy soon pushed out the negative vibes. Gloria pulled craft supplies from the large cabinet at the back of the room and showed the kids how to make a simple flower mask with construction paper, a paper plate, and a popsicle stick. "We need it on a stick so we can pull it down when we are singing and put the mask back up when we are done."

As the kids worked, Gloria played the songs the choir would sing in the background. It wasn't too long before the humming started. Then, the occasional line would slip out while a child focused on their task. Gloria's chest puffed. There was more than one way to learn lyrics. She wandered up and down and around the tables until she stood behind Breanna, who leaned over her six-year-old brother, Luke, and rubbed paste on the end of a stick.

"Are you excited about the play?" Gloria asked her.

Breanna shrugged.

"Is something bothering you?"

Breanna darted a look at her brother, who was now happily drawing on a piece of paper. She stepped away from him. "Dad don't have extra money for costumes or ribbons."

Right then and there, Gloria made an executive decision. She hadn't asked Clara how the church managed extra expenses, but she didn't care. She'd pay out of pocket if she had to. "Don't you worry about that. We're making all the costumes ourselves right here at every practice."

"Really?" Breanna's eyes lightened briefly, but they still held the kind of doubt that came from experience. The kind that knew what it was to be promised one thing yet receive another.

"Really." Gloria squeezed her shoulder. "And it's sweet of you to be concerned about your dad's money, but God always provides exactly what we need just when we need it, often in ways we cannot imagine."

The shadow of a smile started. Millimeter by millimeter it grew into a full-out grin. It took years off the girl. Gloria handed her a paper plate and glitter. "You better get to work."

Breanna trotted off.

"That was sweet."

Owen.

An unexpected shiver tiptoed down Gloria's spine. By the time she faced him, she was sure the same goofy grin that Breanna just sported was pasted on her face. And maybe Sarah's gaga eyes, to boot. "What are you doing here? Isn't Monday your day off?"

Owen's crinkly smile widened as his gaze moved over the busy kids. "I came to see how it was going. I thought you were supposed to be getting them ready to sing?"

"I am."

His eyebrows pulled together.

"Trust me." She reached for both his hands and squeezed them in hers. "They need this."

They stood there, smiling at each other for an uncomfortably long second. For a brief moment, she thought he might challenge her, until his features relaxed. "They look like they are having fun."

The kids threw them covert glances and giggled. Owen pulled his hands out of hers and put a more respectable amount of space between them.

Room for the Holy Spirit, her mother used to say.

"I also came in to check the donations that came in for the roof. After yesterday—well, we need to do something."

"The funds are here?"

"Yeah. The bookkeeper will deposit them later today. For now, they are in my office in a locked drawer. Some more came in yesterday's offering, so I want to see where we're at with it."

Gloria nodded.

"Do you have time for dinner tonight?"

"I can't. Meg, Emma, and I are working on Meg's wedding favors, and after that I have a phone call scheduled with the lawyer. He thinks I'll be called back to the stand for a redirect."

His voice dropped to a whisper and Gloria leaned in before realizing he'd pulled her quiet trick on her. "Do you think they'd notice if I kissed you goodbye?"

Her eyes bulged. The collar of her shirt suddenly felt tight. He was teasing. He had to be.

"Just kidding." He lightly squeezed her fingertips. "I only wanted to see you blush."

She glanced at the window and saw her reflection. Mission accomplished. Blotchy. Flustered. Beet red. Just how every girl wanted to look.

"You're gorgeous." His words dripped with intimacy that couldn't possibly be acceptable in a church. Wasn't the ground holy or something?

Breanna's lips curved, and Gloria's skin prickled even more.

"Until later." Owen's promise caressed her ear. He raised his head and called out, "Bye, kids!"

"Bye, Pastor Owen!"

Gloria distracted herself with opening up a large fabric grocery bag that she'd brought with her. "I think it's time for a treat!"

Hoots and hollers validated her decision.

Gloria removed boxes of pre-made food with no nuts, dairy, or gluten. It cost a fortune to buy everything pre-packaged, but better safe than sorry.

Tommy grabbed fistful of soft, red gummies. "I love these!" He shoved them into his mouth and raced around the table.

Of course, this was when Clara returned with her actors in tow. Her eyebrows disappeared into that sausage roll that forever sat across her forehead, and Gloria suddenly saw the organized chaos through the older woman's eyes.

Tommy had his shirt off and twirled it like a lasso above his head. The twins shrieked like they were having some sort of squawking contest. Luke bellowed out the lyrics of the song, one word behind and completely off key.

Gloria gulped.

So much for her recommendation.

Ten

A harsh knock on his office door jolted Owen from his sermon prep. Janet never let anyone interrupt him during this part of his week. "Come in."

Jason Chalkey entered and closed the door behind him. Not a good sign. "Morning, Owen."

"Hey, Jason, what can I do for you?" Owen gestured to the chair across from his desk. A million questions flashed through his mind, beginning with how Jason had broken through the gatekeeper and ending with why Jason had used his given name. The congregation had always addressed him as pastor. Not that he asked or wanted them to. They just did. Jason's reversal to his given name landed with a hint of disrespect and a passive-aggressive gut punch. "Did Suzy have the baby?"

Jason's neck corded. He worked his jaw back and forth and avoided direct eye contact.

Owen stiffened. Something had happened. Something bad. He fought to reel in his catastrophizing thoughts. Were there complications with Suzy's pregnancy? Did their house finally sink under sea level?

The Chalkey family's money struggles were well known. They'd bought a beautiful home in the country, large enough for their growing brood and well under market value. Then, they found out why the as-is deal that was too good to be true was, in fact, too good to be true. As winter turned to spring, the melting snow filled their basement with water. Every storm or hard rain refilled the space. This past fall, with the series of storms tracking through the area, had been particularly difficult. They'd taken to living on the main floor and blocking access to the basement. Losing half their living space had been difficult. The church was trying to help, but the projected price tag for the fix had come in at close to twenty thousand dollars. No one had that kind of cash, not when the church also needed a new roof. They were praying for a miracle.

"We need to have a discussion about the roof." Jason ignored the offered chair and remained standing, spreading his legs further apart and folding his arms across his chest.

Owen tapped his index finger on the desktop as a tiny release for his pent-up energy. He'd have to chat with Janet later. This was not an interrupt-sermon-prep-day sort of situation. He scrubbed his hand down his face and was just about to say that he didn't have time for this when Jason shifted like a linebacker preparing to pounce. "The money's gone."

Wait. What? Owen's insides momentarily hollowed. He briefly closed his eyes, trying to settle the big breakfast he'd eaten at The Muffin Man that now rolled dangerously through his midsection. "What do you mean gone?"

"Gone. Lost." Jason's nostrils flared. "Stolen."

"I counted the offering yesterday." Owen fumbled for the key to his locked desk drawer. Janet was the only other person who had a key. He shoved the key in, but it didn't unlatch anything. The drawer, already unlocked, opened easily. Busted, actually. "The money was here. All of it."

"Janet called me as soon as she arrived this morning and saw the broken lock." Jason rolled onto the balls of his feet and then back again. Back and forth. Over and over.

She saw the busted lock? What had she been doing in his office? How many times had she poked around in here without his knowledge? But he didn't ask any of those questions. He was too busy trying to remember if he'd ever left sensitive information from counselling sessions out on his desk.

"She called you?" Owen repeated Jason's statement. Why hadn't Janet called him? Why had she acted as if everything was fine when he said good morning to her and sat a coffee from the bakery on her desk?

Then it hit him. It hit him so hard that if he hadn't already been seated, he would have dropped.

They've been here before.

Jason blurred in and out of focus. Owen's tongue thickened, and his throat closed in. They thought he'd taken the money. To do what? Impress a girl already dating him? To splurge on a fancy meal in the city? But Jason's hard lines and stiff posture held no mercy.

Not because Owen wasn't trustworthy, but because the wounds the last guy inflicted were fresh and still bleeding.

"Some of the kids mentioned seeing you at music practice." Some of the kids. So, he'd already called parents. Checked his alibi. Owen stretched his neck on the chopping block and waited.

The ache started at the back of this throat. His chest tingled, and his fingertips went numb. Owen dropped his hands to his lap and clenched them away from Jason's accusingly hard stare.

"What were you doing at the church on your day off?" Jason's angled body and lowered head made Owen want to squirm.

He fought the urge.

Jason's brow wrinkled, and the longer Owen took to reply, the deeper Jason's skin flushed.

"I came to see Gloria." It came out whispery. Owen cleared his throat and tried again. He had nothing to apologize for, and this wasn't personal, no matter how personal it felt. Considering the church history, Jason had to ask these questions, and Owen had to put their minds at ease. "I also checked the fund while I was here. I've been investigating what it would cost to temporarily patch the roof. I wanted to see how much we had. The lock was intact then, so it had to happen in the evening or overnight."

But if it wasn't personal, if Jason standing here, asking these questions was the right next step, why was the room still spinning?

"Suzy said that you and Gloria have been eating in some pretty fancy places. Are the restaurants in Sycamore Hill not good enough?" Jason's arms tightened as if his hands needed to be tucked under his armpits to maintain control. "I'd love to take Suzy to Queens Court, but we have to settle for lunch at the diner."

Owen lifted his chin. That wasn't fair. Under normal circumstances, Owen wasn't obligated to explain how long he saved for that date or how many cans of soup he ate for dinner afterward, but these weren't normal circumstance. Still, he couldn't hide the hurt in his voice. "Stop beating around the bush and say your piece like a man."

Jason's noisy breath whistled through his nostrils. His eyes turned cold and flinty. "Have you dipped into the roof fund to impress Gloria?"

And there it was. All the years invested in this place gone in a single accusation. Shame descended on Owen with such oppressiveness that he couldn't inhale. Not shame over his actions, because he'd done nothing wrong, but shame nonetheless. Shame over what had been done to him. Assumed of him. Doubted in him. He felt *unclean*. Leviticus unclean.

Owen finally understood Gloria's struggles with the trial and people's endless questions because of her association with something tawdry. He felt that same contamination right now. Scripture devoted a whole bunch of Old Testament words to the subject of cleanliness and what it meant to be sent out from the camp.

But unclean was not the same as sinful.

Unclean can return to the community.

But was this the community they wanted to re-enter?

It might not even matter. There might not have been a way for Owen to recover from the accusation, but Owen wouldn't go down without a fight. He held Jason's gaze. "I did not take the money."

"It doesn't look good when the pastor lives a flashy life. Image matters. We're simple people. Most barely getting by."

Flashy? Owen lived in a one-bedroom apartment in the attic of a small house off Main Street. He ate ramen noodles and mac and cheese at least three times a week and walked most places because he couldn't afford a needed vehicle repair. Jason had no right. None. But the twitch in the man's jaw indicated the jury had deliberated and given their judgment.

The words of the apostle Luke in 12:11-12 came to mind. *When they bring you before the synagogues and the rulers and the authorities, do not be anxious about how you should defend yourself or what you should say, for the Holy Spirit will teach you in that very hour what you ought to say.*

Sure, Owen wasn't in front of the synagogue or the rulers, but Jason held authority in this church. This applied. The Holy Spirit was Owen's helper, and boy, did he need help. Right now. In this *very hour*.

Give me words and humility.

Owen held Jason's gaze and refused to flinch. "I understand the church has been here before and that means you have to ask the tough questions. I will not take this personally. I want you to do whatever you have to do to be confident that I've committed no wrong."

Jason's eyes widened. His posture, which had been tense and ready for a fight, relaxed a little. It wasn't much, but it was enough to give Owen the confidence that he was on the right track.

"You have my permission to ask whatever you want, look into my personal finances, and poke around my private life. I have nothing to hide."

"I appreciate that, Pastor. This isn't easy."

"I don't imagine it is."

And while they investigated Owen, it gave him time to do his own digging, because when they cleared him, there'd be a witch hunt. And the only way to protect the unity of the church was to uncover the thief himself.

"I'll be in touch about our next steps." Jason held out his hand.

Owen stood, accepted his hand, shook, and nodded. As the door closed behind Jason, he fell back into his chair and cradled his head. *Lord, help us.*

Before he could pray another word, his inbox dinged with a message from Clara, marked as urgent.

His heart sank further. Gloria had given Tommy a treat with red dye, something he wasn't allowed to have. Apparently, Tommy's parents had called Clara to complain. The boy had bounced off the walls all night long. There was no grace in Clara's tone, but to be fair, tone was hard to read in an email.

He started to type a reply about how this was the happiest he'd seen the choir, well, ever. But Clara's lengthy explanation about how the job of the choir was to sing, not make crafts and eat treats, slowed his fingers.

Maybe if the same kids didn't get the large roles every year . . . Backspace and delete.

Questioning her direction wouldn't help. Clara always put on a respectable show. But frankly, the only kids who ever looked like they had fun were the same crew that starred year after year.

Another email dinged.

Gloria.

He saved his response to Clara as a draft and opened Gloria's message.

Several parents called Gloria to say that the last practice was the most fun their children had at choir in years. Years! Gloria was convinced that Clara would have to give her the recommendation.

He closed her email without answering, pressed a shaky hand to his forehead, and sagged. His gaze dropped to the text he'd been preparing for Sunday. In Acts 6:10-15, after Stephen spoke, the people couldn't withstand it.

So, they killed him.

Eleven

The next few weeks flew by in what Gloria could only describe as a blurred frenzy of activity. A single scene failed to stand out in her mind, just chaotic moment after chaotic moment, split between helping Meg with wedding plans and preparing the kids to be the best, most unique, most *involved* choir this town had ever seen. This wasn't a group of tiny humans relegated to the back, dressed to blend in with the scenery. Nope. They were front and center for their songs. Just as needed to the plot as the main actors.

Gloria had taken the words *complete freedom* to heart and steered this play as she saw fit. Only a small twinge of apprehension twanged, warning her she might have pushed too hard and too far. But later, when Clara and Gloria got the entire group together for a dress rehearsal, the woman would have to agree. It was the exact kind of unexpected twist the musical—and the kids —needed.

It was a good idea.

In theory.

Her gut twisted more.

Breanna had perfected the solo dance that Gloria choreo-graphed, pulling from her younger years of ballet and jazz. Luke was the bee that his little brother absolutely refused to dress as because, as Bethann said, all bees are stupid. And the twins shifted between flowers and stars, depending on the song.

Adorable. Ab-so-lu-tely a-dor-a-ble.

She hadn't planned on focusing so much on the Clarke kids, but when Owen released the fall schedule, she suspected that Nathan had hoped for more opportunities to keep his kids busy. Her non-position in the community didn't give her an avenue to officially help out Nathan with his kids, so she shifted gears. She could give his kids bigger roles that would extend their practice hours so Nathan could have a bit more time to himself. She could use that one-on-one time with them to inject as much fun and laughter back into their life as possible. She could show his kids, and all the others that had believed the lie they were nothing but wallflowers, that they had something more to offer. Something valuable. Something no one else brought to the table. Something she desperately needed to hear as a young girl while her big sister collected first place medals, and Gloria collected participation ribbons. She'd even gone as far as to pull out her old rhyming book.

You are the you that you need to be. No one else can be you, no one else, no siree. If we didn't have you, we'd be missing a lot. You matter. You're wanted. Your company's sought.

She repeated her mantra to the choir so many times they prob-ably thought it was one of their songs.

In a way, it was.

It was her song also. She had something Sycamore Hill Community Church needed. They just didn't know it yet.

· · ·

"Thanks again for picking me up." Gloria hopped into her sister's car and pulled the vehicle door closed quickly before any more rainwater could leak in.

"Anytime." Jessica revved the engine and pulled out of the courthouse parking lot.

If only it were as easy for Gloria to pull the door of her mind closed on all the things her mother said to her this morning before she left the house. Today was her final court appearance in the trial against Emergence. The attorney had been correct, and Gloria was recalled to the stand. But it was Mom's comments that rattled Gloria, distracting her during the closing arguments in the case. When her insides should've been singing with the brilliant conclusion to the drug scandal story, all she could hear was:

Has Owen made his intentions toward you clear?

You're not as young as you used to be. You don't have time to waste.

Translation: Tell that boy to pick up his feet and put a ring on your finger before your uterus expires.

Gloria clicked her seatbelt together and rubbed her thumb over her bare fourth finger on her left hand.

Have the kids learned their songs yet?

Is Clara writing that reference?

Translation: Why are you rocking the boat? Just do things the way Clara expects and be done with it. You can't turn this ship, so just get in and row.

Gloria shifted in her seat, trying to get comfortable in a skirt and blouse that suddenly felt too tight. Mom meant well. But the playfulness in her tone couldn't erase the unspoken implication. Sycamores were go-getters. They accomplished great things. They reached goals. What Sycamores didn't do was get kicked out of school and accused of a crime, change career tracks halfway through university, or struggle to find work.

Unless your first name was Gloria.

Never-good-enough-Gloria.

Gloria didn't have the heart or the willpower to continually challenge her mom. She'd spent the last nine months proving her innocence to the judge and jury, and she was done. Finished. She had nothing left. Her ketchup bottle spurted dust over the French fries of life. The container was empty.

"How did court go?" Jessica flicked her wipers to high speed, checked her blind spot, and changed lanes.

"The closing was fantastic. The attorney did a great job." Now all she had to do was wait for the jury to decide the company's fate. Then, she could put Emergence, Tiff, and the scandal behind her.

"I meant, how was it for you?" Her sister kept her attention on the ever-slickening road, but genuine concern for Gloria oozed from her tone.

The soft beating of the wipers moved back and forth over the windshield in sync with Gloria's heartbeat. It soothed her. "Honestly, it was lousy. The defense made me out to be some sort of disgruntled employee trying to score a quick buck."

Jessica's eyes got that look. The same look she wore when she stepped between Gloria and a bully in elementary school. The same look she wore when Tiff made a passing comment about being innocent in the scandal that wrecked Gloria's life. It shot fire and ice, ready to fight to the death for her kid sister. In proper Sycamore fashion, Jessica stood in the gap with her weapon loaded. "You knew going in that it was gonna be hard, right? The prosecuting attorney prepared you, right?"

"Yeah, she did." But that didn't make it any easier to swallow. No one liked to hear their name dragged through the mud, and the last thing Gloria needed was for a church member to latch onto the crazy notion that she was out for revenge or looking to cash in.

But, of course, they would read it. Everyone in town followed the trial. Everyone had an opinion. Everyone was keeping score.

And no matter what the judge decided about Emergence Pharmaceuticals or her old roommate, Tiff, Gloria was losing. Bad. Gloria felt the weight of Jessica's gaze.

"I get the feeling you think you deserve everything that happened to you."

Pain shot through her jaw, and Gloria unclenched her teeth.

"God has some good words for those who feel like they don't deserve His kindness."

Gloria counted the trees they passed.

"It's not your fault."

Fourteen, fifteen, sixteen.

"You're made in the image of God. For that reason alone, you deserve kindness."

Nice try. Pretty soon Jessica would fall back to the old *God don't make no junk* phrase made popular on cat posters and memes.

"Look at me." Jessica's tone demanded that Gloria stop counting trees. Jessica waited until Gloria turned her face toward her sister. "We love you. We are here for you."

Gloria forced her features into a smile. It was nice of Jessica, but that was a quick fix. Only temporary. Besides this wasn't about her family's acceptance. It wasn't even about God's acceptance. It was about learning to live with the shame that came from the scandal. The shame of never being good enough.

Jessica studied her for an uncomfortable minute, then switched gears. "What's wrong with your car?"

The tightness in Gloria's chest eased. "Nothing. Owen's truck wouldn't start, so I lent him mine. He had a bunch of appointments that he couldn't miss."

"Hmm." Jessica kept her attention on the road as the lights of the city faded behind them. She'd mastered Mom's skill of saying nothing while simultaneously saying everything at the top of her lungs.

Mom didn't trust Gloria's judgment when it came to people, her future, or well, anything. That was the problem with moving back home. Your adulthood got packed away with your stuff, and suddenly, your parents had an opinion on every part of your life. But Jessica? Sisters weren't supposed to judge. They stood with you, shoulder to shoulder in solidarity against parental attacks. At least, that's what a sister was supposed to do.

It was exhausting being the black sheep of the family. *Exhausting*.

A tiny noise erupted from the back of her throat, and Jessica cut her gaze Gloria's way and changed the topic again.

"How are things with Owen?"

"Complicated."

Jessica lifted her eyebrows.

"It's like there's a cloud hanging over him ever since the funds for the roof went missing."

Her sister let out a low whistle. "Have they made any progress? Does Owen suspect anyone?"

Gloria shrugged. She loved that her sister didn't once think that Owen might be guilty. No one in her family even tolerated the idea for one second. It almost made up for their micromanaging ways and strong opinions. "He said that Suzy was in the office after the potluck."

"Jason's wife? I heard they're having trouble."

Gloria sat upright in the bucket seat. "Marriage trouble?"

Jessica shrugged. "We aren't close or anything, but I know money is tight."

Accusing the Chalkeys with no evidence was just as bad as Jason accusing Owen without grounds. Gloria changed the subject as they crossed Sycamore Hill's town line. "How's my favorite brother-in-law?"

"Hopeful." Jessica's face glowed with a secretive brilliance.

Gloria stilled. "Are you pregnant?" Tate and Jessica had been trying to get pregnant for over a year. Jessica had already lost two babies in miscarriages, and since then, struggled with infertility. Emma opening up her walk-in clinic was a gift from the hand of God. Now Jessica had someone local with medical know-how to talk with about her struggles.

Now it was Jessica's turn to shrug. "Maybe. Hopefully."

"Have you taken a test?"

Jessica flattened her lips. She blinked rapidly, so rapidly that when she didn't answer right away, Gloria let it slide.

After a few silent minutes, Jessica cleared her throat. "I ordered two tests online, but both were duds."

"Maybe you peed on the stick wrong."

Jessica snorted.

"Let's get another one. Right now."

"I can't."

The benefit of being the passenger instead of the driver meant that Gloria could watch her sister's every move. The muscles in Jessica's throat contracted as she swallowed. Her rapid blinking, the stiffness of her neck, the way she gripped the steering wheel so hard that her knuckles turned white told a story.

"What do you mean, *can't*?"

"People know we've been struggling to get pregnant. If they see me buy another test, then I'm going to have to answer questions. That's why I ordered online. If I get a local one and the test is negative—"

"I get it. You're not ready to answer questions."

"More like I shouldn't have to answer questions. But hey." She laughed. "That's small-town life."

Jessica's hollow chuckle hurt Gloria's heart. Here she was moaning about a smear to her name when her sister was dealing with literal life and death issues. "Wouldn't you rather know?"

"Of course, I would." Jessica snapped. She cut her eyes to Gloria. "Sorry." She folded her lips inward. "But if it's positive and I miscarry again, I can't go through that. Having to let everyone know. Having to correct people who congratulate us." A tear popped from the corner of her eye and slid down her cheek.

Gloria had no real understanding of how traumatic this past year had been on her sister. Living in the city had insulated her from much of Jessica's turmoil. She didn't want to be insulated anymore. She wanted to be there for her sister the way Jessica was trying to be there for her. The brightly-lit Sycamore Pharmacy sign flickered ahead. "Pull in."

Jessica pulled into the parking lot of the drug store and cut the engine. The rain pinged off the roof of the cab. "What are you doing?"

"Getting you some answers." Gloria hopped out of the vehicle, pulled her jacket up over her head, and jogged into the store. Jessica deserved to know.

The young cashier lifted her head as the door jingled the string of bells hanging from the frame. "Good evening."

Gloria nodded. She didn't know the cashier, which meant the cashier didn't know Gloria. Score one for anonymity.

Gloria trolled the aisles until she found the contraceptives and pregnancy tests. The irony of stocking them side by side on the shelf hit her as ridiculous. She glanced at the curved circular mirror that exposed shoplifters. The cashier's head jerked away.

Nosy Nora.

Gloria pulled a Quick Results test, but it wouldn't come off the shelf. Darn. It was locked. They did this in the city, locked the contraceptives and pregnancy tests to prevent theft, but she hadn't expected that in Sycamore Hill.

The bells above the door jingled, and Mrs. Brisbane's voice carried back to Gloria. "Good evening, Chantelle." Her footsteps grew louder.

Gloria's dinner flip-flopped. She tracked Mrs. Brisbane in the anti-theft mirror. She'd be rounding the corner any second.

Gloria slipped around the corner into the next aisle. Feminine Hygiene. Well at least shopping in this aisle meant no one would think she was pregnant. She moved soundlessly toward the exit. Three more steps to freedom, and her gaze collided with her sister's hopeful one through the vehicle windshield. Gloria froze. Jessica deserved to know.

Gloria held up a finger to indicate that she'd be another minute. Mrs. Brisbane added a few items to her basket and meandered around the corner. Gloria's corner.

She zipped down the next aisle and tried to control her breathing in this weird game of cat and mouse. Gloria pressed her back against the shelving. Her chest heaved. She couldn't leave the store empty-handed. She spun around and slammed right into the cashier.

The young girl's forehead puckered, and her arms were folded across her middle. "Can I help you?"

Gloria tracked Mrs. Brisbane in that tiny mirror. She was on the move again. "No, I'm just browsing." Gloria edged around another corner. The cashier followed.

"If you're not going to buy anything, I need you to leave."

"Everything okay over there, dear?" Mrs. Brisbane's voice increased in volume.

No, Lord, please, no.

"It's fine, thanks," the cashier called.

The older woman poked her head around the corner and

Gloria quickly tipped hers forward so her hair covered her face. The last thing she needed was Mrs. Brisbane reporting to the hens that Gloria was a suspected shoplifter.

Gloria dropped her voice to a whisper. "I need an item that's locked, in the next aisle, but I want to wait until the other shopper is gone."

Understanding lit the girl's eyes. She nodded. She returned to her post at the checkout and rang through Mrs. Brisbane's items. Their murmured words didn't make it back to Gloria, but she caught their good-bye.

Gloria sagged against the merchandise shelving.

Chantelle met Gloria in the family planning aisle. "What do you need?" Her clipped tone had dropped a few degrees from her sympathetic gaze just moments before. The previous compassion in her eyes had vanished.

Gloria pointed to the pregnancy tests.

Chantelle silently unlocked the items and Gloria pulled the closest one from the shelf. No wonder her sister didn't want to do this. Gloria didn't even know this girl, and the judgment oozing from her made Gloria feel dirty.

But she'd done nothing wrong. Gloria lifted her chin. She had nothing to be ashamed of. She had every right to make this purchase and she didn't owe anyone an explanation. Gloria sailed to the cash and placed the item on the counter.

Chantelle followed. She scanned the test. Her eyes paused on Gloria's ringless left hand. That's right, Gloria thought, giving her fingers a wiggle. No ring. And it's none of your business.

"Would you like a bag?"

Really? After hiding in the store, the girl thought Gloria would walk out holding the test proudly to save a measly ten cents? "Yes, please."

"I, ah, noticed you're not married."

"That's wildly inappropriate to point out."

Chantelle's eyes flashed. "I'm inappropriate? You're the one dating the pastor and buying a pregnancy test."

Lightheadedness overwhelmed Gloria. The cashier moved in and out of focus. Gloria stretched her eyes wide open to try and gain clarity. "I'm not," she croaked. "It's not for me."

The girl looked pointedly at the bag in Gloria's hand and pinched her features.

Gloria glanced out the window at the car in the parking lot. Her sister waited. Her sister who needed her privacy. Her perfect sister. The one who always pleased her parents, always did what was right, always performed flawlessly finally needed her.

Lord, help me.

Gloria swallowed her pride, lowered her head, and walked out. She sucked in a deep breath of the cool evening air, but it failed to cool the furnace in her chest. The rain plastered her hair to her head, but she no longer hurried. Somehow, she doubted that Owen would find this as amusing as her dress mishap. She had to get in front of this.

As she passed the only other parked car in the lot, the head-lights flicked on. The sidewalk lit like a stage on which Gloria was the star, illuminating her face before she could turn away. Only shadows moved behind the glare. She kept walking.

A quick glance back revealed Nettie Fry on a cell phone. Her lips flapped a mile a minute.

So much for getting out in front of this.

Twelve

The toe of Owen's boot caught the edge of something, and his arms shot out at the sides to balance him. His to-go coffee cup hit the gravel in the church parking lot. Dark liquid saturated the fabric of his pant leg. He fisted his hands. What had he tripped on? A slice of roofing material.

Several pieces of roofing, to be more precise. Asphalt shingles spotted the property, buried in the grass, pushed up against the brick exterior, and scattered here and there across the parking lot. The sun broke through the clouds, making it easier to evaluate the damage on the peaked roof of the church. The storm from the previous evening had peeled back fresh layers of shingles in several new places, revealing rotted plywood.

Owen unlocked the church doors and grabbed a fistful of industrial sized garbage bags from under the kitchen sink. His mind spun in several directions. Would tarping the sound equipment provide enough protection from the water that was certain to pour in after the next clap of thunder? How many computers were in danger of water damage? And the worst, the church wouldn't be able to meet in the building until the roof was fixed.

He sliced the plastic bags open at their seams with a knife from the kitchen and covered the sound equipment at the back of the sanctuary. He used a few hymnals to weigh down the edges, carefully folding the books under the protection of the plastic so no one could accuse him of ruining the books. He then covered Janet's desktop computer tower, monitor, and keyboard. Owen worked from a laptop that was safely stowed in his satchel, so all he did was poke his head into his office to ensure nothing was out in the open that could be damaged.

His phone! A breath whooshed out. He'd thought he'd misplaced it last night. He snagged it from the desktop and stuffed it into his back pocket without looking at it.

After locking the office door, something he never did before the theft, he hurried outside to start cleaning up. As he stuffed shingle after shingle into the bag, he prayed. *Lord, I don't know what you are trying to teach me, but I have to believe You have a plan. You are not pacing back and forth in heaven, wringing your hands, wondering what to do about the accusations against me, the damage to the church, or about the congregation reeling from a second betrayal. I want to say use me however you see fit, but my flesh wants to be vindicated. I want the people to know I'm innocent. I don't want to leave with this accusation hanging over my head, casting a shadow on the rest of my life.*

Like it did for Gloria.

Irony hit. Now that Gloria was back in town and the trial was leaning favorably toward backing her story and officially clearing her name, Owen might be pushed out.

Thunder rumbled, and a chill zipped down his back. Leaves blew free from the nearby trees. The naked branches rustled. He stuffed another shingle into the bag. The seam split.

It wasn't supposed to be this hard.

Owen stopped. He stopped everything. His frantic actions. His runaway thoughts. His attempts to fix the church, Gloria, and perceptions of the congregation. When had he embraced the idea that ministry was supposed to be easy? Jesus didn't promise heaven on earth. Heaven came later. Right now, Jesus said there would be trouble and suffering. Somewhere along the way, Owen had rejected the idea that random hardship and misery hit everyone. And now, he reaped the disastrous harvest of such a denial. The people in the church simply didn't know what to do when confronted with sin and suffering any more than he did.

Lord, I'm struggling to not just respond well, but also suffer well. I'm tired of jumping through hoops to please people. I'm weary and want to give up. I'm drained by emotional conversations driven by fear. Suffering has brought out our worst. It's exposed weakness and sin.

He dropped to his knees in the middle of the lawn in front of the church. The grass, still damp from the rain, soaked through his pants. He didn't care who saw him. He didn't care who might drive by. This was about him and the Lord. It was about figuring out what it meant to set aside his rights and freedoms to love his brothers and sisters well, even if he suffered as a result. How he represented Christ in the midst of his suffering mattered. *Lord, I want to remove all obstacles to the gospel of Christ, even if that obstacle is me.*

The theft of the funds arrived like smelling salts, making the congregation aware of lingering bitterness and trust issues. It was Owen's job to lead the congregation into repentance for as long as the good Lord gave him opportunity.

His fingers loosened on the ripped bag. With his head tipped back and eyes closed he whispered, "Not my will, but yours be done."

Janet's tiny, compact vehicle pulled into the parking lot. She grabbed a shoulder bag from the backseat and picked her way toward him, avoiding the wreckage.

He stood, brushing away the debris stuck to his wet pants.

She crinkled her nose as she surveyed the lawn. "This doesn't look good."

"Depending on what those clouds do"—Owen gestured to the gray gathering in the sky—"it might get worse before it gets better. I'm not sure where the water is going to pour in. I've covered the electronics with plastic already."

"Would you like me to call anyone?"

Owen didn't really want another confrontation with the deacon board, but this wasn't something he could keep from them. They'd need to make a decision about how to proceed, especially since they no longer had the funds. "Jason, please."

A flush crept across Janet's cheeks. Her head dipped, and she developed an intense interest in the nearest shingle, poking it with the toe of her shoe. "He's already on his way."

Owen's stomach heaved. Something about the way Janet shuffled her feet and avoided his gaze didn't sit well. The air around them stilled. The leaves settled on the grass in an eerie lull. Even the birds quieted. Something was coming down the pipeline, and Owen was standing at the mouth of the tube.

"What's going on?"

Janet rubbed the back of her neck. Her chest rose and fell, and she swallowed excessively. She didn't hold his gaze for more than a second before flicking it away. However, it was long enough for him to read disappointment in her eyes.

"Jason called me when I was on my way in. Someone from church saw Gloria buying a pregnancy test, and they also saw her car overnight at your house."

He instinctively stepped back, craving physical and emotional distance, but not having the luxury.

A low rumble rolled across the sky. The wind scooped up the leaves, and a wet mist chapped Owen's cheek. He turned to face the sudden breeze. It cupped over his ears and echoed. He misheard Janet. That had to be it. His tongue bumped along his lips but failed to relieve the dryness overtaking his mouth. Dullness filled his chest as he fixated on the spire on the summit of the church. An optical illusion made it appear to sway.

"My truck broke down, and I can't afford the repair, so Gloria lent me her car." He pointed to Gloria's vehicle in the church parking lot. "I've been driving it for a few days now."

Understanding filled Janet's eyes as her eyebrows gathered in. "That makes more sense. Hank Sinclair called to ask if Gloria was distracting you at work because he saw her vehicle in the lot every time he drove by. And since I'm not here every day..." Her words trailed off.

"People thought I was alone with Gloria," Owen finished. So much for getting the benefit of the doubt.

Janet nodded. She wouldn't meet his eye. "What about the other thing?" Her chest stilled like she held her breath. Did she really think so little of him? Did she really think he'd stand at the pulpit every Sunday and preach a message that he failed to apply to his own heart?

She tilted her head, waiting.

Apparently, she did.

The wet mist fattened into a drizzle. Owen tugged the hood from his thick sweatshirt over his head. "Gloria had some meetings in the city about the court case. Her sister drove her—"

Her sister drove her.

Jessica and Tate had been trying to get pregnant for well over a year. Gloria must have bought the test for Jessica, to save her sister the humiliation of answering a million questions from a busybody community.

Janet leaned in. Waiting.

Owen wasn't about to out Gloria's sister. Not on a hunch. And not even if he knew one hundred percent that his suspicions were true. If Gloria bought the pregnancy test to protect Jessica, then Owen would honor that choice. "I don't know about that. I can only assure you that I have treated Gloria with the utmost respect, and she is an honorable woman."

Dampness seeped into Janet's eyes, creating a faint sheen. "I knew it couldn't be true. I'm sorry."

"It's not your fault." It was his, and it was time he owned it. The reality was that pastors are held to a higher standard because God has entrusted to them a responsibility for which they are accountable. But he'd been too busy trying to please the people, earn their approval, and prove he was worthy of the title pastor. He'd forgotten who all this was for. Shame descended. Fear instead of freedom.

There is no condemnation for those who are in Christ Jesus.

Conviction? Yes. Condemnation? No.

I'm sorry for how my actions and reactions might have tarnished Your name.

A strange buoyancy lifted him. God was more than able to defend His name, clear up the misunderstanding about Gloria, and expose the thief who smeared Owen's reputation. God could restore this church with a single Word. Owen didn't need to micromanage God. It was long past time that he released it all into the Lord's capable hands to do with as He saw fit. How God saw fit. Not Owen.

Janet's attention bounced all over the property. Her nose wrinkled like she smelled something terrible. "I'm sorry, because it gets worse."

The drizzle expanded into drops. Big, fat drops that splatted at their feet.

"Jason is coming to tell you that the board has decided to remove Gloria from the play. They've decided the constant scandal that surrounds her makes her an inappropriate role model."

Jason's truck turned into the lot and parked, perfectly timed. The bill of his ball cap shadowed his grim expression, but the hard set of his jaw and jerky head movements indicated slapping the scarlet A on Gloria's chest and calling her Hester was merely a formality.

The sky broke open. Rain pellets hit the ground. Janet yelped and dashed for the church doors. Owen followed. He waited in the foyer, rainwater dripping down his face, holding the door for his executioner.

Thirteen

Gloria moved the musical rehearsal to her parents' barn at Clara's prompting. The church was a sopping mess. She could have cancelled practice, but it was the last one before the performance, and Gloria wanted to do everything she could to ensure her little stars shone. Besides, she needed to keep busy, or she'd give in to the temptation to call Owen and see how he was managing. But he didn't need to be fielding calls from her. Not with the roof money gone and rising flood waters rippling across the sanctuary.

Owen would reach out when he could. Until then, she'd push on with her kids and ensure the storm didn't derail their performance. Besides, she'd have to tell Owen about her blunder at the pharmacy if she connected with him. The pressure in her head increased just recalling the cashier's brazen words, her accusing stare, and Nettie Fry on the phone, reporting the news.

Gloria gulped. How could she have been so stupid to go into the *local store* and buy a pregnancy test? She could justify it six ways to Sunday, and it wouldn't change a thing. Her impulsivity bred foolishness, which spawned consequences—unavoidable ones. Appearances mattered. Her reputation mattered because it affected Owen. So she had to confess what she'd done and seek Owen's forgiveness for how it was bound to impact his job. And that conversation needed more than five distracted minutes while he trekked church valuables to higher ground.

It wasn't avoidance. It was wisdom—the opposite of foolishness.

"Beautiful, Breanna." Gloria distracted herself, lightly touching Breanna's shoulder. Breanna extended her leg and bent at the hips, her arms long and graceful. She wore a new leotard that made her look like a real ballerina. It was good. She needed something positive to pour herself into.

Gloria continued to wander, checking in on the various clusters of children working out their parts. Ribbons rippled, carrying laughter along their currents. Everything was just as it should be.

Meg and Emma took the smallest of the crew into the house for a snack. Gloria's mom thrived in her element, surrounded by the choir of garden flowers and evening stars, feeding their bodies and probably their souls the same way she once fed Gloria and Owen after school. But this snack—Gloria had ensured—contained no red dye. No dairy. No nuts. No gluten. No sugar. And, if pressed, Gloria would add, no taste.

"Gloria?"

She lifted her head. Clara stood at the entrance to the barn by the enormous open door. Her age-spotted hands twisted in front of her thick middle, and her face puckered sourly.

Jason stepped around her.

Ah, the lemon in the flesh.

He immediately surveyed the space as if Gloria might inflict some sort of damage on the children under her care.

Gloria huffed. For heaven's sake. Suzy must have spun some tale to cause Jason to track her down like a papa bear on steroids.

"What can I do for you?" As Gloria crossed toward them, the choir spilled in behind Clara and Jason. They split around them and came together again on the other side like a swarm of bees. They buzzed for her attention.

"I'll listen to each one of you if you can talk one at a time, but first, I need to speak with Mr. Chalkey and Mrs. Brisbane."

Her mom, Meg, and Emma herded the kids to the side. "Let's practice the garden song," Mom said.

Emma added, "I've heard you've all made beautiful flower masks."

The children hurried to do their bidding.

"I'm sorry, Gloria." Mrs. Brisbane's rapid blinking couldn't hide her wet eyes.

Sorry? She turned to Jason and arched a brow.

He cleared his throat, and his Adam's apple bobbed. "I'm here to notify you that you've been removed from the play. Effective immediately."

"What?" Everything slowed down, like smoke slogging through her veins. She must have misheard.

Her mom's head lifted, a curious expression pointed at Jason.

"I don't understand." Gloria ignored her mother's unspoken question and sought Clara, who glared at Jason.

Jason's features contorted into annoyance. He jerked his chin up as if to nudge Clara.

"Not a chance." Clara folded her arms across her body. "This is your show. I've already said my piece."

Gloria's insides hummed as if the buzzing students swarmed under her skin. A soft waft of her mom's signature scent bolstered Gloria's courage. Meg joined them. The solidarity emboldened her. Gloria held Jason's stare. She was not speaking first. Not making whatever this was easier.

Jason cleared his throat a second time. His gaze flicked behind her, then to Meg, and landed on her again. "It's come to our attention that you and Owen have been inappropriate." His features tightened." And intimately involved."

Her mom's sharp intake momentarily caught Jason's attention before it bounced back to Gloria. "We cannot have a person of ill repute running our children's programs."

The room fuzzed. Gloria's skull filled with cotton swabs. Her ears throbbed, and she grabbed for the barnboard walls. Romantically involved? They think— Her cheeks burned. Of course, they did. Not once had anyone given her the benefit of the doubt. That she could handle. That she had made her peace with. But to say this about Owen? To smear his name over a piece of gossip before checking the facts?

Twenty pairs of little eyes stuck to her like glue. Twenty impressionable children. Little souls shaped by the adults around them. They waited on her. Waited to see if, when tested, she'd emerge as gold or burn like dross.

She could feel her mother straighten behind her, charging the air like a lightning strike. "Who do you think you are?"

"Mom, don't." Gloria didn't need her mother escalating things in front of the kids, who Emma was thankfully ushering out the side door. Was this God's way of nudging her along? Of confirming she wasn't the one for Owen? Or was this the enemy testing her? Was Owen's church on the verge of a spiritual revival, and all this a distraction? If the cost of reviving this community was her reputation, did she love the people of Sycamore Hill—love the Lord enough—to joyfully pay it? And if not, what did that say about her?

She inhaled until her lungs filled. Nothing held her in

Sycamore Hill. She was not obligated to this town. Self-righteous thoughts piled. Unspoken words burned the inside of her mouth. Graceless words about Pharisees, legalism, and gossip. Hands that shed innocent blood, hearts that devised wicked plans, feet that ran to evil: the Lord hated those things. The Lord hated those who sowed discord in his church.

But that passage in Proverbs also said the Lord hated haughty eyes. Arrogance. A person who looked down on another. The Lord hated it all.

Including her pride.

Her eyes prickled. Gloria swallowed bitterness. "You're wrong, Jason. Wrong to dismiss me without first having a conversation. Wrong to have said that in front of the children. Wrong to assume the worst about Owen."

His jaw twitched. The only indication the man before her wasn't made of stone. The muscle throbbed with a steady pulse.

She wasn't innocent. She got that now. Hadn't she looked down on Suzy and Nettie? Hadn't she hardened herself against them? Hadn't she made thoughtless decisions? She could call it self-defense. She could excuse it and justify it. But if Christ died for her while she was still sinning, couldn't she continue to love others even while they continued to sin against her? Isn't that what Christ-like love was all about?

"I have nothing to be ashamed of, but I do owe you"—she swept her gaze to include her mom, Clara, and Meg—"an explanation."

Her mom shook her head, but Gloria didn't need another excuse to put herself first. After coming home, she'd nudged God from the center of her life and inserted herself in the middle. Everything revolved around her. She needed a job. She needed a reference. She needed to help Jessica. She needed the courts to vindicate her. She needed to prove her worth. The common denominator in all her strivings was her. But nothing she could ever do would make her worthy. If it could, Christ wouldn't have had to die. Her worthiness came not from making a name for herself but from her union with Christ.

Why had it taken her so long to see that?

Her eyes misted at how God used the actions of the Suzys and Netties of the world to peel her eyes off herself and force them back onto Him. God won't share His glory with another.

"I never asked what would be helpful. I just acted. I never paused to seek God's will. That seed of pride grew sin in my heart." She levelled her gaze at Jason. "And for that, I am sorry. Of that, I repent. But the tawdry suggestions you're making here are completely unfounded."

Jason never broke eye contact. He held her stare, fully convinced that he was acting in the church's best interests. He'd already made the decision. She was out.

Gloria rolled her lips in and pressed them together. She wasn't going to cry. Not in front of the children. *Your will be done, Lord.* She handed the folder in her hand to Clara. "All my notes are in there. You'll have everything you need to finish the play."

Clara accepted the folder. Her lower lip trembled, but she remained silent. She didn't need to say anything. Her face and stiff posture radiated displeasure. Whether she directed that displeasure toward Gloria, Owen, or Jason, she couldn't tell. But honestly, it didn't matter.

Gloria was done.

Fourteen

The phone call was quick, succinct, and devastating. Owen disconnected and slumped in a chair at his kitchen table. He cradled his head in his hands. Jason hadn't given him a chance to prep Gloria. Hadn't allowed him to be there for the woman he loved while the people who were supposed to care for her spiritual well-being—the local church leaders—humiliated her.

Meg called minutes after Gloria left the barn. He'd hung up after speaking with her, and Emma rang. If nothing else, Gloria's faithful friends rallied around her.

A gift from God amid ruin. A bright spot in the shadows.

God, what are you doing?

His repeated phone calls to Gloria went directly to voice mail. He understood screening calls. He understood needing time, but shutting him out? He wanted—he needed—to be part of the solution. To be there for her. But he worked for the very people that thrust the dagger of scandal into her gentle heart.

It felt like a million years ago that he stood on the church lawn, broken before God. Yet, it was only this morning that he asked God to remove all the obstacles between the town folks and Christ. But it was one thing to fall on his sword. It was another thing entirely to sacrifice Gloria. That wasn't part of the deal.

Yet, her reputation lay slain, possibly beyond repair. His wasn't any better, but he cared less about that.

That's how Meg, Eli, Emma, and Ben found him. Face to the table. Bible open. Cheeks wet with tears. They crowded around his tiny kitchen that filled a quarter of his apartment. But unlike their typical games night, when hooting and hollering roused his landlord from below to remind him to be quiet, the room remained silent tonight. Their ministry to him was their presence, and it was enough to lift the stigma and shame temporarily. The only one missing was Gloria.

"Do you think they'll fire you?" Ben was the first to break the silence and to ask what everybody had to be thinking.

Owen shrugged. "Probably. They think I stole the roof money. This'll seal my coffin." But he didn't care about that. He cared about Gloria. Who, if his watch was correct, should be here any second. She'd finally answered his call and agreed to come over.

Knuckles rapped on the door and nudged it open at the same time. "Are you sure I can come in?" Gloria's feet remained glued in the hallway. "I wouldn't want people to think we're fraternizing inappropriately." She pulled up short as she scanned the room. Her hands turtled into the sleeves of her favourite sweater. She hugged herself, hiding behind comfy clothes and a scowl. "Chapcrones." Her head bobbed. "Probably a good idea."

Owen pushed the chair back and stood. He didn't get it. He had expected her to arrive in tears. Maybe shout in anger. But this quiet acceptance? He didn't know what to do with it.

Gloria snagged a soda from the fridge and claimed the last chair at the table. "Clara called."

To apologize, Owen hoped.

"She said the rest of the rehearsal went fine. Parents have already flooded her inbox with emails." She gulped back a long draw from the can.

The others might buy the act that Gloria was fine, but Owen saw through it. Her overly bright eyes, heaving chest, and lifted chin contradicted the acceptance she declared. Like a soldier pushing through, wounded, her brave mask never cracked.

"You okay?" Meg nudged Gloria's shoulder with hers.

Maybe they weren't buying what she was selling after all.

Gloria quickly swiped a hand across her eyes. "If I can survive Emergence, I'll survive this."

Meg frowned, and Gloria squirmed.

"That doesn't answer her question," Emma said.

Yeah, they definitely weren't picking up what she put down any more than he did.

"I'm not okay," she finally admitted, focused on her hands twisting around the soda. She kept her head down and rubbed her thumbs up and down the can. "But I will be."

"How do you bounce back from something like this?" The question popped out before Owen could censor it.

Gloria lifted her face. She searched his expression for something Owen couldn't provide. Not because he didn't want to, but because he didn't know what she needed. His gut told him his days were numbered. Overcoming might be possible, but he wasn't sure he wanted to. He wasn't sure he could continue to walk alongside the people who hurt the woman he loved more than anyone else in the world when he wasn't sure he could protect her from it happening again. He wasn't sure if he had what it took to stay. Seminary didn't prepare him for this.

Meg, Eli, Emma, and Ben all faded into the background. Right now, it was Owen and Gloria. And he instinctively understood that whatever she said next would impact him. Something inside her was different. The edge was gone.

"I won't bounce back, but I'll *come* back, because it's not about me." She bit the corner of her lip. "It's not about us, Owen. It never was. Not really. And as long as we keep making it about us, we'll be disappointed."

"What is it about?"

She shrugged. "Power. Control. God's sanctifying work in His people."

"So that's it?" Ben cut in. "They treat you like this, and there are no consequences?"

"Oh, there will be consequences." Owen had already fielded calls from Gloria's sister, ready to storm down to the church and tell off Jason. He'd heard from several parents concerned over Jason's public dismissal of Gloria, who'd won many hearts with her genuine love for the quieter and over-looked children. Even Nathan called, insisting something be done. There would be consequences. For sure. "If I've learned anything in ministry work," Owen said, "it's that God is more interested in shaping us to be like Jesus than He is in taking away the suffering."

Gloria pinched her eyes shut and inhaled through her nose. "Let's talk about something else. Have you made any progress on the lost money?"

"That depends." Owen cut his eyes to Ben. "Is this all off the record?"

Ben chuckled. "Nothing I hear tonight will end up in the paper."

"I've been making a list of all the people who are under finan-cial strain." Owen retrieved a notepad from a drawer in the kitchen. "At the top are Jason and Suzy."

"He could be trying to divert attention from them to cover

their tracks." Emma ripped open a bag of chips Owen had thrown onto the table.

Meg shifted to grab a handful. She popped a chip in her mouth and crunched. "Nathan's financial issues are no secret."

"I can't imagine him doing something like this," Eli spoke quietly. "And I'm not super comfortable accusing people without cause."

"We are not accusing anyone," Owen said. "Just brainstorming. It doesn't leave this room."

"I have to be on list," Gloria said. "It's only fair to include everyone in financial straits. I'm out of a job and living with my parents."

"Hank Sinclair is on a fixed income," Ben added. "I heard that some kids stomped through his garden, and he didn't have the money to hire a landscaper."

"If we're throwing everyone under the bus, I'm trying to get more funding for the medical clinic," Emma said. It wasn't a secret that Emma's new clinic was far from financially secure. She'd established it as soon as she was a fully qualified nurse practitioner, but it wasn't cheap.

Gloria's cheeks puffed out in an irritated breath. "If we are going to list every person with a financial need, the entire town will be suspect. There has to be a way to narrow the search."

"Maybe there is," Owen murmured. Out of all the people in Sycamore Hill with financial needs, only one family showed a significant improvement in their circumstances.

Gloria's upturned face waited for him to explain. Her wide eyes searched him, and his stomach lurched. *How much, Lord? How much can one woman absorb?*

This was going to crush her.

Fifteen

Gloria couldn't stop joyful tears from sliding down her cheeks despite being tossed out of her own production and forced to hide in the corner like a punished child. Her rag-tag choir had morphed from breathing background props to equal stars on the stage. The kids were wonderful.

Well, almost all of them were wonderful.

Tommy pulled his shirt off in the middle of act two and swung it over his head like he was a cowboy trying to rope a calf, but Mrs. Brisbane took it in stride. And for the most part, so did the parents.

Breanna danced her solo flawlessly, and Gloria was sure she saw dampness in her father's eyes. But she couldn't be sure. Gloria's position in the shadowy back corner of her parent's barn didn't provide a great sightline to Nathan Clarke.

Luke buzzed at all the right times in the low-budget costume they made from a yellow pillowcase with painted black stripes. And the twins? Well, they were the stars. Literal stars in the night sky, standing on the bottom riser in the choir and holding high above their heads a hockey stick with a sparkly star taped to the blade. They waved it in time to the music, accomplishing a tiny miracle when they resisted the temptation to clap the sticks in a mock face-off as they had in rehearsals. And Bethann only mooned the audience once when she bent down to pick up her dropped star.

Families from the church filled her parents' barn and spilled out the doors and onto the grass. The cool night hadn't impacted attendance. Family after family sat on the makeshift seats crafted from bales of straw. It was Gloria's idea to cover the straw with flannel blankets and set them up in rows. Her addition of pumpkins, corn stalks, and other farm-friendly fall decor added to the barn's quaint ambiance. It had only taken Gloria about an hour to convince her parents to open their outdoor building to the church, which was also the new Sunday morning location until the deacons figured out how to address the worsening roof situation.

When Gloria's dad heard what had gone down between Gloria and the deacons, he'd come out swinging. And he wasn't the only one. Meg stepped in, insisting on giving a character reference. Emma had been working closely with Jessica, monitoring her brand-new pregnancy, and when she learned what *really* happened and that Gloria wasn't defending herself, she added her voice to the conversation. But it wasn't enough.

It was never enough.

"Are you good?" Meg asked.

Gloria quickly swiped a hand across her damp eyes. The action bought her a few extra minutes to think. Shame had been lying to her for so long, telling her that she was unworthy and alone, pulling her back to her old way of thinking that condemned her by association to Tiff. It said she would never be good enough.

But the truth had something different to say, and Gloria was still grappling with it.

"I'm done living in self-protection." That was just a fancy word for unbelief. Her gaze skipped down the line of children returning to the stage for a second bow. "God has done too much in me for me to keep camping there."

The space thundered with applause and then teetered with laughter as Bethann accidentally mooned the audience a second time.

Jason took to the stage as the clapping died off to say a few kind words about the kids.

"That should be you up there." Meg folded her arms across her chest.

"It's fine," Gloria whispered. "I'm fine." She was better than fine. God had worked mightily in her heart since the deacons expelled her from the musical. God humbled Gloria, and He convicted her that it was time she stopped declaring God had made her this way and the church needed to accept her. The truth was, Gloria needed to compare who she was with who God had called her to be and change as necessary. Gloria wasn't innocent. Her impulsiveness and thoughtless actions had contributed to her struggles.

"Before we wrap up the evening," Jason said, "Tate Wilder has an announcement."

Gloria's head snapped at the mention of her brother-in-law. She raked her eyes over the crowd until she found her sister. Gloria shook her head. Jessica didn't have to do this.

Emma joined Meg and Gloria in the shadows. "It'll be okay." Emma pressed a hand against Gloria's upper arm.

Gloria hadn't been totally prepared for how hard it would be to return to Sycamore Hill. If given the chance, she would definitely have handled things differently, but what she wouldn't do, what she could never do, was tell anyone who she bought that pregnancy test for. Gloria wasn't present when Jessica miscarried and really needed her, but she was here now, and she'd do anything for her big sister.

"I think our church family is in need of good news, wouldn't you say?" Tate's jovial voice didn't need amplifying.

"No, no, no, no, no," Gloria rocked back and forth with one hand over her mouth, muffling her words.

Gloria hadn't told anyone but Owen. A fist squeezed her lungs. Owen kept her secret. He'd insisted he and Gloria were innocent but refused to provide details because it wasn't his story to tell. His resoluteness in the face of tremendous pressure made her love him even more. He valued Jessica's privacy more than his job and more than his reputation.

Gloria held Jessica's gaze. Jessica bobbed her head as if to say it was okay.

Meg and Emma reached for Gloria's hands.

"After years of trying to have a baby, Jessica and I are expecting!"

A cheer rolled like a wave gaining momentum, but Gloria's stomach heaved.

Tate carried on to clarify that Gloria had bought the pregnancy test for Jessica and that Gloria's vehicle was at Owen's overnight because she lent it to him while his was being repaired.

Tate's public announcement was a beautiful gesture. More than kind. But Gloria wasn't here to vindicate herself. She was here for one thing only. To support the people she loved. After everything that had been said about her, logic dictated that she should pack up her bags and leave. But she'd been down that road, and it led nowhere. This time, she'd see it through. This was about modelling perseverance and trust in the Lord. It was about putting her sister above herself. It was about standing beside

Owen and speaking truth as God provided opportunity. Gloria wasn't about to slink away with her tail between her legs after spending the last few weeks lecturing the children on boldness and being proud of how God made them.

"Gloria." Emma poked her.

She snapped back to the present. Someone said her name. But it wasn't Emma, and it wasn't Tate.

It was Jason.

"Gloria, where are you?" Jason shielded his eyes against the makeshift stage lights. "The leadership of our church dealt with Gloria publicly when we removed her from the play, so we need to make it right publicly as well."

Gloria's joints weakened. Meg and Emma's hands moved from her hands to each elbow to provide support. They nudged her from the shadows and into the light.

Jason's gaze locked on hers. "You have my sincerest apology. Some people have been talking"—his eyes cut to his wife, who dropped her head—"and I want you to know that such talking stops today. We hope you can forgive us for assuming the worst and making a hard season of life even harder."

Gloria swallowed, but the lump in her throat wouldn't budge. She nodded her head.

"Pastor Owen, would you close us in prayer?"

She needed out. Fresh air. Freedom lay a few steps away. A tree bent in the breeze, beckoning her, and then a body blocked her escape.

A familiar body. A warm body.

"Where are you going?" He spoke as if his words were only for her. As if the entire congregation wasn't waiting for him to close the night in prayer. As if he had all the time in the world.

Owen.

Everything that had tilted sideways righted itself.

Owen entwined their fingers. He pulled her along to the front of the room. Gloria kept her eyes down. "I was afraid if anyone saw us together, you'd lose your job," she whispered.

The closer they got to the front of the barn, the quieter it grew. Conversations literally stopped. A murmur rippled through the throng.

"Gloria did this tonight." Owen gestured at the decorated barn while he studied her. Not in the familiar way that she understood, but in a quizzical way that said he didn't quite know what to make of her. "After we rejected her, judged her, and excommunicated her, she did this because she loves our kids, her God, and this town more than she loves herself. She suffered silently because she loves us."

Jaws loosened across the room, but none were slacker than Gloria's. Did Owen actually say that? Out loud? In front of everyone?

"God's plan for this church has included suffering, sometimes intense suffering. But that was always His plan A. He hasn't defaulted to a plan B, C, or D. I think I forgot that for a while. God takes no joy in our struggles, but He has ordained our lives from eternity past, and even when it doesn't feel good—when it doesn't feel fair—it's not an accident."

Gloria's heart throbbed in her ears.

"God's greatest concern for the people of Sycamore Hill Community Church is not giving us a roof, repairing our reputations, or providing comfort. It's about teaching us to hate sin and turn to Him. And He'll use everything we face to accomplish that."

Owen faced Gloria fully. He scooped up both her hands in his. "Gloria Sycamore has suffered well. Not perfectly, but well." Owen's gaze sought Jason's. "Jason's humble and public plea for forgiveness is an example to us. We can learn from these two, if we're willing."

Mrs. Brisbane started a slow clap. Soon, others joined in.

Owen led the crowd in a closing prayer. Afterward, people broke apart to mingle.

Clara threaded her way toward Gloria, pulling her into a grandmotherly hug. "You did a tremendous job with the musical. It was perfect. I'm certain you'll get the job at the school and stay in Sycamore Hill where you belong."

"You're giving me the recommendation?" Gloria's eyes stretched. "But Tommy took his shirt off within ten minutes of starting the play."

Clara patted the air with her hands. "I sent the recommendation in days ago."

Days ago? Before Tate cleared her name in the pregnancy kerfuffle?

Mrs. Brisbane nattered on. "As for Tommy? Well, that's nine minutes longer than usual. It might be Tommy's record." The people closest to them tinkled with laugher.

Clara hugged Gloria again, not giving her time to sort through her conflicting emotions. "Maybe you can join Meg and me for our weekly Bible study? She mentioned you ladies were meeting regularly."

"I'd like that." The Lord was so gracious.

As soon as the attention moved on, Breanna found Gloria. "I'm glad you came," the girl said. "You should have been up there with Mrs. Brisbane."

"I didn't want to cause any more trouble for Owen. You—" Gloria placed her hands on Breanna's shoulders as she looked the girl up and down. "You were brilliant. Beautiful. Stunning. I don't have enough adjectives to capture it."

Breanna glowed. Gloria wasn't sure, but she thought she even saw a smear of light lip gloss on the girl's lips.

Gloria hesitated. She bit the inside of her cheek. She hated to do this, to spoil an evening that had been a magnificent victory for Breanna, but it couldn't be helped.

After Owen ruled out suspects for the theft one by one, he shared his suspicion about the one family in better financial shape. Gloria recalled all the people who might have heard her and Owen discussing the money, who might have heard where the money was stored. Who suddenly showed up in lip gloss, a new leotard, and a fresh haircut. "Breanna, I have to ask you something."

Breanna folded her arms across her body. A worried glance to her dad erased all doubt in Gloria's beaten-down heart. They'd found their thief.

"I think I understand why you took the money, but this is not the way the Lord wants to meet your needs."

"You said He provides in strange ways. And then I heard about this money just sitting there, and we needed it so much." Breanna clutched Gloria's hands. "Dad's trying, but he doesn't see it. Luke didn't even have underwear that fit him. We needed it."

Gloria met and held the girl's eyes. "I believe you need it, but this is not the way."

"What do you know about need?" Breanna gestured to the twinkle lights and portable heaters to ward off the autumn evening chill. "Your barn is nicer than our house."

"I know that all of us need to depend on God and wait on God, and that includes you. Owen could have lost his job."

Breanna's cheeks lost their pink hue.

"You didn't make this decision in a vacuum. It impacted the people around you."

"Are you going to tell?"

Gloria hesitated. "Not tonight."

Tonight, Breanna could have her moment to shine.

Sixteen

Gloria fisted her hands on her hips. She surveyed the jam-packed storage unit. Correction. Overflowing storage unit. But she didn't see the boxes she needed to sort. Her mind drifted from the task at hand.

A lot had happened since the musical. Gloria's throat closed up just thinking about it. Breanna confessed, and Nathan returned the funds. Nathan hadn't attended a church service since his wife died, but the congregation's gentle response to Breanna and their enthusiastic desire to help Nathan manage better had wooed his battered heart. His wife had to be rejoicing in Heaven over her husband's reengagement with the community and, Lord willing, his faith.

Thankfulness clogged the back of her throat, and she shifted her focus. It fell on the top half of the storage unit that still housed boxes she needed to sort. Gloria didn't have the upper body strength to get them down, and Owen was late.

Again.

Gloria tapped the auction app on her phone and scrolled to

her listing. The items she'd already posted had bids that were climbing. An unexpected release of tension loosened her muscles. She'd convinced the church's fund-raising committee to let her take over their planned rummage sale and move it online. After Suzy explained their biggest hesitation had been that an online auction stopped people from coming into the church building and that their favorite part of the rummage sale was chatting with buyers, they compromised and set aside an entire Saturday for buyers to schedule their pick-ups in person. Everybody won. And if the sales trend continued, by the time Gloria added the rest of her contributions of big-name clothing, accessories, footwear, and purses to the auction, there would be enough money to pay a roofer to fix the church. She just needed to get the clothes in the box at the top of the stack.

Gloria pushed up the sleeves of her sweater and pressed her shoulder against a stack of boxes. They slowly scraped along the floor.

"Need a hand?" She heard Owen's smile, and it made her insides swell. The soles of his shoes scraped along the floor with a scuffing sound.

"Sorry I'm late." His apology caressed the back of her neck, and she shivered from the warmth of his breath. He wrapped his arms around her middle and tugged her until her back pressed against his chest.

"You're worth the wait." She turned in his arms and lifted her face. "Did Jason tell you about the benevolent fund?"

All the lines on his forehead softened as he looked down at her. Wonderment replaced his playful banter. "He told me *someone* received a generous settlement from the courts and donated it to the church."

Joy rippled down her spine. "There's enough to help out Nathan's family, and Jason and Suzy, and still have a cushion leftover to keep in reserve for future needs in the church family."

His neck bent forward. A tingle started in her chest. "And you want to donate it?"

Her lungs expanded to their fullest. "All of it."

He pressed his lips to her temple and a whisper warmed her earlobe. "You are amazing."

She tucked herself into his arms, resting her cheek against his chest. The steady thumping of his heart promised her that she'd come home for all the right reasons. He cinched his arms tighter and rested his chin on the top of her head. They fit perfectly like that for several glorious seconds, then he untangled himself from her. The hint of a secretive smile tipped up his lips. "Let me move these boxes for you."

Gloria tilted her head to the side and wrinkled her nose. "I only need the top one for now."

He ignored her instructions and effortlessly transferred several boxes to the nearby trolly cart and pulled them out of the unit, revealing another set of boxes. A row of four boxes. Each labelled in black marker with one word.

Will

You

Marry

Me?

She swung back to Owen, who'd dropped down on one knee and now held out a modest diamond ring. "I know I let you down, and I know it'll happen again. I'm going to mess up, but I will never walk away from you. I will always fight for you. I will defend you."

Gloria moved her gaze over the face of the man she loved. The remnants of the last few difficult weeks carved crevices in the corners of his eyes and across his forehead. Her throat squeezed.

"Frank Brisbane once told me my wife only gets one husband and my kids only get one father, but the church can always hire a new pastor. I know that now in a way I didn't understand before."

Heat filled her chest, cheeks, and head. *His kids. Her kids. Their kids.*

"This is probably not the romantic proposal you've dreamt of your whole life—"

Wrong.

"—but I didn't want to share this moment with anyone else—"

She tried not to think about who might be in the car crawling down the nearby road at a snail's pace.

"—in a town like ours, this is pretty much the only place I could be sure we'd be alone, and privacy trumped romance."

Oh, this was romantic, all right.

He cleared his throat, but instead of reading the script he'd scrawled onto the boxes behind her, he launched into rhyme.

"When life pours me lemons, I'll think lemonade.
When the sun gets too hot, I'll be thankful for shade."

Her eyes tingled. She blinked fast. Her gaze zipped to the open box that held her preschool materials, and sure enough, her favorite book was missing.

A secretive grin snaked across Owen's face.

"No matter how awful or ugly it gets,
I can be thankful for something, I'd bet."

He'd memorized her poem. *He'd memorized her poem. HE'D MEMORIZED HER POEM.* Pressure grew behind her eyes.

Owen never broke eye contact.

"You are the you that you need to be.
No one else can be you, no one else, no siree.
If I didn't have you, I'd be missing a lot.
You matter. You're wanted. Your company's sought."

She blinked, and dampness spilled over her cheeks.

"Be true to what's you, be you all the way.
They can't take from you what you won't give away."

His voice cracked. The last few words tripped over one another, but he'd never sounded so eloquent. She couldn't breathe. She couldn't speak. But she could remember.

That first raspberry kiss in the clearing behind the church. Their first date. Owen taking her to prom and slipping that ridiculously huge corsage onto her wrist. Standing with her against the town, declaring her to be honest and upright when Tiff claimed the opposite. Not pushing when she pulled back. Giving her space when she retreated. Seeking her out when she tried to return to town in secret. Calling in Ben and Emma to carry on the task of exposing Emergence when she couldn't. Driving to the city to see her and take her on dates. Eating soup from a can so he could treat her to dinner. Standing up for her when her character was challenged. Loving her when she wasn't being loveable. Loving her like Christ loved His church. Owen would give his life for her. She had no doubt.

He had not failed her. Never.

"Gloria Sycamore, will you marry me?"

With a gulp and a short cry, she hurtled toward him. "Yes!" She buried her face into the curve of his neck and inhaled his familiar scent. She held it deep in her lungs. "Yes," she repeated. "Yes, I'll marry you."

Owen pulled back just far enough to slip the diamond onto her finger, and they stared at the representation of his promise to her. "I love you."

All tension of the previous weeks drained away, and he pressed his lips against hers in the sweetest, most chaste, most wonderful kiss ever. They lingered like that, both anticipating all the Lord had for them in the future. Eventually, Owen pulled back. He rubbed his hands up and down her arms, creating delicious friction. "You're trembling. Are you okay?"

She nodded. After all that had happened, she knew, beyond a shadow of a doubt, she was not a worthy woman, but that was okay. God loved the unworthy. He sent His Son to redeem the unworthy, and He made them worthy through Christ. "I'm more than okay."

God had replaced her shame with honor.

STACEY WEEKS

VOLUME 2

RETURN TO
Sycamore
HILL

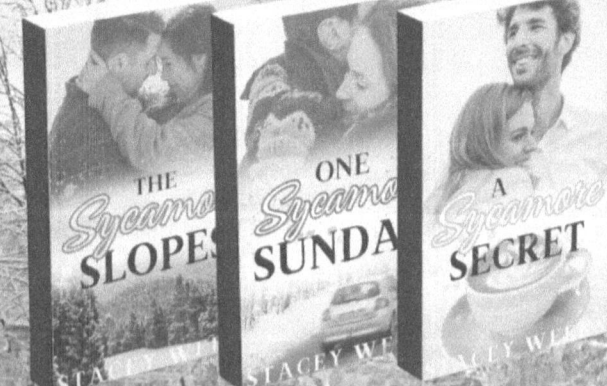

Return to Sycamore Hill

Don't miss the final three books set in Sycamore Hill. Visit StaceyWeeks.com/books to order.

THE SYCAMORE SLOPES

When a family is torn apart, the battle lines are drawn and the fight to control Sycamore Hill heats up.

Ben Sawyer gives the vulnerable a voice and strives to protect them, but he can't stop the avalanche of trouble descending on his nephew. His strongest opponent isn't the grumpy Grinch stirring up the community, but the one person he believed would always side with him: Nurse Practitioner Emma Powles.

Emma Powles is busy in her newly established medical clinic as the fallout from sledding and skating accidents fills her clinic. When she treats the suspicious injuries of a local child, she's forced to intervene for the girl's safety. Her actions rouse traumatic memories in Ben; will their relationship survive?

ONE SYCAMORE SUNDAY

It starts as a normal Sunday, but one horrifying moment changes everything forever.

When a group of men abduct her son, Kim Jansen turns to the only person she can trust—Jackson McGregor. Officer McGregor would trade his life for the boy, but it's not McGregor the kidnappers want. They want a woman Kim helped disappear, and they've taken Kim's son as leverage. As McGregor races to save the boy, Kim faces an impossible choice—protect her friend or save her child.

A SYCAMORE SECRET

His custom coffee blend, paired with her social media following, brews a latte of trouble.

When the Fan Favorite Choice Awards include Kathryn Withers's independent web show as a finalist, the internet trolls slither out from under their bridges. Kathryn livestreams daily, growing her following and improving her chances of winning, but trending on social media backfires. The generated buzz connects an unwelcome guest in Sycamore Hill to a shameful secret in Kathryn's past. A secret she'd do almost anything to keep hidden.

Ethan Roberts invested every penny in expanding his bakery, The Muffin Man, to include on-site coffee roasting. When Kathryn streams from his location, the increased visibility boosts his confidence that everything he has ever wanted is at his fingertips. But the frenzied online comments and lingering paparazzi prove that mixing a tenacious morning show host, an entrepreneurial baker, and a decade-old secret only percolates trouble.

Acknowledgments

Writing is never a one-person adventure. Despite the hours I live inside my head working on a story or book, countless others invest in the project. I would have never created Sycamore Hill without the encouragement of my writing friends in the Brantford Writers Group. Thank you, Karen, Sandy, Heather, Tara, and Deirdre for your enthusiam and belief in me. You believed these characters had more to their stories.

Thank you to an extraordinary editor, Olivia, from LivEdits. You helped tie the threads of this story together.

And thank you to my family for always believing in the stories I want to tell.

You Can Make a Difference

REVIEW WELCOME TO SYCAMORE HILL

Did you enjoy this book? You can make a difference. Honest reviews of books bring them to the attention of other readers. If you enjoyed this book, I would be grateful if you could take a few minutes to leave an online review or star rating where you purchased the book. You can also post reviews and star ratings on Goodreads and Bookbub.

About the Author

Stacey Weeks writes contemporary romance and romantic suspense filled with strong women, honorable men, and just enough heart-pounding sweetness to keep you turning pages. Her stories are rooted in hope and grace.

She's also the author of non-fiction titles like *Glorious Surrender*, *Chasing Holiness*, *Season of Wonder*, and *Unceasing Prayer*. A ministry wife and homeschooling mom of three, Stacey holds graduate certificates in Women's Ministry and Biblical Counselling from Heritage College and Seminary.

When she's not writing or speaking, you'll find her with a cup of tea and an open Bible, sharing hope (and laughs) with women. She a child of the "play until the streetlights turn on" generation, she loves fixing old things, and above all, she follows Jesus, her greatest joy and deepest hope.

facebook.com/writerSWeeks

x.com/writerSWeeks

instagram.com/writerSWeeks

www.ingramcontent.com/pod-product-compliance
Lightning Source LLC
Chambersburg PA
CBHW020933260626

47169CB00006B/1706